Reckless Desire

Reckless Billionaires Series

Maxine Henri

"The best way to find out if you can trust somebody is to trust them."
Ernest Hemingway

Chapter One

Sydney

"And then I watched him talking about himself with a full mouth, or remains of seaweed between his teeth." I shudder internally at the memory.

London laughs. She sounds like a pack-a-day smoker despite a fairly healthy lifestyle—aside from the quarts of margaritas she consumes at times—and as much as I love her, I wish she wouldn't draw attention to us. I'm on my first cocktail, not yet relaxed enough.

"Oh my God, don't be so sour. One shitty date... so what? I'm sure there is someone on that app who clicks with you." She leans forward and winks, amusement tugging at her lips, which is concerning by itself. Lo cultivates a permanent scowl.

We're at the cocktail bar in the lobby of The Ritz-Carlton, which isn't my normal social scene, and it feels like the whole place is staring at us when London cackles like that. And, of course, my sister has maneuvered the conversation around to my unfortunate Tinder dates. I suspect she might have encouraged me to try dating apps for her own distraction, even though I don't really have any fun or exciting stories to share with her.

"Of course, I've chatted with several reasonable-looking and intelligent men, but once we meet it's a disaster. One guy called me seven times within an hour after our dinner. Just to check on me." I cringe. "Needy. Or the one who forgot to take off his wedding band."

Hmm. Maybe my dates are a cause for laughter. Why do I even bother? "Oh, wait, there was a guy who was so annoyed I was a few minutes late, he practically didn't talk to me for the first half of our dinner."

London snorts.

I take a sip of my drink. God, this strawberry margarita tastes good. The only good thing about this evening.

"And those who're the most interesting only want sex." Online dating is depressing.

"What's wrong with that?" London narrows her eyes and shakes her head like I've just said something ridiculous. She's not interested in love, but she doesn't shy away from a hook-up. Ruthless during the day and fun and loose at night. I envy her. Well, some of it.

"Not exactly the way I want to start a relationship. I'm not on that stupid app for one-night stands." Jesus, I may need another cocktail.

I love hanging out with London. I'm closest to her of all my siblings. Perhaps because we have a similar, practical, realistic—some say pessimistic—outlook on life. We live in different circles because London manages her money more aggressively than I do, but we still spend time together regularly.

She is sensitive to my financial situation—not that she knows much about it—and we usually choose somewhere less posh, less ostentatious, and more comfortable for my budget.

Today, we're catching up on my birthday celebration—four months later—and London insisted we meet here since it's her treat and all. The location surprised me because Lo is the last person who wants to spend money on things. Experiences, yes, but things are a waste for her.

This being my birthday outing, I wish we were somewhere I'm not reminded of how ordinary I am. But knowing her, I bet there is some experience planned.

London is wearing a beautiful navy blue jumpsuit

hugging her tall figure in all the right places. I'm pretty sure it's from a secondhand store, but she wears it as though it was tailored for her. She's not curvy like me, but nevertheless very feminine. Her dark hair is styled into effortless-looking waves and her makeup is perfection.

Me, on the other hand? My brown hair is in desperate need of a retouch and in a bun—*styled* by necessity because I didn't have time to wash it. In my green wrap dress, I'm acutely aware of how not glamorous, not attractive and very average I've become in the last three years.

Perhaps the margarita is not that good after all, just spiraling me into melancholy. This entire bar isn't good for my self-esteem. Why did she even bring me here?

"You need to loosen up. The whole point of signing you up on that site was to get your coochie serviced finally."

I roll my eyes and take another sip. No amount of alcohol can drown out London's well-meant and utterly annoying efforts to find me a man.

"I'm perfectly fine in that department." Not entirely true.

She throws her arms up. "Oh please, a vibrator wasn't invented to replace a man. Just to carry us over. But your dry spell is concerning. It's been three years since that asshole husband of yours died. Three years!" She raises her eyebrows.

My stomach tightens at the mention of Jeremy. How could you love someone so much only to discover you didn't know them at all? Yet I'm offended on his behalf that she called him an asshole.

"Come on!" London shakes her head. "Enough with the sour face. Whatever happened to my fun and carefree sister? I want her back." She pouts like a spoiled child.

She is no child, or spoiled. Lo was Bianca's—our stepmother's—sweetheart. Always willing to go shopping, get manicures and do all the other things daughters do with their mothers. Until she wasn't. She lost her spark and belief in love over several horrible months when she was seventeen and her darker side won over.

Frankly, she is the last one who should call me out on not being fun and carefree anymore.

"That girl is gone, Lo. I'm a deep-in-debt, responsible adult now."

She twists her lips, unimpressed. "Point taken. Still, you're an adult who needs her lady parts taken care of."

Two men, sitting at the table beside us, turn. Not with shock. With interest. One of them openly checks me out as if I was a piece of meat on display in his favorite steakhouse. What the hell? Heat rises in my cheeks, and I try to hide my reaction behind my drink, emptying it in one gulp.

"Sex is not a universal solution to all the world's problems." I put my glass down with a clunk.

"But we're not solving the world's problems, we're solving yours, Syd. And while you don't allow me to help with the financial disaster your dearly beloved late husband caused, I'm not giving up on other areas of your life. You've been stuck somewhere in the land of solitude. Not moving forward is the worst way to live your life. You have to start trusting people."

"You're one to talk." I frown at her.

"I'm living my life fully. Perhaps not to other people's expectations. Yes, I'm frustrated about the world's injustices, but I try to help where I can and I've been reasonably content for years now. And I'm not planning to change anything. Your trust issues sprouted three years ago and you need to move on."

She's right. I hate her for that. Well, not really, but I'm perfectly comfortable suspended between no longer having a husband and my next chapter. The next stage scares me, so I'm in no hurry to reach it.

I had my future planned. And it didn't involve anything that is a part of my life right now. So I'm not looking forward anymore. What for? Just to have my plans crushed?

"I don't have trust issues." I lean back and glare at my sister.

"You're right. You don't have trust issues." She nods, her tone mocking. "And there are no protective walls. None at all. That's why you're a substitute teacher *by choice*. You're scared to get attached to a school, a class, those kids. You've arranged your life in a way that prevents any lasting relationships. You don't need to remember the names of your colleagues or the kids you teach because everywhere you go is temporary."

"And you're different? You don't even know your doorman's name and you see him daily." I'm defensive, which only proves how right she is. What nerve. She's preaching against the very life she lives.

Lo runs a charity and a palliative care center and is constantly pissed at the world for all the loss and pain that confronts her daily. To survive, she doesn't get attached. Ever.

"I'm not as miserable as you are," she quips.

"I go to some schools more often. I know the names of other teachers." One or two. "I'm happy with my job. It's never boring, always changing." I wish I could raise my voice, but this place is so deadened.

"Oh, that's the reason you haven't taken any of the permanent positions they've offered you? Because you *want* constant change instead of a better salary and a stable position in a job you love?" She is baiting me, but I refuse to bite. "And when was the last time you hung out with any of our siblings?"

"I'm hanging out with you, and you know how busy they all are." I spoke to Paris last... Has it been over two months now? Shit.

"Yes, but let's face it, I'm the only lasting relationship in your life, and that's only because I force myself on you."

I'm not going to admit she is right. But London stuck around even after I refused to see anyone else. When I was sure I was going to die from grief and disappointment. In the darkest moments of my life, when I closed the door on her, she simply returned through the window.

"And having sex would help me regain trust in humanity, especially the male portion of it?" Why am I indulging her?

"Definitely not, but it's a start. It would snap you out of that ugly cocoon you wove around yourself as protection." She raises her glass. "Let's toast to burning down those fucking protective walls and enjoying life fully again."

I lift my glass by the stem and dip it toward hers. The crushed ice settles and I fake a smile. As luck would have it, I don't have any drink left to toast to fully enjoying my life. Because the universe is too aware I don't know how.

London rolls her eyes and waves at the server.

The bar is half-empty. All the other guests look like business-people, in the full swing of their working week, probably having meetings. Come to think of it, there are mostly men here. Oh God, is this London's ploy to pick up men? Or, more specifically, hook me up with someone?

"I'm starving. Are you going to feed me anything but alcohol? Let's go have dinner." I try to get us out of there. "This birthday sucks, by the way."

The man at the next table is visibly watching me now. He didn't even notice me before London shouted the comment about my lady parts needing servicing. And they do. Oh God help me, they do. But this douche is not my type.

Not that I have a specific type, but a man with a wedding ring is definitely not it.

"Don't be so impatient. Let's have a cocktail or two, so you're in a better mood before you get your present." She smiles and her eyes sparkle with mischief. I get an uncomfortable feeling she's planned something I won't like.

"You didn't need to worry about a present. You paying for an extravagant dinner here is more than enough."

She waves at the server and orders another pitcher of margaritas.

I can't stop her plans, so I better drink up to get into a more festive and receptive mood.

"I'm sorry I unloaded on you, Syd. I worry about you." She reaches over and squeezes my hand and then turns to the two men next to us. "And you, stop drooling. It's not happening."

I laugh. She really does have my back. As the server brings our pitcher, the two ask for their bill and clear out, not giving us another glance. London rolls her eyes and we both burst into giggles.

The next hour is lighter on conversation and heavy on drinking. We laugh and I'm grateful she forces me to do these things because, as sad as my life is, she snaps me out of my funk occasionally.

I know it's her way of dealing with the darkness in her own life, but I let her work the magic on me as well.

A few men try to make contact and join us, or order a round for us, but London scares them off with her signature ice queen look that can freeze hell. That helps me relax even more. It's nice to have a girls' night out. Perhaps I should have more of those.

"So when will you give me my present?" I hunch my shoulders in glee, margaritas hugging my insides with a warm and fuzzy feeling.

She checks her watch. "In about half an hour."

I giggle. "What did you get me? Is it going to be delivered here? Are you going to embarrass me?"

"Excuse me." She pretends to be offended, but immediately smiles and wiggles her eyebrows. She's having way too much fun with this. "You're having dinner with your present."

I frown. "You got me silverware?"

Her laughter gets attention around the lobby and perhaps on the other side of the street. "No, silly, but if you need silverware, I'm buying you some for Christmas."

We both snicker, more courtesy of our drinks than the conversation itself.

"My darling Sydney, I got you a dinner date and a room for the night here." She smiles, scanning me with expectation.

"What do you mean? You set me up with someone? On a blind date?" And it was shaping up to be such a great evening. The worst part is I realize I'm not as opposed to the idea as I should be. I've definitely had too much to drink.

"Kind of." She bites her bottom lip, the picture of innocence.

"And it's quite presumptuous to assume we would end up sleeping together. What if I like him?" I gulp down what's left in my glass because I can't possibly imagine dealing with this sober. Though I'm quite tipsy already. She got me drunk first on purpose. Oh, she's good. I frown at London, trying my best to imitate her stony stare.

"Oh, you *will* like him." She gives me such a knowing look. Oh, for fuck's sake, has she set me up with someone she knows well?

"Cancel the room." I'm not hooking up with someone I've never met, and especially not if she knows him. Oh God, has she slept with him as well?

"Whatever for? This date is for your coochie."

A woman passes by and turns to us, half appalled, half interested. She winks at me. What the hell?

"Don't be ridiculous, Lo. Oh my God, did you tell him I'll sleep with him? Is he coming assuming we would..." I think I just sobered up.

She smiles and shrugs nonchalantly.

"Oh my God, London, that is the worst birthday present ever. How could you? And why did you assume I'd even go along with that? A spa certificate would have been a reasonable gift. I'm not having sex with him."

"Don't be so dramatic. I'm not setting you up with your future husband. It's just to get you interested in men again. He has absolutely no expectation beyond tonight."

"What do you mean? He could like me." This evening is a nightmare.

"It's against the rules, I think. Or just unprofessional, so you can relax and enjoy a perfect night, no strings attached. No bullshit Tinder dates. He comes highly recommended."

"Highly recommended? Is he some sleazy player? Who recommended him?" Oh my God, a part of me wants to laugh, but I don't think this is a prank. And London seems perfectly pleased with her present.

"His other clients," she whispers, raising her eyebrows, as if I'm the unreasonable one here.

I want to ask her to explain, but the words spring into comprehension and I freeze. I'm not even sure if I'm shocked or angry. Or a little bit curious.

"You got me a male prostitute?" I whisper, looking around to make sure nobody can so much as read my lips.

"Don't be ridiculous." London swats that idea out of the air. "I got you an exclusive male escort."

Chapter Two

Hunter

I lift the weights one more time, breathing through my teeth. Shit, lately I've been so busy with clients and family I haven't had time to work out properly. I haven't had time for myself in ages.

"Losing form, dude." Ash snickers and helps me place the heavy bar on its stand.

You can always rely on friends. Annoyingly, he's right. I swing my legs over the bench and sit with my elbows on my quads to catch my breath.

"I'm still far better than you, loser." I stand up and punch his biceps.

"Yeah, but the way you're running around like a

headless chicken, soon I'll be the king of this gym." He flexes his arms and admires himself in the mirror.

Two girls in sports bras and tiny shorts steal glances and giggle on their way to the changing rooms.

"You just officially became a laughingstock." I chuckle.

"They were ogling me." He glimpses his reflection again with a grin.

"Sure, and now they're trying to shower off the horror." I shake my head, throw my towel over my shoulder and go to make myself a smoothie behind the bar.

"Make me one two, bro." Ash climbs up on the stool on the other side of the counter.

"Sure, asshole, your order is coming up."

By the time I finish blending, the girls from earlier have ambled over to chat with Lea, the receptionist. I place a glass in front of Ash as he checks them out.

"Who is ogling now?" I pour the protein drink for him.

Lea comes over and swats at me. "Get out of here. Employees only."

"I work here." I raise my hands in mock surrender.

She grabs a dirty washcloth and I dash to the other side of the counter before she throws it at me.

Sitting beside Ash, I reach over to get my drink. The girls are now clearly eyeing us.

Ash extends his hand. "Hi, I'm Ash, and this is Hunter. I haven't seen you here before."

While I think they look young for us, I can't ignore how attractive they both are. And very eager to hang out with us while they wait for their smoothies. After they introduce themselves, Ash chats with them.

Nursing my drink, I stay silent. These interactions used to be my jam, but there is no point in getting interested in someone if I can't date. Two jobs and a family are as much as I can manage.

And it's not like my career is conducive to maintaining a relationship. No woman would ever accept my work. I'm fine with that. I need money now, and I've made peace with my choices.

However, I enjoy letting Ash make a fool of himself as I sip my drink.

"What do you do?" the shorter one asks. Shit, I didn't even listen when she told me her name.

"We're personal trainers." Ash flexes his biceps again, the idiot, and the girls titter.

"You train here? We may need some help." The taller one bats her lashes.

Lea hits the button on the blender and glares at Ash. I hide a chuckle. He answers something, but I can't hear it over the ruckus. I hope he isn't setting up a training session with them.

"So you go to people's houses to train?" I hear the question as Lea finally pushes the off button. Good, it seems he didn't offer my services to them. My calendar is full.

I check my watch. Shit. "Sorry, ladies, kindergarten pickup waiting."

The taller one chirps away with Ash, but her friend's face falls. If she only knew what choices I had to make in my life, she'd be less disappointed I'm leaving. She might even thank me for leaving her alone.

My lifestyle doesn't allow a normal relationship. There are important women and commitments in my life already. The most important one is waiting for me right now.

I leave quickly and speed walk the few blocks to the school.

"How is my favorite girl?" I squat and Caroline runs to me and wraps her arms around my neck. I inhale her scent of innocence.

She wiggles out of my arms. "You're late. Nico's mom is gone. And you're sweaty."

Every time I come after Nico's gone home, she gives me shit, my little angel. Nico is her best friend.

Caroline's teacher leans in the playroom's doorway, smiling at us. Another woman—one of the helicopter moms—is grinning as well. Both are looking at me.

Stepping into a kindergarten as a single man is akin to swimming with sharks. Not as deadly since most of the moms are married and their flirting is harmless, but it still requires careful navigation.

Particularly in the case of Caro's teacher, Ms. Eliza, who is single and drools when she sees me. She is a lovely woman, I think. And a good educator. Caro adores her, but she hasn't taken the hint, or the hundred that I've given her in the last month since Caro started here.

"I'll try to be here sooner on Monday." I stand up, giving both women a grin, as fake as possible not to encourage them. "Get your shoes and let's go. I'm in a hurry."

"Why?" Caro doesn't move.

Oh, for fuck's sake, again with the whys. "I have to work tonight." She opens her mouth to undoubtedly kill me with another why, so I quickly add. "And we need to hurry if we want to get ice cream first."

That shuts her up. Her eyes widen with excitement and she runs to get her shoes, her ponytails bouncing. My heart flutters. How this little person can stir all my warmest emotions and melt me into a puddle every time is beyond me, but she does. And I love it.

"She's a lucky girl. Don't mention i-c-e-c-r-e-a-m

out loud here because the rest of us will be in trouble, forced to spoil our kids as well," the helicopter mom teases me. Her smile is so wide, her jaw might crack.

"I think Caro is the luckiest girl," Ms. Eliza chimes in, staring at me with glassy eyes as if I was a saint's apparition.

As far as I'm concerned, very little in Caro's life could be described as luck, but I won't point that out. We do the best we can with the cards the universe has dealt us. I scramble for words to respond to them as both women stare at me in expectation.

I indulge them because good relationships are critical. I'm glad Caro has settled here, because there has been enough uncertainty in her life and the last thing I wanted was to rip her out of the environment she'd known since she was barely a year old. However, I had little choice.

Since the school runs have become more my responsibility, we made the tough decision to move her closer to my work, so I could pick her up without canceling trainings.

"Ladies, I'm the lucky one here. One of these days, I should get more parenting advice from you." I wink at the helicopter mom, my sarcasm successfully covered, and turn to Caro's teacher. "Ms. Eliza, Caro adores you." I smile as color floods her cheeks.

Sometimes I think I should act like an asshole to fend them off, but my mood is always brighter around Caroline, so here I am, killing these women with semi-kindness, encouraging their advances. Instead of *acting* like an asshole, *I am one.*

"How many times do I have to tell you to call me Eliza." She breathes the words and I shudder internally. Even if I was attracted to her, she has no chance. I'm not on the market.

"Are the children alone in there, Eliza?" The helicopter mom raises her eyebrows and jerks her head to dismiss the teacher.

"Two scoops?"

I look down. Caro is glaring at me, her hands on her hips, ready to negotiate and get out of here. Not as ready as I am.

"Ladies." I nod to the two women and take the hand of the only woman that matters here. Well, she has years to become a woman—and thank God for that—but she is the most important person in my life.

"One scoop, pumpkin." We cross the yard and turn onto the sidewalk, Caro bouncing and me slow-walking beside her.

She stops. "I'm not a vegetable. My name is Caroline." She cocks her head, glaring again, frustrated I don't remember.

"Sorry, cookie," I tease. She draws the line at all endearments related to food.

"Hey," she protests.

"Sorry, Caroline, I'll behave, but if you keep stopping there will be no ice cream." She flinches and starts marching. With all the power of an almost-six-year-old.

We find the ice cream truck in a park and of course, the sucker I am, she gets three scoops. On a bench she licks diligently, while getting most of her ice cream all over her wrists and skirt.

"What are we doing after this?" She swings her legs, the ball of energy that she is. I think ice cream time is the only time she is reasonably motionless.

"Remember, I have to work. Granny will stay with you." I lean in to kiss the top of her head.

"Where is Mommy?" She looks up at me and I exhale, trying to be as casual as possible. I don't want her to pick up on my emotions. She deserves a carefree and happy childhood. As much as possible in our situation.

"She needed medicine again, so you're having a sleepover with Granny, but tomorrow you need to help Mom when she is back." She nods solemnly, understanding the responsibility she shouldn't even know about at this age.

"Okay," she says and returns to her ice cream.

Two boys kick the ball and a toddler trots around while his mother follows him. A couple is enjoying double scoops on a bench beside us. In the middle of a city that pulses with activity and chaos, time, noise and reality cease to exist here. This peaceful patch of grass in the middle of a concrete jungle seems unaffected.

But it's these moments, these snapshots of normal in our lives, that piss me off the most. Without hesitation, I would give all my organs to provide more ordinary moments for Caro and her mom, but I can't. I'm helpless. Powerless. Useless.

Fucking cancer.

"Nico pulled my hair today." Caro's ability to switch into another topic is something I wish I could learn from her.

"He certainly shouldn't have done that, but perhaps he likes you, sweetheart." I chuckle, not really sure how to handle this. With Caro in my life, I find myself helpless too fucking often.

"He should kiss me then." She looks at me for confirmation and fuck, I don't know what to say. Where does she get this shit from?

"Well," I say with a shrug, "sometimes we men don't know how to show someone we like them."

"I'll ask him to kiss me tomorrow." She stretches her hands in front of her, done with the ice cream.

I won't comment on the kissing. Let Mrs. Eliza deal

with that. Part of me hopes the little fucker will kiss her because she doesn't need more heartbreak in her life. A much bigger part prays she won't be kissed for at least another twenty years. Even thirty. Shit. Can she stay a baby girl forever?

I wipe her palms and wrists. And elbows. Then I try to salvage the skirt and her T-shirt before I glance at my watch. Fuck.

"Caro, I'm late. We really need to go now. Can I carry you?"

She is very adamant about walking by herself, her need for independence a cause for admiration and disdain, but luckily she agrees, so we make it to the subway and across the river quickly.

We get to my building and Mom opens the door before I find my keys, already waiting for us.

"Granny!" Caro hugs Mom's leg.

"Oh, here is my favorite girl. I baked cookies. Go wash your hands."

"I have to shower and get changed." I give Mom a quick peck and move past her.

In my bedroom, I lay my suit on the bed. I check my watch again. No shaving tonight. A quick shower and off I go.

Caro sits on the floor in front of the TV, her hands already stained with chocolate.

"Mom, she's just had ice cream," I call before I

enter the bathroom.

The kid is spoiled thanks to our efforts to overcompensate for her not having a normal family. I need to stop the regular ice cream runs with her. I chuckle inwardly, picturing her facial expression if I suggested a fruit cup. God, that girl has us all wrapped around her finger.

After the fastest shower in history, I rush to get dressed and am struggling with my tie when my phone rings.

"Hey, my friend," Ash greets me, sounding too nonchalant considering I just fucking saw him. He'd better not have set us up on a double date.

"What do you need, asshole? I'm in a hurry." I balance my phone between my shoulder and my ear, trying to fix the knot.

"You should have stayed. Those two are fun. We agreed to go out next week. I promised you'd join us."

"Not happening." I put him on speaker and finish with my collar.

"Hey, no need to be snappy. Listen, I need a favor."

"Of course you do. I'll put it on your tab. Shoot." I tousle my hair a bit to give it that purposely unkempt look women like.

"I have a client tomorrow morning. An older lady, mostly stretching and some light cardio, but I'm going away for the weekend."

I roll my eyes. "And your weekend plans have just materialized, so you couldn't make arrangements sooner?" I shouldn't complain. Ash is disorganized and I usually make money out of his double bookings.

"Come on, can you help me out? I'll owe you."

"I have a thing tonight. I can't have an early morning." I need the money, though. "Can you push her up to the afternoon?"

"What thing?"

"Seriously? A dinner. Focus." I pull my suit jacket from the hanger. I'm going to be late because of him.

"By the sound of it you plan to stay for breakfast, too."

"Do you want my help?" I growl. I need a new friend.

"Yes, yes, I do. Drinks are on me next time. She is a long-term client. I'll call her now and text you the details. Have fun tonight. We should go out together soon."

"So you can buy me all the drinks you've promised?"

He laughs as if I made a joke. "Perhaps next week with the girls from the gym."

"Have a nice weekend, Ash."

I don't have time for this shit. I hang up and put on my jacket. This is my favorite suit. Usually my wardrobe is more casual, but tonight is a fancy affair. I check myself in the mirror. Game time.

In the living room Caro is bouncing around, watching a show while pulling out books from the shelves and using them to build a fort. Half of the covers in my library have suffered under her treatment, but this is her favorite game, so I let her.

She notices me and moves my way. "You leaving already?"

Her face is smeared with chocolate and I glance at her hands. Oh, poor books. "Stop right now, cookie monster."

She halts, looks at her hands and promptly hides them behind her back. I bite my lip, stifling a laugh, and approach her gingerly. "Don't move." I lean in and kiss the crown of her head, staying as far back as possible. "I love you, sweetheart. Have fun with Granny."

"Before you go, do you think I can get a new scientist Barbie?" The concept of being late is completely lost on her.

"Sure, let's add it to your list for Santa, okay?" I rustle her hair.

"But the delivery guy comes more often than Santa. Can we ask him instead?" She cocks her head, her eyes shining with excitement.

I chuckle. "You're a smart girl. We'll talk about it tomorrow."

She hops away and I almost collide with my mom. Her eyes glisten with emotions as she dusts my lapels.

"You look so handsome, darling." Mom raises on her toes to kiss my cheek. "I'm so proud of you."

Kill me now. If only she knew.

Chapter Three

Sydney

For some reason, I haven't run away. I should have. I still should. London is having way too much fun with this, and I'm trying to flush out the conflicting emotions with the last drops of margarita.

Accepting her gift would solve my dry spell, and perhaps—in theory only—she might be right about sex snapping me out of my idle state. It's not like I'm paying for it after all. Nevertheless, it's paid for. Even if I ignored my moral objections, I don't think I would enjoy it.

Isn't he contractually obliged to pretend he likes me? Is there even a contract? He must sleep with so many women. What if London's present leaves me with an unwanted gift? Like chlamydia. I trust she screened him well. They must produce a health certificate at the time of hiring.

Morals and health concerns aside, it could be just like a one-night stand. I'm not sure if that's what I need. I had one of those before Jeremy and it left me feeling lonely and empty. And doing it now with a man who is only pretending—getting paid—to like me, I would for sure feel even more deflated.

Why am I even thinking about it at all? Sex isn't on the menu tonight. What was London thinking?

She takes care of the bill and practically drags me to the reception area near the entrance to wait for my stupid present.

When we were kids, London was an instigator and got me involved in some sick shit. Okay, some of it was my idea. But overall, I was the good girl forced to step into the role of caretaker after my mom passed, and London was the on-paper well-behaved daughter who rebelled on every occasion.

We had lots of fun together and frankly, over the years, I've appreciated how she's always stood by me. How she didn't let me sink into premature adulthood after I was left with three younger sisters, her included, and a grieving father. Then, she was there, again, to pull me out of depression after Jeremy died.

But this prank-like gift is next level fucked up,

regardless of how much she considers it perfectly appropriate for me. I'm regretting it, even knowing there is no way I'll go through with it.

"Geez, don't be so tense." She elbows my ribs and then perks up, smiling in the direction of the entrance.

I take a breath to tell her I'm leaving, but then I follow her gaze and freeze. Henry Cavill is pushing through the revolving door. Only once he steps in is it clear that he is no Superman. This man is real. Breathtakingly handsome. Magazine-cover hot.

His black hair swings playfully across his forehead. A tiny smile softens his square jaw. Or maybe it's a smirk, but it gives him a cocky handsomeness that makes my pulse dance.

He is wearing a navy blue suit and it must be tailored, because I don't think an off-the-rack piece would ever hug his broad shoulders and torso in such a flattering way. Maybe he *is* Superman.

He carries himself in a way that causes all women —and, to an extent, men—to turn. And he's only been here for a split second. His other leg is practically still on the street, and everyone here seems affected.

Or it might be just my imagination. The soft, organized buzz of the hotel flows unconcerned. Shit. Even the romantic music has only been playing in my head.

What an entrance. I lick my lips, but my mouth remains dry. The man sucked in all the air and humidity. It's a desert here now for sure, because I'm sweating way more than the margaritas warrant.

And just my luck, he ambles toward us, slicing through the room with a confident gait. My resolve to leave wavers. How can walking be this sexy?

"London?" He smiles, and I'm not only parched anymore. I'm blinded.

"Hello, that's me." My sister offers him her hand and he kisses it. Kisses it! While staring into her eyes. "This is Sydney. Promise me you'll take good care of her tonight."

I'm focused on willing the ground to swallow me, so it takes me a moment to realize he's now extending his hand to me.

His eyes are the most unusual gray color, like silver with sparkles of amber. Hot and cold at the same time.

I shake his hand vigorously, almost ripping his arm off. "Hi." My greeting is a squeal. Yes, I'm perspiring, my heart is palpitating, my mouth is my only dry cavity and I squeal. Perfect.

"Hunter Stuart, pleased to meet you." And apparently that playful smirk is his permanent countenance, and flickers in his eyes as well. His voice drapes around my skin like silk—strong, yet soft and luxurious.

"Which one is your first name?" I spit out, due to my brain apparently being broken. Along with my self-respect because I'm still standing here. With my sister.

And with a male escort. Though I have to give it to him, with his looks he must have a very successful career.

"Hunter." He frowns and shakes his head slightly, as if he startled himself, but then his smile is back. "London, I promise Sydney will enjoy tonight, and perhaps even remember it fondly." He winks.

London wiggles her eyebrows and gives him a card, the key to *our* room. I look around, half expecting the police to burst in and arrest us. Geez, is this even legal? Am I going to do this? What if a parent of one of my students recognizes me here with him? *Don't be stupid.*

"You have a table at the restaurant waiting for you. The staff knows to bill it to the room. Have fun." London smiles at Hunter.

He nods and then turns to me, scanning me up and down. Not in a sleazy way, though, in a very discreet way. His gaze scrapes my skin, exposing feelings I haven't felt in a long time. If ever. It's like my body came alive, alight, ablaze under his scrutiny.

He's probably wondering what kind of nightmare client I'm going to be, regretting he took the order. Assignment? Transaction? Jesus, this *is* a nightmare. What am I doing? Or not doing?

Damn it, I'm sick. I shouldn't have drunk anything.

"Happy birthday." London hugs me. "Loosen up, silly, it's just one night," she whispers into my ear.

I watch her leave, scheming how I'm going to repay her for this. Accidental acid spillage on her new shoes? Vomiting in her favorite bag? Oh, I know! I'll sell the nudes she secretly took to the media.

I'm not even sure if I'm mortified or annoyed when Hunter offers me his arm.

I glare at him and he winces, raising his eyebrow. Yeah, buddy, I have many questions as well.

"Let's go." I ignore his gesture. Why am I going through with this? Because I'm going to get the most expensive champagne and caviar. Not that it's any punishment for London. She probably won't even notice it on her statement, but I'm hungry and this poor asshole will just have to sit through dinner with me.

Or I can send him away. He'd get paid and London would never know. A smile finally tugs at my mouth and I lace my arm through his. Let him have dinner and send him on his way. I can use a peaceful night in the gazillion thread count sheets here.

Hunter

Why did I tell her my name is Hunter? My real fucking name. I don't use a fake name for these encounters because it only adds to all the cover-ups I have to invent to keep this gig discreet. I simply let my clients call me Stuart. It's less personal. And on some occasions when things progress, the last thing I want is for a client to scream my name. That's too intimate.

Yet I was so taken by her glowering, I used my real name. Fuck. I should abort this mission. It wasn't just the glowering that distracted me. Those emerald eyes, while cold as a frozen lake, pierced me with an intensity I don't want to examine.

As I walked to her in the lobby, and now as I guide her to the dining room, I let my eyes wander for longer than appropriate. The way her simple green wrap dress hugs her curves is sinful by itself. I've just met her and I've already undressed her in my mind. Abort. Abort.

Even if I'm attracted to a client, I don't normally get so caught up in it. This level of attraction is not good in my line of work. Though I'm probably safe because she clearly doesn't feel the same. Most of my clients seek connection. Sydney looks like she doesn't even want to be here.

The restaurant isn't very busy and its silence echoes too loudly in my mind. I'm never uncomfortable during these dates, but shit, I don't have a good feeling tonight. There are only a few people dining, and the clatter of the cutlery reverberates around us.

My lack of comfort is surely caused by this pretentious place, not my companion. I'm used to ridiculous luxury because my clients pay for it, but this restaurant is too impersonal.

Perhaps Sydney feels that too. Maybe that's why she is so edgy. I should read the menu, but instead I'm searching her face, trying to figure out the reason for the short circuit in my brain prompting me to tell her my real name.

She is studying the menu like it's the most intriguing novel. Thick lashes cover her green eyes, but I can still recall their glimmer from earlier. The emeralds in them are intriguing, but it was the layers of sadness seeping through them that startled me.

There is loss and resentment written in them. I know because it's the look that confronts me in the mirror every morning.

The waiter comes and takes our order, and with no menu in front of her Sydney's eyes dart around, trying to settle on anything but me.

"You must be starving," I comment because she ordered several appetizers and two main meals.

"I'll have it wrapped for later. This is just to make a dent in London's credit card. Vengeance." She runs her finger up and down the butter knife's handle, still not looking at me.

"Vengeance?" I reach across to stop her hand from fidgeting. As my fingers connect with her soft skin, she stiffens. I regret reaching out because the jolt of electricity that the feather-like contact sends through me is unexpected. And welcomed. I mean unwanted.

She looks up finally and bites her lip. I'm not sure if she's struggling with the same influx of heat as me or if she's considering how to turn me down, but I smile at her and she relaxes.

"Look. It's not personal. I just... I didn't know... I'm not interested in this." She cocks her head and shrugs, her face ridden with apology.

"I've noticed you don't want to be here. I'm sorry I'm not what you expected." I squeeze her hand briefly and let go, leaning back in my chair.

"Oh, no, it's not you. You're very attractive." She winces at her own words and a blush spreads across her face. And fuck me if that doesn't increase her allure. "I mean, obviously you do look good. It's part of the job, after all. You probably work out all the time and go to the spa and take care of yourself because your body is your..." She widens her eyes and I bite the inside of my cheek to stop myself from laughing. Her blabbering is adorable.

And she finds me attractive. Why that makes me feel like the king of the world, I don't know. This is too similar to an awkward first date. Snap out of it, idiot.

This has never happened to me. I need to maintain a shallow interaction with clients, so why am I feeling like I want to dive deeper? I can't afford stupid mistakes.

Shaking her head, she continues. "What I'm trying to say is... it's not you, it's me."

She plasters her hand over her mouth and we both burst out laughing.

"Really, we've just met and you're already giving me the *it's not you, it's me* speech? My feelings are crushed." I mock horror.

"Jesus." She relaxes a bit. "I'm sorry. I don't want to come across as judgmental."

Her throat bobs up and down a few times. The air between us has changed too many times already. From the chill to an inferno and back. Her confusing messages are giving me whiplash. I don't think she even knows what effect she has on me. What I'd like to know is: why? What the hell is happening?

"So what do we do?" Sydney asks, color spreading through her cheeks.

"We talk." Her discomfort is kind of attractive. I need to snap out of this strange infatuation with a woman I don't know. Not good for business.

"What about?" She narrows her eyes, her tone so genuine it makes me chuckle.

"Whatever you want to talk about. Usually women talk a lot on these dates."

The server brings our water—flown in from some

European glacier—and a bottle of Dom Perignon. Sydney wasn't joking about her revenge. She fiddles with the butter knife, avoiding my eyes until the server leaves.

"Okay, but usually women book you. I'm still in shock here." She looks around, as if being seen with me is a crime.

"You don't enjoy having fun?"

She jerks her head back like she's offended by the suggestion. Or maybe surprised by the concept of having fun.

"I'm just not okay with this. With paying for sex. Technically, London is paying, but you know what I mean."

"There doesn't have to be sex."

She drops the butter knife and leans forward, studying me, dissecting the truth behind my statement.

"How is it supposed to work?" Even the slight exasperation in her tone is attractive. I'm fucked.

"What do you mean?" Watching her squirm may be my new favorite activity.

"Correct me if I'm wrong, but your job, or hobby or whatever it is, doesn't really have the best reputation. So I'm just wondering how it all works?"

"It's an honest transaction. A woman pays for a service and I deliver it. Usually she's just looking for a companion. In this case, since you're not paying and you seem very uncomfortable, why don't we have some of this champagne"—I raise my glass—"and talk a little."

She smiles and takes a sip. "What do *you* want to talk about?"

"You," I say without thinking and Sydney swallows visibly. Her blush spreads even further. So much for my excellent conversation skills. "Or whatever you feel like," I add in a desperate effort to make her more comfortable. Or to erase my stupid suggestion. I don't want to know more about her. What for? I won't see her ever again after tonight.

I'm already attracted to her physically more than I'd like. I don't need to find her interesting as well. Perhaps she isn't, but I already sense she is.

"What's your favorite color?" She looks at me through her lashes, playing with her glass, and I'm relieved she found a way to ease the tension. It's a ridiculous question that single-handedly lightens the situation for both of us. I like that she asked it. Fuck.

"Blue, of course. It's the best color. From baby blue to indigo." I play along, content we are finding shallow ground. Shallow. Superficial. Meaningless. That's where I need to keep us.

"Seriously?" She widens her eyes. How would she react if I said turquoise with a hint of yellow and ten percent of aquamarine, which is Caro's current favorite color? "Blue is my favorite, too."

She almost sounds disappointed. Maybe having something—even this trivial—in common is embarrassing. Or I'm reading her wrong.

"What's your favorite book?" We'll play twenty questions.

She tucks a strand of hair behind her ear. It's a simple gesture and perhaps driven by her discomfort, but she executes it with such grace that I stare at the delicate whorl of ear.

"Oh, I have too many." She shakes her head.

Just like me. "Okay, your favorite author."

"Jo Nesbo." She smiles. "You probably haven't heard of him."

"Harry Hole is my favorite detective." I gulp down my wine. So what? We have things in common. Two things actually. And really, blue doesn't even count. It's too common. So why am I wishing this was an actual date? Only a part of me wishes that. A tiny part. Insignificant.

"You read Nesbo?" Her eyes glitter with excitement as she stares at me with her mouth open. This is the first time tonight she is all animated. Oh, I want more of that. And of that mouth.

She purses her lips, making me unreasonably excited about kissing that mouth later. Hopefully. It's full and red without lipstick. I wonder how she tastes. Perhaps a bit of sweet and sour, just like her mood.

What's wrong with me? I have never fantasized about a client before. And she might not even be a client because she still looks like she's ready to bolt.

"His plots are pure mind fuck. His writing is such a joy. Simple, yet—"

"Powerful," we both say at the same time.

A hint of a smile brightens Sydney's face and my cock twitches. I really hope she decides to go through with this and unwrap her birthday present.

And if she does, I hope to God one taste will be enough.

Chapter Four

Sydney

I ordered a ridiculous amount of food. We haven't even finished the appetizers sampler and I'm already full. We've been sitting here for two hours already. Just nibbling and talking, waving away the servers who are impatiently circling around our table.

Where did the time go? I don't remember the last time I had this much fun. Not crazy, laugh-out-loud fun, but a stimulating, thought-provoking conversation that is playful and flirtatious at the same time.

This is the best date I've had in a while. Perhaps ever. We've covered so many topics, and after the initial awkwardness the energy has flowed so effortlessly I don't want the dinner to end. It's good that I ordered so much.

The only cloud hanging above us is the nagging reality of what this is. It's not an actual date.

Hunter is clearly very good at his job. Most—or all—of his clients are willing participants and he doesn't need to put them at ease. Yet, he managed not only to relax me, but to move me past the dread. I'm enjoying myself. I haven't enjoyed myself in forever.

I keep reminding myself it's his job. He might be telling me lies for all I know. He's getting paid to make this a pleasant experience for me. It makes me wonder how good the other half of the night would be. I mean, his body is impressive, even dressed up. My heart pulses with anticipation and heat spreads up my neck at the idea. Jesus, I need to stop thinking about this.

"If you had a time machine, which time period would you go to?" Hunter asks and gestures to the server to refill our glasses.

I cover mine. After all the margaritas and two glasses of champagne already, even with all the food, I need to stop drinking. A clear mind is what will save me tonight. Save me from what? Or rather, who? From Hunter? From myself?

"How many trips would I have?"

"For the purposes of this conversation, one trip."

In the dimmed lights of the dining room, the silver

in his eyes is darker. His irises change color as he speaks.

Sometimes they are gray and sometime the speckles of whiskey shine through, giving them a distinct glint. I'm drawn to them. There is more behind them than a playboy who sells his body for money.

"I think I'd go back to the nineteen twenties and thirties, the decade in between the two wars. The glamour of the era, Art Deco, Hemingway, Picasso, Modigliani. Everything fascinates me about that time period. Well, not the financial crisis and the suffering related to that. But being rich back then and possibly in Paris. I'd love that." Nobody's ever asked me that.

"Interesting." He studies me intently, his eyes like hot coals on my skin.

"Don't tell me it's your favorite period?" We have already discovered seven things we have in common. If he says yes now, I'm going to take it as a confirmation he's just saying what I want to hear. My theory isn't bulletproof because he answered at least half of the questions before me, but I'm sticking to it. I need to tame my interest in him.

"No, but when you describe it I want to time travel there."

Those eyes, fanned with those thick lashes, are going to be the death of me. And why isn't the air conditioning working here? It's like we're seated next to a furnace. A bead of sweat rolls between my breasts and I want to use the napkin to pat myself, but I resist.

"And I love that you traveled outside your lifetime," he continues. "Usually people want to travel to fix their past or find out what's in their future." He spreads foie gras on a piece of toast and takes a bite, all the while never moving his eyes away from me.

If his voice is silk, his gaze on me is like fur—hot and decadent. I don't think I've ever experienced so many physical reactions to a simple smile or look.

I'm unreasonably pleased he liked my answer. But he obviously asks the same question often. We've been playing twenty questions, and while I'm having fun he is following a scenario he's probably played out too many times.

I call the waiter to clear the appetizers. If Hunter notices my change of mood, he doesn't let me see it.

We have been connecting and we haven't touched on any personal topics. We didn't talk about our families or work—well, my work. That's not what this is about. He doesn't need to get to know me. Yet I let myself fantasize it's real.

I've been so lonely and bitter that a bit of fake attention screws with my ability to see things for what they are. An honest transaction, Hunter called it. Honest, my ass.

He leans back in his chair, relaxed, his hooded eyes scanning me.

"Beach or mountain vacation?" He changes the dynamics of the conversation. So he must sense something is different. *Yeah, Hunter, I sobered up.*

"Mountains," I lie. That's the game, after all.

He jerks his eyebrows up, as if calling me on my bullshit. "Movies or a play?"

"Both." I might prefer movies, but he doesn't need to know that. He doesn't care, anyway.

"Dogs or cats?"

"Fish." I shrug and he narrows his eyes.

Our main course arrives and I attack it, though I'm not hungry. Anything to avoid those eyes. I'm really annoyed. I let myself believe this was something. It's nothing.

We eat in silence. It's not a comfortable silence because I'm fuming inwardly. I steal a few glimpses at Hunter, but each time he catches me our eyes lock, and I wish he wasn't who he is.

Why does he do it? Paying off student loans? Mortgage? Gambling debts?

I want to ask him why. Is it a side hustle? What is his actual job, if he has one? I'm perversely interested in finding out more details about him.

I like him. I need this dark part of him to have a

profound reason. I want a positive spin, so I feel better about tonight.

What? Tonight is about to end. We'll finish our meal and I'll send him home. Won't I?

I like him. Perhaps London is onto something. There is no chance I'll ever see him again. And even lesser of this becoming more, so I have nothing to lose. I'm pretty sure sex with him would be amazing.

I like him. Can I set aside my useless morals? I protested the idea strongly before, but now, even if this connection is fake, I'm having a good time. What's stopping me?

"What's your favorite dessert?" Hunter breaks the silence. I want to snap "enough with the fake interest", but if I'm going to go through with this, I should just play along. Because that's what we're doing. Playing.

"Obviously, all of them," I answer honestly.

He grins. That self-confident smirk on his face is attractive and annoying at the same time. "Obviously?" He shakes his head. "Because you're so sweet?"

Smooth, Casanova. "I know you haven't seen me naked yet, but my hips are visible." I point downward to emphasize my point.

He frowns. "You think you have big hips?"

I laugh. Seriously? "I know I do. And I'm fine with it." I put down my cutlery. I'm stuffed. If I'm going to consider the post-dinner itinerary of this evening, I'll need to walk off the meal before any other activity can occur.

"I think you are perfect."

The compliment hangs between us, sucking away all the air and setting my skin on fire again, while simultaneously sprouting goosebumps down my spine. I'm trying to ignore it.

Hunter is waiting for my reaction. I fidget with my hands and look away. I wish I could remain casual and lighthearted, but his gaze may as well have X-ray qualities. We're in the middle of a restaurant, fully dressed with a table between us, and I feel completely naked and alone with him.

I'm faintly aware of the hum of the few conversations around us, the soft lounge music, the clinking of glasses and clattering of the plates and silverware. All the sounds are almost imperceptible in the background as my heartbeat travels from my temples to my toes in a frantic beat.

When Hunter gets no reaction from me—I'm hoping my internal squirming is not visible—he speaks again.

"You said yet."

I blink a few times, but it does nothing to ground me. "What?"

"You said I haven't seen you naked *yet*."

I swallow, but my mouth remains dry, so instinctively I lick my lips. His eyes fall to my mouth and I'm pretty sure the sparkles between us could power this hotel, if not the entire block. I kind of wish we'd returned to the former awkwardness.

"No, I didn't." My voice is hoarse, the words barely passing through my parched vocal cords.

"Okay." He smirks.

The server comes to clear our table and recites the dessert menu.

"I'll take my dessert to the room," Hunter says, burning me with his gaze. The server runs without waiting for my order. Not that I want to eat anymore, but Jesus, the innuendo is coiling around, separating our table from others. Everything else is in a different dimension. Between us the air crackles, robbing me of oxygen.

"What now?" I push the words out with effort, more sweat breaking on my nape. The few loose strands of my hair are glued to the back of my neck.

"My terms don't allow refunds." He pauses, daring me to suggest the direction of this conversation. Will I bolt or will I continue? The latter would give him the upper hand, control. No way I'm allowing that. He can be hot, but I don't want him to know what effect he has on me.

He must know already anyway. If anyone is new to this game, it's me. His cards are well hidden and even better played. I'm out of my depth here. I want him, but I don't want the circumstances.

He continues staring. Daring. Challenging me with those impressive gray eyes.

"What is it going to be, Sydney?" I love the way he says my name. "I'm your birthday gift. Are you going to unwrap me? Use me?"

Oh God. I make a sound that could be interpreted as a cough or a shriek and try to cover it with a generous gulp of water. I should have had more wine.

"Maybe I can put the gift away. Not use it, but not return it." Am I asking him for another date? I don't even know what I'm saying anymore.

"Are you telling me you want to re-gift me?"

I say nothing because my brain has reached its capacity and I can no longer string words into sentences. I have no words. The entire conversation is ridiculous, but the person asking—the eyes piercing through me, the faint masculine scent wafting across the table, the body that any woman would die to touch.

And the electric current zapping through me just from his look. Jesus. I'm royally screwed. I'm so sex-deprived, a single look, a simple dinner with a man, and a fun conversation and my body is out of control.

"What are you saying, Sydney?" He pushes, confidence oozing from him. Bastard. "Do you want to spend our night talking, watching TV and just hang out?"

Is that what I want?

Before I can contemplate any further, I nod my head yes.

Why do I do this? It's just like me. Too afraid to go all the way, so I play it safe and I opt for the middle ground.

Somehow I've moved from my initial complete refusal to entertain this to wanting it with everything that I am. So I settle on this halfway mark that's neither one. Only, it seems more dangerous.

He regards me with a long, scorching look that I can't interpret, but it makes my heart beat faster. I hope this restaurant has a defibrillator.

"Okay, Sydney, as you wish. No sex."

I'm relieved and disappointed at the same time. Until he continues and my body tenses. His words, like a referee's pistol, set my heart to racing.

"It's so much more intimate."

Chapter Five

Sydney

It will be okay. I'm sure we will have a great time together, even if we just talk.

My overactive sweat glands chilled during dinner to a level acceptable for a normally functioning adult. For the most part. But now that we're in the elevator, they are back to working overtime. And why does this elevator shrink with every floor we pass?

Hunter stands beside me, our backs against the rear wall because a family jumped in before the door closed. A little girl stares up at everyone. Her eyes connect with Hunter's and he gives her a wink. She giggles and he contorts his face into a ridiculous grimace. She hides behind her father's leg and keeps peeking at Hunter, her face alight.

Apparently he charms the entire female population regardless of age. Their silent interaction, the impromptu peek-a-boo, warms my heart.

The family gets out and we end up standing closer to each other. It makes no sense because the large car is now empty. Yet the back of Hunter's hand is brushing my wrist. His eyes are set on the changing numbers above the door, seemingly unaware of the light link between us.

His closeness is overwhelming. It sears the edges of my resistance and I can't remember why sleeping with him is a bad idea. My brain energy must be channeled into the meal digestion and nothing is left for reasoning.

All my nerve endings tingle with anticipation or anxiety—whatever the feeling fluttering its tiny wings around my stomach is.

Would sleeping with him be okay? Am I just being too uptight? It's not like I'll see him again.

I *won't* see him again.

The realization punches me in the stomach and the tickling wings fly away, making room for the persistent indigestion that settles there. What is wrong with me? I've known him for three hours. I won't miss him.

But will I regret it if I don't let him do his job? Argh. I roll my eyes inwardly. The desire mingles with my objections—ones I can't articulate properly with him this close—as heat rises to my cheeks. I don't—

I don't finish the thought because Hunter whips around, pushing into the panel and the elevator jerks into a halt. It happens so quickly I instinctively step backward and my back hits the mirrored wall.

He glides to stand in front of me, engulfing me with his masculine scent and warmth. I thought he was close before, but now I don't know which breath is his and which is mine. I can't look up because if the dinner was any indication, holding Hunter's gaze challenges my willpower. My ability to remember basic functions.

I'm panting in short, shallow bursts. For a moment, or an eternity, we don't move or speak. My body exhibits involuntary reactions to his heat—my mouth is dry, my heart is palpitating, my knees are shaking, and I'm sweating and shivering with goosebumps at the same time.

I'm a thirty-three-year-old widow and I've never been this riled up by a man.

Hunter stands there and waits. If I took a deeper breath, my nipples would touch his chest. At least they made up their mind easily and are almost painfully hard, begging for attention.

He is too close. Yet we're so far apart because I'm afraid to take the leap. Shit, I'm not even willing to look at him.

I push my hands against his chest. His jacket is open and my palms feel his sinew through the thin fabric of his shirt. I think I was going to push him away, but I'm barely touching him.

I'm not shoving him away because I don't want to. Even though my rational mind is discounting the energy between us. This is real. I can't deny the attraction. We have a connection I haven't felt with anyone in a long, long time. Could he really fake it? Is he like this with all clients?

Hunter touches my temple with his index finger. The butterfly brush sends a current down my spine. He slowly trails down my cheek and his breathing synchronizes with mine. Our chests heave in unison. Maybe the ventilation is off in here and we're both suffering from oxygen deprivation.

His exploratory finger reaches my bottom lip and I stagger, a soft gasp escaping me. My nerves might as well be attached to a detonation device. He traces my lip back and forth. Languidly.

Still unable to look at him, I scrutinize the tiny lines of his tie. They are red. I didn't realize that during dinner. How I notice a fabric pattern at this moment is beyond me, but here I am, grasping at anything that might snap me out of the tension. I fear if I look at him, I'll lose... I'm not sure what I'd lose at this point.

And then he moves his finger below my chin and I

close my eyes because only one of two scenarios can follow. He will nudge my face up or he will continue his exploration downward. Or he might stop and push the elevator button instead of all my buttons. But I know he won't stop.

I don't want him to. Can I possibly experience this night with him and leave unscathed?

He rests his finger there, either deciding which direction he'd take or waiting for a sign from me. Waiting for a reaction, but I can't react. Giving him that green light would signify surrendering control.

I can't give that up. As much as there is a part of me that wants to let go and enjoy this, I know deep down it won't end well. Hunter might leave unaffected, but I will wake up tomorrow full of regret or guilt. Or both.

Hunter smashes his other hand on the wall behind me, beside my head. I wince and open my eyes. It wasn't a violent move, but it startled me. Sudden and fast, it contrasted with the previous stillness.

If he wanted to get a reaction from me he didn't really succeed, because aside from the startle I keep stubbornly staring at his tie.

He leans into his hand, moving even closer, taking up all the space around me.

I'm not the only one affected. His heart hammers against my palm. He can fake the flirting, his interest, the conversation, but his heartbeat is real. And it pulses deep into my core.

He allows me another beat to decide. I'm not sure why I'm not reacting. I should just push him away. I'm not going to fuck him, so what am I waiting for? For all my organs to melt in his heat? A brain aneurysm would be handy right now. Perhaps I suffered one already, since my muscles are experiencing some weird form of paralysis.

And then it comes. He nudges my chin up. It's gentle yet firm. And in a very mature way, I shut my eyes.

"Look at me, Sydney." The words grate past his throat and they rush through me like an earthquake, leaving devastation behind.

I pry my lids open, and if I thought his gaze was intense before... My God, this man can see deep inside me. It must be entertaining for him to witness all this confusion and turmoil. He holds my gaze, studying me as if trying to read my thoughts.

"What are you thinking, Sydney?"

My name from his lips is a rasp, dirty and sensual.

Why does he want to know what am I thinking? For fuck's sake, he is getting paid anyway. He doesn't need to work overtime.

"I think you're very good at your job." It's just a whisper, but it could have been a tornado because he flinches like my words caused him pain. My mind spirals to a new level of confusion.

"You think it's just business to me?" He snorts.

He shakes his head and pushes off the wall. Losing his warmth impacts me more than I care to admit. As much as I'm grasping my belief that this is not a good idea, my body is not in agreement. And now Hunter acts offended?

"An honest transaction, you called it." This time my voice is steadier. My conviction not so much.

His Adam's apple bobs up and down and he opens his mouth, but then changes his mind and pushes the button without saying a word.

The elevator lurches up and I grab the sidewall rail for balance. I wish there was a bar to settle the war between my mind and body.

The core of my problem is my mind not being a hundred percent on board with the abort mission either. The physical attraction is undeniable, but the conversation downstairs left me craving more. I want to get to know this man.

Sleeping with him would lead to regret, but talking to him might lead to a deeper connection. And he was right. That is so much more intimate. How does one shake that off?

Hunter doesn't look at me anymore. He drums his fingertips on the sides of his legs while standing a step ahead of me. Even though his previous closeness and his later reaction left my mind scrambling in all sorts of directions, I'm trying to use the time to gather myself.

When the door dings open, he steps out and slides his arm in, to keep them from shutting again, so I can exit safely.

His smirk is back, the one he carried into the lobby when we met earlier. It seems tense, but it's there. That confident grin is a part of his toolbox. A professional mask. Devastatingly handsome, but still only a mask.

I wish I had an inventory list of all the tools of his trade so I could find the ones that belong to the man himself, not the professional. Would I be pleased or disappointed?

When he places his hand at the small of my back to lead me toward the room, the tingling in my core returns.

Hunter opens the door. "After you, Sydney." Again, he kind of hisses the S in my name. Nobody has ever said my name with so much steam.

Oh my God. London really went out of her usual frugal way and picked decadence over anything else. This isn't a room. It's a suite the size of a ballroom, and I can only see the living area from my place in the doorway. The level of luxury is beyond reasonable. It's tasteful, I think, but definitely not understated. No, this is opulence in your face.

Money has never been an issue in my family. My mother was from an old family that made a fortune in the financial district. And while her parents had never approved of my blue-collar father, we lived comfortably. And the family's finances improved further when my father met Bianca Cassinetti two years after my mother's passing.

Most of my siblings are wealthy, either successful entrepreneurs or managing their trust funds sensibly. I chose to be a teacher, but it wasn't my choice to spend most of my money to pay off Jeremy's debts. But I've made my peace with that.

Places like this room are not my thing. As though this whole encounter isn't uncomfortable enough, the room is not going to make me feel relaxed.

"Your sister wants only the best for you," Hunter says, and walks to the coffee table where a bottle of champagne is waiting in a bucket of ice. "Would you like some?"

"Yes." I take off my shoes and, all my hesitations aside, the softness of the carpet is unbelievably soothing on my feet. Perhaps there are some advantages to this kind of luxury.

There is a long sofa in front of the window and two love seats on each side of the table. We take one each, sitting across from each other. His heat reaches me despite the glass coffee table between us.

"Do you gamble, Hunter?" I take a sip.

He doesn't answer right away. He supports his glass on his thigh, rolling the stem between his fingers. I don't think he is contemplating my question. He suggested this isn't just business to him and that indirect admission of his interest in me hangs heavily between us, but I'm not going there.

"I guess I gamble in some areas of my life, but if you're asking in the literal sense, I don't. Do you?" He continues twirling his glass, not looking at me. Strangely, I wish he would.

It's not the intensity of his burning gaze I miss. But penetrating me with those hooded eyes seemed his sole mission this whole evening, so now it feels like he's backing away from... well, from whatever this is.

"I've been to Vegas a few times, but I can't say I gamble. I do have gambling debts, though." I snort at the irony. Shit, why did I even admit that? I asked him the question because I want to know the motivation behind his line of work, not to share the gory details of my life.

"You went to Vegas a few times and ended up with gambling debts? They must have been some trips." He takes a sip of champagne and looks at me finally, but his look is guarded now.

I achieved what I wanted with my comment in the

elevator, so why do I feel like the villain here? Like I'm the losing party?

"No, I inherited those from my late husband." I shrug. He lifts his eyebrows. It's an almost imperceptible reaction and I'm not sure what surprised him more. The fact that I'm a widow or that my husband was a scumbag who left me with trouble I'm still sorting out. "Do you have debts?"

I don't want to talk about myself. Also, I have an acute need to understand his motivations. It may be just my misconception, but I assume a gigolo would be a shallow man. The man across from me feels all sorts of deep.

He puts his glass down, stands up and takes off his jacket. He drapes it over his seat, moving with the grace of a predator. Hunter. It's fascinating to watch him glide around as he gets closer to me. He loosens his tie and pulls it over his head. While he works the first two buttons of his shirt, I scoot to the farthest corner of my love seat.

It's a protective move, but he takes it as an invitation and sits down, rolling his sleeves up. I didn't know forearm muscles could be this defined. He leans forward and scoots my feet off the floor.

Instinctively, I extend my arm and the wine sloshes over the rim. With his burning palms on my ankles, he yanks me to angle my body to face him. He relaxes against the sofa's backrest and puts my feet into his lap. It's strangely familiar and domestic.

I'm focusing all my mental faculties on breathing and swallowing. I've been doing a lot of the latter, but the lump in my throat keeps swelling.

Trying to get back to our conversation, I'm about to repeat my question when Hunter pushes his fingers into the ball of my foot, massaging it, and I melt into the soft cushions behind me.

This room is over-the-top elegance, but Hunter's hands kneading my soles with just the right amount of pressure is exactly the type of luxury I appreciate. I close my eyes and a moan escapes me.

He's very generous with his caresses. God, what those hands could probably do to other parts of my body.

I'm deep in a blissful oblivion when his voice jerks me back to reality.

"I have medical bills."

Chapter Six

Hunter

Sydney snaps her eyes open and straightens, shoving her feet into my crotch. As her heel connects with a sensitive spot, I double over, pain vibrating through me. She realizes what happened and swings her legs to the floor.

"Oh my God, I'm so sorry." She jumps up.

I wince and stretch my arm. "I just need a moment." I lean back, tilting my head backward and releasing the pain with a long exhale.

When I open my eyes she is standing above me, biting her bottom lip, and it takes all my willpower not to pull her into my lap.

"I'm so sorry. Do you need an ice pack?" Her

cheeks are crimson, her face a grimace as if we shared the pain.

"No, it wasn't that bad. I didn't mean to startle you."

"And I didn't mean to dig my heels in…" She gestures with her hands and then covers her face. "God."

I chuckle. "Come on. Sit down. I'll be fine."

Her shoulders shake. I can't see her face, but God I hope she's not crying. "Sydney?"

"I'm sorry." Her voice is strangled with laughter.

I rest my head back and laugh as well. "I'm glad my misery is a source of entertainment for you."

She drags her hands down and bursts into laughter. The sound of it spreads warmth in my chest. A woman's laugh has never been a particular attraction for me. I didn't even know it could be a thing. But Sydney's laughter moves me like an emotional musical score.

I'm kind of grateful for the painful interruption. Not because the conversation was getting too personal, but because for some reason touching her feet had a direct line to my cock. The last thing I needed was to sport a boner. This woman is affecting me enough already. Fuck.

Sydney apologizes a few more times and finally sits beside me again. She folds her legs under her and turns with her arm over the backrest. She is closer than she was before. We stare at each other for a moment and a sparkling tension replaces the lighter mood.

"You never told me where you would like to time travel to." She swallows and I have a hard time tearing my eyes off her neck. I want to kiss her there. To sink my teeth into the hollow above her collarbone.

I'm relieved she abandoned her interrogation. I don't know why I told her about the reason behind my moonlighting as an exclusive escort, but she pissed me off with her comment in the elevator. Am I the only one feeling the connection between us?

Sydney is trying to stop herself from having fun and I don't understand why. It's not my place to push her, to provoke her. She believes dinner was simply a job performance for me. She doesn't believe the confusing feelings are honest. Real. Too real for my comfort.

Though I'm trying hard to chalk this up to just a mutual physical attraction, I wish I could take her out on a few dates. Something I can't do. Something I've accepted I can never do because of the situation that's led me to this job.

"Ancient Rome. Atlantis. Any other civilization that vanished. I'd like to be there to see and understand firsthand what happened. And why."

A smile lingers on her face and I'm ridiculously pleased she likes my answer.

"You want to prove the historians wrong?" She raises her eyebrow, taunting me.

"At the end of the day, all the records are just interpretations of those who'd taken them. We don't know what really happened."

She smiles at me and I'm glad she's relaxed again. "And let's not forget, most of the *facts* were recorded by men." She leans over to pick up her glass again.

"You don't trust men?" I tease her, but the smile disappears from her face.

"I can't say past experience has reinforced my confidence in the male population, but I trust my father. And to a certain extent my stepbrothers, I think."

"Doesn't that leave you lonely?" She mentioned her late husband and debts, so I guess I know who to blame for her attitude.

I wish I could ask her about her father and brothers, but I've made too many exceptions tonight already, and talking about family would be another lapse into forbidden territory. I only venture there as a listener if the client needs it.

Sydney averts her eyes with a frown. "It leaves me in control." She looks back at me, probably seeking understanding.

"If you don't trust people, you have control? Explain that to me." I have dealt with many lonely clients, but I don't think I know anyone who's chosen loneliness.

"My husband betrayed me and I only found out after he died, leaving me with consequences. I lived with him for over four years, and I didn't know him at all. I had my future planned out, and because I trusted him, I lost it. I lost control over my plans because they had to be adjusted due to his betrayal."

"Would you have proceeded with your plans if he died without betrayal?"

Her expression tells me she's never thought about it that way. She opens her mouth and closes it again, and then takes a generous gulp of her wine.

I get the feeling she doesn't appreciate me challenging her. I don't even know why I did. I should listen and support. That's the key to success in this profession.

"I think having control over your life is important to be content," she says finally.

"But we don't have control, do we? You can't plan for a disaster, a robbery, a disease. What you can do is live your life every day the best way possible. As if it was your last one. Because regardless of how well you think you're prepared, the only control you have is over your attitude. How you respond to all the bad shit life throws your way. And choosing to exist instead of live is not an option in my book."

We stare at each other for a long time. I see the war brewing inside her, but she doesn't share what she's thinking.

Finally, she says, "I can live my life fully without a man in it." Her words ring with regret.

Still, I get that. Hell, I'm living it, but it wouldn't be my first choice. I don't tell her that. "I'm sure you can, but sometimes the walls we build to protect us grow so high and impenetrable, they isolate us."

A sad smile crosses her face, and she stands and refills her glass. She gulps it down, possibly searching for courage. To do what?

"I miss dancing." She puts the glass down.

I didn't expect that. "You'd like to dance, Sydney?"

"Jeremy was an excellent dancer. I miss little about our life together because it's all tainted by his deception, but I've always loved dancing and I haven't danced in such a long time."

There is vulnerability in her admission, and I want to kill her husband all over again for robbing her of this, among other things. I pull out my phone and find a slow love songs playlist. The music pours gently into the large space.

I stand up, place the phone on the table and kiss Sydney's hand. "Would you do me the honor?"

She chuckles and curtsies. "I'd love to."

As soon as I pull her closer, she gasps. It's a soft sound, but it sends electricity down my spine. My cock twitches. I've had a semi several times since we met down in the lobby. Where I lost my self-control tonight, I'll never know.

I hold her tight, enjoying the warmth of her body, the way she fits against me. Lowering my head, I bury my nose into the crook of her neck, inhaling her essence. She smells of citrus and something very feminine.

I don't think she meant this when she suggested dancing because we have barely moved, locked in each other's arms, swaying to the rhythm of the sensual music.

A realization hits me, shocking me to the core. I don't want to sleep with her. I don't want to ruin the tender connection by jumping into bed with her. It's a strange concept for me, but I want to spend time with her.

I don't want her to think she is just a client. Because somehow over the course of the last few hours she stopped being one. And that's not a plausible scenario in my case.

Since I checked out from the dating scene, I've been doing just fine. Tonight is the first time in three years that I'm regretting how little I have to offer this woman. Who would want to date a gigolo, after all?

Another song starts and I twirl Sydney around, push her away and then pull her back, moving around the room and creating a subtle distance between us. I need to snap out of my attraction so I'll give her the dance she missed, rather than hanging onto her like this is a real date.

She seems to enjoy herself, which scares me because my needy side—one I didn't fucking know I have—interprets it as her interest in me. She was close to bolting at first, yet here we are. I'm treading on ice too thin for anyone's good. I need to let her lead. And keep her in a playful, safe zone.

"You're a wonderful dancer." Sydney laughs as I pivot and dip her, her hair brushing the carpet. I get a vision of those brown strands splayed across the pillow as I fuck her and I almost drop her. Shit.

"Not as good as you." I pull her back up, but step away immediately. We can't dance. "I need a drink." I dash for my glass and walk to the window. As far away from her as possible.

The lights of the city sparkle below me, teasing the promise of fun and entertainment, the never-ending joy of life. I wish I could absorb some of it.

The double door to the bedroom slides open and I stiffen.

"You don't have to stay the night, but you can if you want to." Sydney's voice tickles my ears and my stomach. I don't know what she is doing, the soft carpet not revealing much, but another door clicks open and then closed, and soon water runs in the bathroom.

I close my eyes. Perhaps, I should sleep with her. Get her out of my system. She practically gave me the option. Why am I thinking about it?

I watch the nightlife below, realizing this situation is going to end poorly regardless of my or Sydney's next move. Any way I slice it, we can't see each other ever again because I can't offer her what she deserves. I can't win her trust, and not only because someone before me already made that into an uphill battle.

Why am I even analyzing it? I'm desperately trying to find a win in this losing situation, but there isn't one.

I gulp down another glass of champagne. A cone of light shines from the bedroom as Sydney opens the bathroom door. Her silhouette moves around as she pulls the bedcover back. She's a vision. A towel covers her body, a secret waiting to be unraveled.

The light from the wardrobe casts a warm glow on her and I step into the doorway, scanning her beautiful figure. Droplets of water are scattered across her shoulders and I want to lick her dry. The curve of her neck is begging to be kissed. She pulls the bathrobe from the hanger and drapes it over her shoulders, sliding her arms into the sleeves.

The towel drops and I inhale sharply. I want to pounce on her and not move at the same time. Fastening the sash, she walks around the bed and climbs in. She doesn't say anything, just curls into a ball, pulling the cover over her ankles.

For a woman who claims not to trust men, she's just put a lot of trust in me. The question is, what does she trust will happen? That I'll take good care of her? Or that I'll leave her alone? The former conviction to not sleep with her weakens and grows stronger at the same time.

Dressed, I get into the bed beside her. She doesn't turn, doesn't initiate anything. Like in the elevator earlier, she is stubbornly waiting for me to decide. For some reason, whatever I decide makes me feel like an asshole, so I go for the golden middle path.

I turn to her and pull her closer. She stiffens but relaxes when she realizes that spooning is all we'll do.

I don't plan on sleeping because there is no way I'll loosen up enough with her against me, but her breathing is like a relaxant for me, and as I feel her drifting away, I close my eyes too.

I wake up with a start. We didn't draw the drapes last night and a newly-awakened Manhattan sun is piercing through the window.

I'm curled in the same position, my limbs rigid from the weirdest night I've ever had. What is it about this woman that has me all conflicted? I should just get going right now. In the light of day, my lapse in judgment is growing exponentially.

Sydney lies on her back. The morning rays render her hair a mahogany hue. Her robe fell open, unveiling the swell of one breast, and my cock immediately springs to attention.

She is beautiful, and so peaceful. I gently pull her robe to cover her and can't resist leaning in to brush her temple with my lips. She utters a soft moan and wiggles closer, wrapping her arms over my shoulders. Fuck.

"Good morning," I whisper to make sure she is fully awake and aware.

Her eyelids flutter open and she smiles contently, only to realize where she is and who I am. She jerks up to sit, pulling her robe tighter. "Good morning," she blurts and it sounds like an accusation.

A blush spreads over her face. I better give her time to recover. "I'm going to take a quick shower. Would you like me to order breakfast?"

"No, I'm good." She shakes her head vigorously, and then she freezes. "I mean, unless you want something." She glances at my raging boner and bites her lip.

"I'm not hungry. I'll go take care of this situation." I gesture to where her eyes landed and then leave quickly for the bathroom.

Take care of the situation? What the hell? *Real smooth.* Did I just tell her I'm going to jerk off? Fuck. *Am I?*

I let the cold water pound my tense muscles, staying as long as possible to will my cock to stand down, which proves difficult since the idea of Sydney on the other side of the door continues to excite me. Goddammit. Quite the professional I am.

Dressed in my shirt and pants once more, I find Sydney in the living room, standing by the window in her green dress.

"I had a great time, Hunter." She faces me, pursing her lips, all business. It's a tense announcement, not really an exciting proclamation.

I put on my jacket and shove the tie in my pocket. If someone sees me leaving they would never guess what happened in this room. That I spent my night fighting my attraction to this woman.

"I'm glad, not only because you had a hard time accepting this date to begin with, but because I want you to have a great time. You deserve to have fun."

She sighs and I erase the distance between us in a few fast strides. I tuck a curl behind her ear and leave my hand there, cupping her face. Her cheek is soft under my thumb. Before I can change my mind, I pull a card from my inner pocket.

"I'm breaking all sorts of rules and going completely against common sense, but if you ever want to... I don't know, hang out..." I cringe inwardly. Idiot. I push the card into her hand.

She blinks a few times. "You're a personal trainer?"

I need to leave now before I say or do something stupid. But I will regret it if I don't at least...

I cup her face with both hands. My eyes drop to her mouth and her breath hitches. It's the softest sound, but it's enough to silence the world outside, all the voices. The voice of reason included.

I capture her lips. And it's not gentle. I don't give her a chance to respond or to protest. I kiss the hell out of those beautiful, full lips that teased me unknowingly all night.

She goes rigid at first. I almost step away when Sydney parts those lips for me, inviting me in. I devour her like a man starved. Her mouth is sweet and warm, a tease and a regret, just like she is.

She grips my lapels, holding on to me and pulling me closer. There has been little joy in my life in recent years, so I treasure moments like warm dinner rolls with melting butter, or new words Caro mispronounces, or the fresh air after the rain cleans the city. All those moments combined don't come close to the overwhelming sense of joy and rightness this kiss evokes in me.

A feeling I try to push aside because it's not right. It's not joyous. It's an exploration of what could be, but never will.

When we finally come up for air, her eyes are bewildered and lit up with desire. Or maybe that's what I want to see in them. But I've kissed many women in my life and not once has it felt like this.

"I better go now," I say, not only because my cock is saluting again. Reluctantly, I walk to the door. I don't like that our future is impossible. That she might never call. That even if she calls, nothing real can come out of it.

This is goodbye. Once and forever. I turn and take in the beauty of the woman. The sun is shining behind, accentuating her curves. Our eyes meet.

I take a mental snapshot before I find my voice. "This was the best date I've ever had."

With that I walk out, knowing this will remain a beautiful memory, but nothing else.

Chapter Seven

Sydney

I stare at the closed door, waiting for my brain to finish its aimless tour around the world and finally do me some good inside of my head.

What was that? How have I walked through my life and never once experienced this? That kiss was hungry and decadent, leaving me breathless and wanting more. If that kiss suggested what could have been last night, I'm already torturing myself with regret.

Ironic, considering I wanted to prevent the regret by avoiding sex last night. My efforts fell flat because something beyond physical connection sprouted between us. Just as Hunter predicted. Intimacy.

And now it's not just regret. Need and want filled

my veins at his touch. Jesus. *Okay, Sydney, snap out of it. He is a good kisser. He made you feel heard, safe and beautiful. He challenged you and made you laugh. It was the best date I've ever had.*

Hunter said the same thing. Did he mean it?

Why am I so insecure? London's gift sucks. Big time. It turned my beliefs upside down. It's much easier to believe all men are assholes when you stay away from them and only sample here and there from the often pathetic pool of online dating.

My lips tingle from Hunter's kiss. I want to ignore it, but instead I reach to touch them. At least I get to keep this memory. Maybe there is a man out there who is as interesting and hot as Hunter, and has a boring job that doesn't include fucking other women.

By my feet, I spot the card he gave me. It must have landed there in the heat of the kiss. I pick it up and trace the letters of his name with a smile.

What's wrong with me?

I drop the card into my purse and leave the room. I'm kind of glad he left before me. I've been feeling strangely nervous since I opened my eyes this morning. What was I thinking when I didn't send him away last night? And why did he act like a gentleman after he joined me in bed? Damn him. The man makes it diffi-cult to dislike him.

The only moment I disliked him was before I met

him. Solely on the basis of his occupation. Hobby? Whatever it is. He was going to tell me more. Medical bills? The conversation got lost in the awkwardness of me kicking him in the balls. Shit.

Is he sick? Is he dying? Does he sell his companionship and body to women to pay for medicine? Oh God, he was going to share the details and I interrupted his confession.

The elevator opens to the lobby and I step out. I approach the concierge, but I realize I don't want a cab. I want to walk for a few blocks before I take the subway.

I'm rested because I slept well. Better than I have since Jeremy passed. Even all wound up by indecision and Hunter's presence, I felt safe and calm enough to sleep deeply.

He really is good at this. I only wish I could file this encounter away. Will I call him? I might, if only to find out if he is okay. How did I change the subject so quickly and not ask about the medical bills?

I step out of the revolving doors at the same time that Hunter is jumping into a cab. Instinctively, I gesture for another car and it immediately pulls to a stop.

"Could you follow that car, please?" What? Why am I following him? I need to know he's okay. I wish I'd asked him about it. I pushed him to share and when he was about to reveal something so important I completely side-tracked the conversation.

I pull out his card again and stare at it. If I'm so interested in making sure he's not dying, I could just call him. This is so not me. I became a stalker overnight.

I don't tell the driver to take me home and I give up on finding justification for my behavior. We drive over the bridge. He lives in Brooklyn, like me. Another thing we have in common. *Stop it.*

I assumed he lives in Manhattan. Where his clients are. But I guess he really doesn't do this to improve his lifestyle.

Slowly we navigate through Brooklyn Heights, and when we turn a corner I spot Hunter getting out of the cab.

"Stop here. I don't want him to see us."

In the rearview mirror, the driver raises his eyebrows and a flush of heat spreads across my face. What the hell am I trying to accomplish here?

"The meter is running." The driver shakes his head.

Well, it's not like we can turn now and risk getting discovered.

The street is lined with brownstone homes. It's a great neighborhood, probably paid for by London's wealthy friends who are his clients.

I slide lower in my seat as Hunter, several houses ahead of us, takes two steps at a time. He doesn't even have his keys out when the door opens and my stomach tightens. A little girl bounces into his arm, followed by a woman.

Hunter holds the girl in one arm and snakes the other one around the woman's shoulders. He kisses the crown of her head and they disappear inside. A happy family.

The street blurs in front of me as tears pool around my eyes. I blink them away and swipe at one that escaped with the back of my hand. I'm not going to shed a tear for that man.

I don't know him after all. That fact carries more gravity in light of my discovery. I thought I was crazy to have followed him. I don't understand what possessed me to do it, but I'm glad I did.

I had so many reservations about his work and now I know it's much worse. He has a wife and a daughter and he fucks wealthy women all around Manhattan. London said he came highly recommended.

I lower my face into my hands, shaking like an aspen tree. I want to focus on my anger, but disappointment and sadness top the chart of my emotions.

"The meter is running," the driver repeats.

* * *

I push the sofa away from the wall, swearing as my nail bends then breaks. Sweat trickles down my spine. I have been at it for hours now, and I swear by the time I'm done this apartment will be spotless like never before.

One result of Jeremy's betrayal was a significant downsizing of my home, but I've learned to like my studio. I keep my things tidy overall, but today I'm channeling my frustration into chores with the utmost vigor.

The mission is to overwrite my thoughts. I vacuum the corner and then push the sofa back into its space. All the least visible and accessible corners are spotless now.

I don't think my cleaning therapy is having much of an effect, but it's at least bringing fatigue, so I won't stop.

As much as I want to erase the bouncing little girl and the gentle, chaste kiss Hunter gave his wife, it flashes in front of my eyes. How could I have let him fool me so much?

I store the vacuum in the tiny closet by the entrance then look around my now sterile museum of an apartment. Kitchen cabinets next. Better to attack them than my self-esteem or sanity. Both are at their lowest.

I empty the cabinets. There aren't many things to

pull out, which is oddly disappointing. I have been living alone for three years, and I sold or donated most of our things before I moved here.

I polish the shelves, so now they are not just clean, but they sparkle. I don't feel accomplished, but I keep going. I wash every dish in the sink and then dry them with a hand towel before putting them away.

As stupid and unnecessary as the activity is, it keeps my mind occupied. Barely, but it does. At least I know I can survive this. It's nothing. I had one date with Hunter. I got over Jeremy and that accounted for years of lies, so Hunter's betrayal is... Well, it's not even a betrayal because it's not like the two of us were involved.

I was a client. I wonder if his wife knows where the money comes from. *Stop!*

Somehow I make it through the day, and desperate to keep the kitchen clean, I order pizza. As soon as I hang up, I regret it. Cooking would have given me something to do. Cooking and tidying up again. Therapy at its best. If it worked.

What is wrong with me?

One kiss.

One date.

One lie.

Followed by one case of ensuing insanity. I try to read a book while I wait for my pizza and decide that a glass or a bottle of wine is exactly what a doctor would prescribe to snap me out of this funk.

I'm on my third glass when my dinner finally arrives, along with an epiphany. I'm hurt.

It might not be logical because I don't actually know the man, but somewhere between Hunter introducing himself and kissing me the following morning, despite judging his way of life, I trusted him. Or at least I let my guard down. Never again.

Hunter was right—protective walls eventually isolate you. He didn't feel like he was on the other side. He was right there with me.

Seeing me.

Hearing me.

Making me laugh.

I finish the bottle and two slices of pizza, flipping through the channels with the dedication of a binge watcher chasing a new hit series. I have no idea what's on, but I don't want to go to bed.

A couple of hours later, I stare at my ceiling. A lonely tear rolls down my cheek. I'm so freaking lonely I even consider calling Paris, who is my least favorite sister because her sunshine personality depresses me.

London wanted to cheer me up, to give me a therapeutic orgasm and an unforgettable coochie service. All her gift achieved was to remind me how lonely I've been.

I toss and turn all night, unable to find peace. Not that I'm a peaceful sleeper by nature, but the turmoil of my thoughts is as bad as it was during the weeks after Jeremy's death.

That realization pisses me off. One date—not even an honest one—doesn't compare to a marriage and the loss I experienced after Jeremy.

I swing my legs over the edge of my bed and cross the room to make myself some coffee. The polished kitchen pisses me off further because it reminds me that I cleaned it to stop thinking about the asshole.

At last, somehow, it's morning again. I take my cup to the armchair by the window and pick up my book. But it remains closed on my lap because my mind wanders, repainting the memory of Hunter's body against mine, reviving the feel of his lips on my mouth, replaying his words, his voice, our conversation.

I must be too starved for attention if one date could stir this many emotions. If I didn't know better, I would say I'm broken-hearted. The thought makes me snort.

Okay, I had a good time. Perhaps a great time, but the man gets paid to orchestrate that. And after the string of mediocre to plain awful dates I've had recently, it's only natural last night stood out.

I sip my coffee and try to focus on the page in front of me, but I have no idea what I'm reading. Great. Now he's ruined my lazy Sunday reading ritual. I finish my coffee and abandon the book. If I had a regular class, I'd be prepping or grading exams. But I don't.

Maybe London is right and I should try to get a permanent position. I can't shy away from all commitments forever. It's been three years since Jeremy deserted me—because yes, I think of his death as a desertion—so perhaps it's time for me to move on. To move past the hatred, resentment and fear.

Having a job would also help me find new friends, my circle. People who don't know how gullible I used to be, how I made choices that led me to a situation I wouldn't wish on anyone. A permanent job would definitely help with my debts.

I fire up my laptop to check the permanent positions available with the school board. But instead, I type Hunter Stewart into the search. Or is it Stuart? The search engine produces multiple results, but before I can go down that rabbit hole my phone rings and I snap the laptop closed.

Busted.

Jesus, it's not like whoever calls can see me. Or understand who I am trying to cyber stalk. Or whatever I was doing.

I check the phone's screen and groan. I don't have it in me to listen to London or avoid her questions. I'm so deeply embarrassed about the way that stupid date impacted me, I don't want to discuss it with my sister.

But I have to face her inquiry at some point, so I may as well rip the bandage off while the wound is fresh. That makes no sense. I shake my head and answer the call.

"Hey, Lo, you're up bright and early on a Sunday morning." I hope I sound like myself, but I'm never this chipper, so she's probably already figured out something is up.

"What happened with Hunter?"

Geez, no preamble. But then I realize she sounded as if she knew something was up.

"What do you mean what happened? We had dinner, we talked, and as you may have assumed, knowing me, we didn't have sex."

"Why the hell not? I source someone who can safely take care of you—"

"Stop it. I can take care of myself."

"Clearly. The combination of the vibrator and your failed dates is doing wonders for you. But back to my question. What happened?"

I roll my eyes. "I just told you."

"What I don't understand is why he returned his fee? Have you robbed the man of reason and turned him into a monk like you are?"

"He returned his fee? Why?" My heart hammers so hard I fear it'll burst inside my temple. It's a good thing I'm sitting because my limbs go weak. I use all my remaining strength to hold the phone, but even that seems too much.

I drop it into my lap and tap the speaker button. What the hell? Why did he? Is he expecting me to call him? He doesn't know I've seen his wife and daughter. Oh God.

"Well, I called him to ask." God help me, London has no shame gauge. "In his words, 'I don't want Sydney to be uncomfortable when we meet again.' Why would you be uncomfortable? When are you meeting him again?"

"Never." The events of my life are like domino blocks. As soon as I carefully place one, it tumbles and takes down everything else. Not that this Hunter thing could be compared to my previous disasters. It can't. Why do I need to remind myself of that?

"He seems to think you'll see each other. Why?"

"We kissed and he gave me his card. He said it was his best date yet." The numbness spreads through me like mercury, poisoning me with detachment. I might as well tell her everything.

"How unprofessional. It's not like you would ever date a male prostitute. What was he thinking?"

"It's not like that. We really had a great time." My voice shakes.

"Damn it. Okay, let's have breakfast. I'm downstairs."

Wait, what? "You're here? In Brooklyn?"

"I was in the neighborhood." *Unlikely.* "Put on something casual and we'll find pancakes somewhere."

I don't want to go out, but I want to stay home even less. I put on jeans and a simple black T-shirt and drag myself outside. London gets out of her car and hugs me.

"I'm sorry my present achieved the exact opposite of its intent. You were supposed to fuck him, not start a relationship."

I lean into her embrace because it feels so good to have someone on my side. "You know the worst part? I was considering giving him, us, a chance, but he's married."

And the dam breaks and I cry into London's sleeveless cashmere top. I cry because Jeremy robbed me of any joy. Because I've spent the last three years like a hermit. And I cry because the night I started opening up to the outside world turned out to be a big fat lie.

Chapter Eight

Three years later

Sydney

"Good morning, Mrs. Lowe."

The soft voice penetrates the last remains of my dream. The sheets are so warm and cozy, I don't want to open my eyes and get on with my day.

But then I remember what kind of a day it is and I push myself to sit.

"The sun isn't up yet." I rub my eyes. The drapes are open and outside it looks as if twilight still reigns.

"I woke you up early, so you don't have to rush and stress." Dan smiles at me.

Of course, he thought about all the aspects of this

morning. I didn't want to stay over. We only do sleep-overs occasionally. But I preferred staying with him instead of dealing with my anxiety alone. It's an important day, after all.

Dan's bedroom is small, but at least he has one. That might be the reason he prefers us hooking up here and avoids my studio at all costs. Soft, neutral pastel colors blend with his white furniture. There is nothing masculine about this bedroom. It's gentle and calming, like Dan's personality.

He is reliable, kind, and like the colors of his bedroom he blends well. With my life. My plans for the future. My expectations from a friend with benefits. He makes me feel safe. We're good together, but not too attached. He is the perfect solution to my loneliness.

And he spoils me. I spy the tray he is holding. "So you rob me of sleep and make me breakfast? Good morning to you too, Mr. Ravinski."

He plants a kiss on the crown of my head and places the tray in my lap. The smell of coffee mixed with fresh croissant makes my mouth water.

"It's a big step, finally getting your own class. And I'm hoping I can steal a moment with you in the broom closet after school." He sits on the edge of the bed.

"A broom closet?" I laugh and take a sip of the coffee.

"The gym lockers?" He winks.

"Ew, you better get more creative." His eyes sparkle. "Or no, don't. I can't believe I'm even discussing it. If my day goes well, you might get lucky. Here in your bedroom."

I take a bite of my croissant and Dan grabs my wrist, kisses me and takes a bite himself, the crumbs sprinkling his light gray sheets.

"I'm going to take a quick shower." He swipes the mess around the tray into his palm and leaves.

My own class. It's taken me a while, but after four years as a sub, I spent the last two years on staff, covering someone's leave, at a private girls' school on the Upper East Side. And today I'll get my class of third graders.

I've finished my breakfast by the time the water goes off in the bathroom. In the kitchen, I put the dishes into the dishwasher.

"Would you like another coffee?" I call as the door clicks and the scent of Dan's shower gel spreads through the apartment.

I pour myself a cup, but there is no answer. "Dan?" I return to the bedroom and find him standing there, a towel around his waist. He is holding something in his hand, but closes his palm promptly when he sees me. "Are you okay? I asked if you wanted another coffee."

"This might be the worst timing ever. I know that

your head is probably in your classroom already and I wanted to wait for the afternoon, but today is an important day for me too and I'd feel much better if I knew..." His eyes are darting around.

"If you knew what?" I lean against the door frame. Levelheaded Dan is never nervous. I squeeze my cup with both hands, a film of sweat covering my palms. God, what is he up to?

He opens his palm and I frown.

"A key?"

"It's a key to my apartment." If someone needed to portray hope on a billboard, they could use Dan's current expression. Only it makes no sense.

"Dan, I don't need a key, I come over when you're at home." I step closer and cup his face with one hand. "What's going on?"

He turns his head and kisses my palm, closing his eyes briefly with a long sigh. "I'd like you to move in with me."

My hand drops as if his words burned. And they do. They've scorched a hole in my stomach and the croissant is screaming its way out.

I think I blink a few times, but the situation doesn't change or disappear.

"You are right, Dan. This is the worst timing." My voice is bitter even to me. "We are both teachers and today is the beginning of the school year and you chose to mark it with such a significant decision? How dare you spring it on me like that? We have never discussed this before. I like things the way they are."

I can't look at him. Not because he caught me off guard, but because his stunned expression shows signs of hurt and I can't cope with that. I'm overreacting. I'm not being fair here. And his face shows it all.

But how did he even get the idea? How do friends with benefits turn into a living together situation without a prior discussion?

I'm not ready to give up on my independence. I'm not ready to move in with him. I love having my own place. My place lost its wasteland of loneliness stamp after I started hooking up with Dan, so I have that to thank him for, but that's what this has been. Convenient hookups.

How did I not see his head was somewhere else? Our relationship has been perfect... or so I thought. Once again, I didn't read a man correctly. Again, I misinterpreted everything.

Dan reaches out and pulls me into a hug. It's awkward with my arm outstretched to stop my coffee from spilling. "I'm sorry, sweetheart, you're right. I should have waited. Let's talk about it tonight."

Or not at all. I don't want to talk about it. I want to forget the option because I'm not ready for such a commitment. Why do we need to change anything?

I nod and kiss him because my communications skills are worth a pile of shit.

Dan breaks the kiss quickly. "Let's get ready."

Leaving my unfinished coffee on the side table, I dive into my overnight bag and lay out my dark blue skirt on the bed. I ironed and hung my white blouse last night. In the bathroom, I try to avoid Dan's eyes. He seems busy dressing up, but before I disappear, he mutters, "You wouldn't need the stupid overnight bags."

It might be meant for him only, but I hear it. The practical comment coils around my stomach and builds my resentment.

What started as a lovely morning with breakfast in bed continues on autopilot with the two of us dancing and side-stepping around each other in a choreography of hurt feelings and annoyance to the score of passive aggressiveness.

"Do you want to grab lunch together?" Dan asks as we enter the elevator.

He is wearing a gray suit that brings out his blue eyes. His light brown hair, longer on the top, is styled to perfection. Instead of his contacts, he pulled out his thick-rimmed glasses today. He's so handsome and put-together, and right this moment I know deep in my bones I'll have to break up with him.

"I'm not sure. Will you have time to come over to

my neighborhood?" I fidget with my purse, trying to avoid eye contact. Jesus, I should have stayed at my place.

"I'll be in your neighborhood." He rubs my arm gently and I almost recoil.

"You will?" That makes no sense. "Why don't you text me and see how I'm doing?" I should have lunch with him, just to tell him we're over. I don't think we can go back to casual after this. His hope for more would hang above our heads and it's not fair to him, or to me, for that matter.

"I'll text, and perhaps we can find that broom closet?" he whispers darkly and kisses my temple.

Luckily the elevator stops, and I push out before I'm forced to break up with him right here right now.

I sit at my desk in the front of the classroom. The doors of the school won't open for another thirty minutes, but I need a moment to adjust, to get ready, to accept that I'm really committing to something. To believe it's a good move. In the world I created—one where nothing is permanent—this is a huge step. I'm excited but more anxious.

I open the folder with the list of my students. There is one new girl coming in. It's good it won't be just me. I've been working here as a long-term sub teacher, but I haven't taught in this class before.

Normally what the students think of me doesn't matter. For the most part, they like me. So why am I so worked up? Perhaps I should have blow-dried my hair?

Jesus, it's eight- and nine-year-old girls. They can be mean at that age already. I groan.

My phone chimes.

Martinis to celebrate the new school year? Love. L.

London might be the only non-parent celebrating the beginning of the school year, but then London finds a reason to party all the time.

I'm about to type "raincheck" when another message comes in from Melissa at the principal's office. *Teacher's lounge now.*

I grab my purse and walk out, running into Lara who teaches the second-grade class next door to my room. "We better hurry."

"What's going on? I thought there would be an informal get-together tomorrow." I follow her down the corridor.

"The chair of the board is here to introduce our new boss."

"I thought she couldn't start until October."

"I heard she took another job and they called in the runner-up. Melissa told me it's a man and he is handsome." Lara wiggles her hips and shrugs her shoulders.

I laugh. "The last thing we need at an all girls' school is eye candy for a headmaster. Thank God I teach little girls."

We rush into the lounge along with some of our other colleagues, but I stop in my tracks in the doorway. The chair of the board stands across the room, her white dress blinding against the sun streaming from the windows behind her. But it's the man beside her that causes my mind to backfire.

Someone bumps into me as more people try to push through. I stumble inside and my eyes meet with Dan's. *What the actual fuck?*

Chapter Nine

Hunter

Clack. Clack. Clack.

The sound snaps through the darkness, invading the warmth of my dream. I struggle to ignore it, desperately fighting to stay asleep. I'm so fucking tired.

Clack.

Clack.

What the hell is that? I'm definitely more awake than asleep now. The clacking continues and I have no idea what's going on. What time is it even?

I pry one eye open and find Caro on the floor near the window. The shutters are tilted up slightly so she has better light for her torture device. Papers are strewn around her and she is stapling them. *Clack. Clack.* Fucking *clack.*

"What are you doing, honey?" I rasp.

"Honey is food." *Clack*, she snaps two papers together.

"What are you doing, Caroline?" I roll on to my back, knowing sleep is done. I run my hand over my face and push up on to my elbows.

"Stapling." *Clack.*

"I see that. Why are you doing it here, in my bedroom while I'm asleep?" I'm afraid to look at the clock because the five a.m. wake-up calls weren't fun when I had early morning fitness clients at the beginning of my career. And they are even less fun now when I have a full-time business to run.

"Don't you want to know what I'm creating?" *Clack.* She doesn't even look at me, busy with her project.

"Please tell me." I yawn.

"It's my magazine. I wrote and drew it yesterday and I made copies this morning in your office—"

"Caro, I asked you to stay away from my office." I need to start locking that room.

"I didn't move anything. I just made copies, and now I'm binding them together so I have an issue for everyone important." She lifts her eyes to me and, as always, my annoyance disappears.

"And we are all eager to get the next edition, but why are you doing it here? How long have you been up?"

"Long enough." She collects the papers, clutches them to her chest and comes over. I lean in for a kiss and she gives me a peck on my cheek.

The morning is getting better now.

Until I glimpse the clock on my nightstand. "Caro, we're going to be late!" I spring out of bed, almost toppling her over. Fuck.

I overslept on the first day of school. And it's a new school. A private one, but I have no idea if that makes any difference. Shouldn't they be more forgiving since we're paying them?

There has been so much to navigate since the inheritance. I grab a T-shirt from the floor. I wore it yesterday, but with a bit of deodorant, the snobby parents and teachers might not notice.

"Perhaps we can skip today and I'll start tomorrow?" The small voice behind me pauses me in my frenzy. I let out a long breath and squat in front of my little girl.

"Caro, sweetheart, I know it's hard to start a new school. I understand you didn't have a good time in your old one, but you have to go to school, and why not start today when it's a lazy welcome day. That way, tomorrow will be easier." I squeeze her shoulders.

She scrunches her lips to the side and thinks. I count my breaths, but we're late already so a few minutes won't make a difference.

"I don't want to go." Her voice is a whisper and I almost give in, but I know tomorrow will be harder if I give her an out right now.

"It's a short day. And there will be other girls who are anxious like you and you can support each other. I'm sure your new teacher is all excited to meet you."

I pull her into my arms and inhale the scent of her shampoo and gummy bears—I guess she had breakfast already. How many times do I have to tell my mother to stop leaving candy here?

"She or he doesn't even know me." She leans in, her lips tickling my neck.

"Well, then we need to fix that. They are missing out."

She smiles. "Can we go for ice cream after?"

"Deal. And now show me your fastest possible deployment. See you at the door in five."

"What is a deployment?"

"Get ready. Now." I pretend-frown at her and she giggles, running out of my bedroom.

We take another fifteen minutes because Caro decides she doesn't want to wear her uniform. The girl has been wearing gray and black for two years now, but I don't have time to argue, so I hope her street clothes won't draw unnecessary attention at school. I let her wear what she wants and we run out.

"Good morning, Mr. Stuart," the concierge greets us. "Aren't you late for school, Miss Caroline?"

"And you're right, Karl, we're very late. I hope Suzanne is feeling better."

"Thank you for remembering. She was discharged last week and recovering nicely. You have a lovely first day, Caroline." He winks at her and opens the door for us.

After we moved here, I refused his help. It's fucking ridiculous to have someone open the door for me, but it became obvious I was hurting his pride by not accepting, so I gave up fighting and just let him assist us. In fact, sometimes I invent an errand just to make him happy.

The school is walking distance. It was one of the deciding factors for me, but today it feels like the distance doubled overnight. Partially because Caro is dragging her feet.

"I don't think that ice cream is happening if you walk backward, sweetheart."

She stops and puts her hands on her hips. "I'm not walking backward."

"No, right now you're fu-freaking not moving at all. Caroline, I understand you don't want to go to school and you have every right to feel that way, but I'm begging you to give this school a try."

"What if they are mean?" She looks down. In that simple gesture I sense the suffering she's already experienced, and a wave of fury sweeps through me. She doesn't deserve all the shit life has dealt her.

I scratch my nape. "I'm not going to tell you they won't be mean because I don't know that. But I'll do everything I can to make sure you feel comfortable there. Promise me you'll tell me if something or someone scares you. I want to know, so I can help you. Can you be brave for me?"

"I'm not brave. I'm scared."

"Courage means we do things we fear. This is a great school and I'm sure you'll love it there."

"I doubt that," she grumbles and starts marching.

I would give my kidney to change the first eight years of her life, but even if I donated all my organs, it isn't in my power to make things better for her. Not enough. At least now we can go to a school where our money hopefully buys us understanding and support.

"Will you wait for me?" Caro slides her hand into mine. She's fiercely independent, so this gesture is telling.

"Granny is coming to pick you up. I have three meetings today and I don't know when I'll finish."

"What about that ice cream? I'm not going

anywhere if there is nothing to look forward to." She stops again, tugging at my arm.

I pull her forward. At least we're at the school already. We ascend the stairs, painfully slow.

"Granny will take you for the ice cream, and knowing the two of you there might be cake or some other poison included."

She giggles. "Will Granny stay the night?"

"She will, because I'm meeting Uncle Ash later." I drag her behind me, hoping no one assumes I'm kidnapping the kid. She really is resisting. I hope the little girls here aren't auditioning for *Mean Girls* 2.0.

"Aren't you with him at work all day?"

"Unfortunately, yes."

"That's mean. Oh, no!" She stops, her eyes wide open.

"What happened? I was just joking, Caro. I like Ash just fine. Let's go." The silence emanating from the school confirms our lateness. The last thing Caro needs is to be noticed this way. How did I miss my alarm?

"I forgot to make a copy of the magazine for Ash," Caro whimpers.

"You'll make him one after school." She started it to record her memories, her version of a journal. The magazine is important to her. "Come on. We need to find your class."

"Or we can come tomorrow?" Her large eyes shimmer with hope.

"Oh, you're coming tomorrow, but you're also staying today."

She trudges through the polished floors. Laughter sounds from behind a door. That's good. Kids are laughing here. Hopefully Caro will too.

We make our way to her class and I squat down. "Remember, you're a very smart and kind girl. And if you feel overwhelmed, think of the ice cream."

I knock on the door and open it. Many pairs of girls' eyes turn to look at me. And one more pair. Emerald-green eyes I've worked hard to forget.

Several things happen at the same time.

I swallow a swear word, trying to ignore the pull at my chest.

Sydney drops a binder she was holding and papers go flying.

A couple of girls scramble to collect them.

It all takes the longest second of my life before I realize the small punching sensation on my leg is Caro's fist.

I look down and meet her face. Her eyes are wide and her lips are pursed. So much for helping her transition seamlessly.

"Our alarm didn't go off," I say. "Caroline is late, but I take full responsibility."

I want to say nice to see you or why didn't you call, but thank God some of the blood flow returns to my brain and I act semi-normal. I kiss Caro's head and she grabs my hand.

Luckily, Sydney recovers and smiles. Fuck, I forgot how sexy her smile was. Mostly because she isn't aware of it. It's not staged sexiness. It's just her.

"Nice to meet you, Caroline. We're so happy you made it. Come on in and we'll find you a seat." She offers her hand to Caro who reluctantly steps forward, but immediately seeks my encouragement or permission to bolt, her eyes pleading.

I nod and beckon her forward with my head and stumble back into the hallway.

What are the odds?

Chapter Ten

Sydney

Despite my better judgment, I agreed to meet Dan in Central Park. For lunch. I'm not even hungry. I sit at a bench where we've eaten before, hoping he won't bring me a turkey Reuben from my favorite deli. I don't want a delicious sandwich from him. I want an explanation. An apology.

Who am I kidding? There is no way we can continue this relationship. I would be misleading him. Have I been misleading him already?

Children stroll around, enjoying ice cream and September sun. Everyone is celebrating the beginning of the new school year. Well, okay, not all the kids. And perhaps most parents are relieved that the responsibility of bringing up their offspring is now shared with people like me.

Irony really. Because what do I know about living life? Nothing. I've spent almost ten months with a man in a no-strings-attached relationship and he invites me to move in and forgets to tell me he's my new boss. I guess I shouldn't complain. I could be suffocating for real, after all.

I should probably be relieved he fucked up. His omission gives me a bit of an upper hand here. I'm so mad I don't even know how I feel about him being my boss.

We met when I was a sub for a week at his previous school. He was well-respected by his colleagues, I think. I don't mind that he is my boss. That isn't the problem. I hate that he didn't tell me about it.

I channel all my energy into the issue with Dan because I'm scared to think about the other man who wrecked my balance this morning.

What are the actual odds of Hunter's daughter starting in this school? In *my* new class. Shit. I won't think about that. I won't think about that. I repeat the mantra while I think about his tousled hair, the surprise on his stupidly handsome face. I won't think about him.

Since when does a simple black T-shirt scream sin?

And he has tattoos on his biceps. I didn't know that. I wish I still didn't.

Okay, I established he was an asshole three years ago. Period. Damn him for gliding back into my life and my mind. At least if he wasn't so impossibly attractive. I'm an adult woman. I'll be professional. And avoid him at all costs.

"I told you I'd be around for lunch." Dan startles me from my failed attempt at not thinking about Hunter. From now on, I'll refer to him as Caroline's father.

My new boss looks half-amused, as if his being around was an excellent inside joke, but he's scanning my face for my reaction, half-anxious. He sits down and places the lunch bag between us. Of course he got the Reuben. And smartly, he used it as a barrier between us.

"I got you your favorite." He points to the sandwich.

"I'm not hungry." Really mature.

"Come on, Syd, let's talk about it all." Dan pulls out his chicken salad on rye. His usual.

One quality I always appreciated about Dan was how predictable he was. Until now. I didn't predict the move-in invitation, or the omission about his new job.

"You found time to ask me to move in with you, but you didn't think of mentioning you're my new boss?" I fold my arms across my chest and turn my head to face him. There's remorse on his face, but a light smile as well. Is he mocking me?

"I didn't want you to feel more nervous than you already were. The offer came only last week, it was a surprise. It was a complicated situation because I didn't want to let my old school down on such short notice. And you were fretting about the beginning of the school year already—"

"Don't use me as your excuse. Yes, the job is important to me, but your news impacts me as well. Have you even checked the ethics policy?"

He winces. I'm not even sure why I point that out, because there is no way we're staying together.

"You don't need to check it anymore, *boss*." The snarl in my voice surprises even me. "You lied to me."

"No, I didn't." Dan drops the sandwich back into the bag.

"Semantics. You kept something important from me and that's almost like lying."

"Don't you fucking compare me to your late husband." He stands up, daring to tower over me. It pushes me up as well.

"Don't you fucking act like him."

We glare at each other as the air fills with frustration and anger, their teeth sinking deep. Dan sighs and steps closer. A small part of me wants to rise above it all and forgive him. It would be easier. Could we just fall back into our predictable routine?

I dismiss the idea as soon as it comes and move back. The distance between us is negligible, yet we have never been further apart.

He has a minor cut on his chin from his morning shave, but otherwise he is perfect. Almost too perfect to be true. Have I idolized him all this time because he pulled me out of my years-long funk?

He didn't share a big life decision and I blame him. But over the ten months of our relationship I've only let him in marginally. To a safe depth. That way he couldn't hurt me. And yet he stuck around.

A little girl giggles behind us and I turn, breaking the moment. The tension. The fragile hope.

A man has her over his shoulder and they bounce around, laughing. I want to be that carefree. But I'm not.

I turn back to Dan. "I'm sorry, but I don't think we want the same thing from this relationship."

He frowns and blinks a few times. "What are you saying?"

I don't even know what I'm saying. A war wages inside me. The comfort of Dan against the fear of loneliness. But I can't draw my happiness from another person. It's not like Dan has even made me happy. He just... He was around. Available. I took advantage of it, so I didn't have to stare at the ceiling every night, alone.

I took advantage, but I also really believed we were on the same page. "I think we shouldn't see each other anymore."

He opens his mouth, but I raise my hand to stop him. "I'll see you tomorrow at work." A ridiculous statement in light of not wanting to see him anymore.

I turn and leave Dan and my Reuben sandwich behind, a sole tear keeping me company, mostly sad I let things progress this far.

"I thought you didn't want to celebrate the fucking beginning of the school year." Lo slides into the booth at a cocktail bar near her condo. I've been sitting here for an hour nursing a drink as I waited for her.

After I got back home, the walls started closing in on me. Or my thoughts did. I don't want to think about Hunter. I want to rewind back to my simple life when Hunter was the asshole I hadn't seen since our date.

London looks me up and down and raises her eyebrows. "That bad. Are those girls mean to you?"

I snort. That's another thing Hunter and Dan took from me today. The first day was actually fantastic, but I didn't get a chance to absorb and enjoy that.

"One of my students is Hunter's daughter. And Dan is my new boss. He also asked me to move in with him and we broke up." I wave at the server.

London slouches deeper into the beige leather bench like she's at home watching a boring movie. In her white button-down and jeans, she looks like a model.

"Who is Hunter?" She cocks her head.

If I hadn't finished my cocktail while waiting for her, I'd hurl it into her face right now. Geez, ending a stressful day with a dose of aggression. "The man I've tried not to think about for the past three years."

London sighs. "Fuck. I was really hoping it was a different Hunter."

The server comes over and Lo orders us six drinks.

"Is someone joining us?" I frown.

"No, but this place will be packed in half an hour and it'd take ages to order."

I shake my head. "It's a school night."

"You're welcome." She grins, adjusts her top and scans the long bar lining the wall across from us. I know that predator look, so I wait. She scrunches her nose and shrugs before she returns her attention to me.

"What am I going to do? I can't see him every freaking day and pretend he didn't rip my heart out."

"Don't be so dramatic. You spent one night with

him." She swats her hand in my direction. "*Sans* sex," she deadpans.

No one really understands this. I can't understand it. Why has a man I barely know left such an impression? One innocent night that remains the best, most intimate experience of my life.

His lips left a permanent memento tattooed on my mouth and my brain. He lied to me, he pretended the whole time, and yet my skin tingled the minute I saw him today.

Even if I somehow figured out how to avoid him, seeing his little daughter every day will be a constant reminder of a man I can't have. What? A man I don't *want* to have.

"Maybe it's a good thing. Maybe the universe sent him back to you, so you can explore your chances."

Our drinks arrive. Thank God.

"He's married, London. Why is everyone pissing me off today?"

"Pardon me, but have you considered the possibility he might not be?" She raises her eyebrows and her glass, sipping while laser pointing her expectation my way.

"Even if he isn't married anymore, he was three years ago and lied to me. He's been probably lying to his wife the whole time while sleeping with your rich friends." I gulp down my drink.

Lo rolls her eyes and raises her hands in surrender.

"He gave me his card—not his gigolo service card—and asked me to call him, while there was a woman and a child waiting for him. So even if he wasn't a male prostitute, he is a liar."

I grab another drink and the clear liquid sloshes over the edge. I lick my fingers. I should stop drinking. It's a school night, but it's not like my boss has the moral ground to do anything about it.

"Hunter is back in your life. His daughter is an innocent bystander, you need to pull your shit together and decide how to handle the situation. Given his extracurricular activities, he'll probably play it low key, so you might not need to worry. What interests me is that Hunter shows up and you immediately get rid of your boy toy." She scrunches her lips to the side, assessing me with a sharp look.

"Boy toy? Jesus, London." I shudder. "Argh, why do I hang out with you again?"

"Because you love me. Okay, spill it. What's up with Dan?"

"He is my new boss. He didn't tell me about it. I found out at work, along with all my other colleagues." I sound like a petulant child, but that must be the alcohol, because my complaint is valid.

"I see." Lo purses her lips like she knows something I don't.

"What?" I snap because that seems to be my favorite mode of expressing my feelings today.

I was supposed to celebrate my new beginning tonight. Okay, it's just a small step in hopefully the right direction, but it's huge for me. And here I am. Mad at Hunter. Mad at Dan.

Kind of mad at London, though I'm not sure why. Most of all, I'm mad at myself. Because I'm acting like I have the emotional intelligence of the little girls in my class. Great.

"You're not pissed he's your boss. You're hurt he didn't tell you about it. It's a Jeremy move in your books." She weaves her fingers together and rests her chin on them.

"Exactly. I mean, no. Not exactly. This has nothing to do with Jeremy. This is Dan keeping important information from me." I take a generous sip. The last one.

"Why did he?"

London stirs her drink with the little paper umbrella. The bar is getting busier and a few men have been eyeing our booth. It's a large table for two women. Lo scares them off with one look. For now.

"Because he didn't want me to stress out on my first day." I hear the meaning of my statement deep in my stomach. It rolls there like a boulder. Heavy and undigested.

"So he did it to protect you, not to betray you." London raises her eyebrows.

"Which side are you on?" This day keeps going downhill.

"I'm on your side. I've always been." Lo takes a sip and swings her finger to deter another hopeful companion. He scurries away.

"I know." I sigh. "I can't believe he asked me to move in with him."

London raises her eyebrows, barely able to hide her gleeful smirk. "Ooh la la. Though moving in together would be a natural progression of your courtship."

"Ooh la la? Courtship? Which century did you come from?" I shake my head and try to articulate my feelings. Who else could listen without judgment if not London? Though right now, she's having a bit too much fun. "He asked and I realized, in that moment, we're in two different relationships."

"Frankly, I'm surprised it lasted this long. But for the future, you either have a hookup—my rule is three at most with one guy—or you set up rules at the beginning." London nods.

I roll my eyes. London's freestyle way of living scares me more than commitment.

"I wish being celibate wasn't so lonely."

For a split second, I almost wish I was still grieving for Jeremy. While that was a horrible period of my life, at least there was some comfort in the sameness of it. I moved on, somewhat, but I always seem to push in the wrong direction, cornering myself rather than progressing.

"For what it's worth, I'm glad you broke up." Lo raises her glass. "Cheers to that. I never really liked him. He didn't make you spark."

I stare at her. "You never told me that."

"I was just glad you were out of that post-Jeremy funk, but I hope you didn't break up with him because seeing Hunter today made you a bit irrational." Lo pulls the menu from the holder at the edge of the table. She's so casual, as if we're discussing new shoes. Unconcerned.

I technically broke up with Dan after seeing Hunter, but I know I would have done it regardless after he blind-sided me twice with major news. "I may admit to being irrational, but all the shit with Dan happened before Hunter waltzed back into my life."

The moment I say the words, as though to accentuate what a surreal day I've been having, the man himself waltzes in again.

Chapter Eleven

Hunter

"No way. That's just your luck." Ash puts his feet up on the desk. "You find your girl a fancy school after those little fuckers did a number on her, and now you'll face the woman who broke your heart every day."

"She didn't break my heart." The memory of her and our night messed with me for a moment—or a few months—but that was it.

"You were insufferable for a year, dude." Ash clicks the pen he is holding.

Hammering and drilling echoes in the large room behind us. We're in a half-furnished office of our new location. I'm leaning against the wall because we only have one chair here so far.

This Tribeca gym is our second location within a year. I spend most of my time in our primary space on the Upper East Side. Since I was forced to accept the generous inheritance, our former lives have been a distant memory in the rearview mirror.

Ash is now my employee, but he's been more of a partner and soon he'll be managing this location. Between full-time parenting and building our empire, I haven't had the chance for much else.

But I did occasionally wonder what would have happened if Sydney called. But she didn't, so there wasn't much to ponder.

"It wasn't a year, and besides, she made it quite clear she wasn't interested and that's good. I don't have time for women, anyway."

"That's something we should correct because you'll turn into a brooding bachelor. Also, with you officially off the market, I would enjoy all the attention of our clients."

"Stop it right now. We agreed you'll keep your hands off the clients. We can't afford a lawsuit. Things are going too well. And *I am* off the market. I'm happily committed to Caroline and my work."

"Talking about work—"

I push off the wall and move to the window. I've been full of restless energy since the school drop-off.

"Why do I feel you're about to head in a direction I won't like?"

"Delaney talked to me." Ash swivels in the chair. "Again."

"She won't give up, will she?"

Delaney Rielski, a producer, has been on my case to get me work with celebrity clients in a new reality show.

"Would you at least meet with her? That kind of publicity might help us expand further. Move to LA, San Fran, Chicago, Florida."

"We'll expand there without a reality show."

Watching the commotion on the street from this place is therapeutic. The two-story space—a construction site for now—already has positive vibes. It took me some time to come to terms with the inheritance, but it makes me happy to offer these sanctuaries to our clients.

"Could you at least talk to her and hear her proposal?"

I put my forehead on the glass. "Okay, but next month. With the construction and Caro in a new school, I don't have the mental capacity for much more."

He jumps up and pumps a fist in the air, as if I agreed to do the show, but I guess I've been dodging

Delaney for long enough that even vague commitment sparks his enthusiasm.

"Let's go for drinks." He grabs his keys and phone.

"I'm not staying long. We overslept today. I can't risk that again tomorrow."

"Isn't your mom staying over? She'll drag you out of bed, hopefully mortified by the sight of your companion." Ash winks.

I shake my head. "We're going to have a beer and talk shit, not pick up women."

"They might pick up us." He flexes his biceps. "What's not to like?"

"Oh, there is plenty to like." I pat his shoulder. "But then you open your mouth and the magic is lost."

"Asshole."

"Takes one to know one."

We laugh as we walk over the floor around the area where the steam room with spa will soon be.

The golden brown paneling is not yet fully installed, but I can see we made a good choice with the slightly overstated decor. We stop to get an update from the foreman and then head out.

"Let's go to check the gym and then we can grab something to eat at the place on the corner," Ash suggests.

"Are you trying to earn employee of the month?" I

chuckle. I keep teasing him, but I've been amazed by his dedication. He still acts like an immature asshole, but he takes his job seriously and has been a tremendous help.

We didn't speak for two months after the inheritance, but we patched things up after I offered him a role with my company, and our friendship won over any resentment.

"I want to catch up with the new trainer. He had several bookings canceled this week. We should find out what's going on."

It takes us almost an hour in the cab to get to the other side of Manhattan, but we finally arrive. Our Madison Ave club caters to wealthy clients, but we also offer services to the busy white-collar professionals commuting to Manhattan. They deserve a nice gym as well.

We don't find the new trainer, but Ash walks through the facility while I peruse the mail by the front desk.

"Well, well, well, if it isn't my favorite trainer." That soprano voice—entitled attitude masked by false sweetness—makes me stiffen.

"Gigi." I nod curtly.

"I'm so glad I've run into you, Stuart. Have you lost your phone? I've been leaving you messages, darling."

Her flowery scent turns my stomach. She puts her hand on my chest and I instinctively step back only to hit the counter. She has me cornered. Goddammit.

"Did you have a good workout?" I ignore her question. I wouldn't answer her call even if she were the last woman on Earth.

Her phony smile fights against her Botoxed skin, not really succeeding in moving her numbed facial muscles. She also ignores my question. "I have theater tickets for Friday night and I'd like you to join me."

Gigi was one of my first clients when I really needed the money. Her loneliness made her bitter, or perhaps she's always been like that. I was new to the gig and crossed some lines with her.

I have successfully avoided her in the past few years, but occasionally we run into each other. Especially since she's fucking joined my gym.

"I'm busy on Friday." Being polite is useless. I've turned her down gently before and kindness only encourages her. She smells weakness and latches onto it.

She might squint now, or perhaps try to smile, but it looks more like she's constipated. Her duck-like lips quiver. "Anytime this weekend? I'll double your rate."

"Gigi, I quit a while ago, so there is no rate to double." I speak through my teeth. How dare she mention my former livelihood so freely? Someone could overhear. I need to cancel her membership.

Luckily Ash shows up and I use it as my out. "I have to go. We have a meeting we're late for. Take care, Gigi."

She crosses her arms over her chest and glares at us as we leave.

"What was that about?" Ash asks into the sound of a siren outside. The city drills into my brain, giving me a headache. This has been the longest day ever, but at least Caro had a good day at school.

"Gigi Lafontaine, a socialite and wealthy widow who doesn't take no for an answer."

"She seemed pissed at you." Ash looks back, checking she isn't around anymore. Gigi has that ghost-like effect on people.

"She'll be okay." She might be overbearing, but she isn't dangerous.

We push the door open into a full bar. I wish I was home in bed, but I can use a drink after a day that started with Sydney and ended up with fucking Gigi.

"Damn it, this joint is full." Ash turns to me. "Get us drinks and I'll find seats. I'm not squeezing in at the bar."

I get two beers and scan over the heads of other patrons. Ash waves at me from a booth. He's chatting with a vaguely familiar woman in a white shirt. She doesn't have the typical happy hour crowd vibe about her. She might be simply dressed, but she oozes style and wealth, laughing at something Ash said. Where do I know her from?

I reach the booth and the mystery is solved. Out of all the people in this crowded bar, in this busy city, Ash found us seats with Sydney and her sister. Both women widen their eyes as if they were attempting a synchronized pantomime. It would be funny. Only it isn't.

I slide in beside Sydney. She looks like she wants to throw up.

"This is Hunter," Ash introduces me, oblivious to our companions' reactions. "London and Sydney." He grins and takes a sip of his beer. "I have never been to Sydney, but London is cool." He winks. Can he be any more lame? "What?" His eyes dart between the three of us. "Do you guys know each other?" Maybe he's catching up.

"We met Hunter a few years ago, but we haven't seen him since. How have you been? How is your family?" I don't know London much, but that smile is phony. And why is she asking me about my family? What the fuck is going on?

"Nice to see you again. We're good. Caroline started at a new school today." I look at Sydney.

She fidgets with her hands and then smiles. "Yes, and she had a great day."

Ash catches up for the second time and sprays the beer across the table. "*You* are Caro's new teacher?"

"What a happy encounter," London chimes in, glowering at me.

Sydney gulps down her drink and I attack my beer with the same enthusiasm. London turns to Ash and runs her long red nails up his biceps. "So how did you get these, Ash?"

They both proceed with flirting like we're not here. It's disturbing and nauseating, but the two of them seem to have a good time.

Perhaps this is the right moment to clear the air with Sydney. We'll be seeing a lot of each other for the next ten months.

After I finally left the classroom, I briefly contemplated finding a new school, but Caro has had enough changes in her short life. She doesn't need to deal with another one because I freaked out.

There is nothing to worry about, after all. I've protected my family from any potential backlash from my former lifestyle. Mostly by luck. But I don't think Sydney would drag that cat out of the bag.

She made it clear she wasn't interested in me when she never called. I can keep my wits in my head, as much as my dick would like to have a vote.

She is uncomfortable though. Perhaps she feels guilty for never calling me. Fuck. This isn't high school.

"I'm glad you never called," I whisper to her. Hopefully that will relax her. Instead, she scoots further from me and makes a choking sound.

"So what have you been up to in the last three years?" London pulls me into conversation. Thank God. My mind was already going in a very dangerous direction.

"I opened a gym, and I'm about to open a new one in Tribeca. Ash manages the day-to-day." Ash winks at me, probably grateful I'm making him look good. "Do you come here often?"

I need to find out if this joint is off-limits for the foreseeable future. I don't go out often, but I'd like to restrict potential Sydney-sightings to the school grounds.

"I live a block away. We've been here a few times. Where is your gym?" London's eyes jump between me and Sydney.

"It's just a few doors down. Hunter's Club," Ash answers. "Not very creative with names." He chuckles. "Looks like you work out." He rakes London's figure with his eyes. Kill. Me. Now.

"I go to a gym, but maybe I should give Hunter's club a try." For some reason, she addresses this to Sydney.

"We have a private VIP membership. You can enjoy the facilities at certain times without the crowds," Ash pitches. I should be glad he's working overtime, but it's clear his motivation is far from our business.

"We have a tiered membership," I cut in, "and we built the facility in a way that we can accommodate wealthy clients who have certain expectations in terms of service and privacy. But it was important for me that the gym be affordable for people who come to work here. Premium club for a reasonable price. We lose some more prestigious clientele due to that, but I'm fine with it."

As I speak, Sydney shifts in her seat. I can't be sure, but I sense her eyes on me now. I find her face and I swear for the first time since this morning she seems genuinely interested, or impressed even. Or I'm just making up shit because I realize I *want* to impress her.

I don't want her to think of me as a gigolo. Maybe it's just because she is Caro's teacher now. I've never been ashamed of what I did. I had good reasons for it. And it was fun. But she was scandalized even as she went through with the date.

I don't want to care about her opinion of me, but I do. Fuck.

"So would my membership include personal

training from you?" London asks Ash, talking into his ear, but not trying to keep her question private.

He turns and I swear their faces are only inches apart. I can't hear what he answers, but based on London's languid smile, I think they are back to flirting.

Sydney is staring in front of her, tapping her fingers on the table. If she was a pianist, a rock beat staccato would deafen us for sure.

She grabs a glass that sits in front of London and takes a generous sip. There are four empty glasses on the table and London has only taken a sip here and there from hers. Has Sydney finished all these drinks?

As she raises the glass again, I seize her forearm. She lowers it but doesn't look at me.

I lean in, her scent causing all sorts of reactions in my body. She tenses against me. "I don't work as an escort anymore," I whisper in her ear.

She whips her head around and glares at me, her eyes flaming. She shakes her head, as if trying to rid herself of a disturbing image. Why is she still pissed at me? It's not like I didn't call her. I thought she was uneasy about facing me after she never called me, but now I'm almost confident she is angry with me.

"Are you just going to ignore me all night, Sydney?" She winces. She fucking winces. "Or shall I call you Mrs. Lowe?" I add to provoke her. Because now I'm pissed too.

Screw. Her.

"I have to use the bathroom." Her face suggests urgency. She looks at London, but her sister ignores her plea for company. What is it with women going to the restroom in groups, anyway?

I stand up to let her out of the booth. She stumbles and I grip her elbow to steady her. Her skin is smooth and warm and something cracks between us. Our eyes meet and there is a moment of... I don't know of what. Goddammit. I'm regrettably attracted to this woman.

She looks at me bewildered and jerks her arm away.

I sit back down and watch her push around people. Just before she gets sucked into the mingling crowd, I admire her swaying hips. That ass.

Stop it. She's Caro's teacher for fuck's sake. Besides, she is clearly annoyed by my company.

"I'm going to get us another beer." I stand up. Ash thumbs up my way, but his attention is fully on London, the two of them having a great time.

I weave through a group of suits to reach the bar. It takes a good fifteen minutes before I order and return. Ash's tongue is down London's throat.

"Where is Sydney?" Has she left? She can't have been in the bathroom this long.

"She went to get us more drinks." London pulls

away from Ash and adjusts her top to cover her cleavage.

Fuck. Sydney doesn't need more drinks. I look around and spot her gulping down a cocktail before she clutches four more to her chest, trying to make her way back to us. The drinks are sloshing all over her hands and shirt. She keeps bumping into people and I leap forward to help her.

I snatch the glasses from her and she stumbles into me. Now the drinks are all over my clothes. I drop them on a high table beside me, the party around it not paying attention. I snake my arm around Sydney's shoulders to help her.

She smiles at me but loses balance again after tilting her head. But the smile was genuine. Don't they say drunk people are sincere? She lowers her forehead to my chest and wraps her arms around my waist.

She mumbles something. "What?" I lean in.

"The ground is swi-sw-swirling," she slurs.

"I'm sure it is, sweetheart," I say, as my macho genes kick in and all I want is to take care of her. She clings to me tighter and I try to ignore the warmth spreading around my chest, the feeling of peace and the twitch behind my zipper. Damn it, she feels good against me.

"You smell so good, Hunter. Did you know I went

to the perfume department a few times, sniffing the bottles, trying to find your scent?" She giggles.

I kiss the crown of her head as her admission free-falls into the crevices of my soul. Sydney Lowe will have a hangover tomorrow. My symptoms might be more severe.

Chapter Twelve

Sydney

Someone must have fed me glue. I would investigate further, but a headache is pushing behind my eyeballs. I don't think I can open my eyes. Shit. Is it morning? I peek with one eye, but it's dark. Good. I can still sleep.

What day is it? Saturday? No. Shit. Tuesday. School.

I sit up, but the wave of nausea and throbbing in my forehead throws me back to the pillows. Why am I so sick? And disoriented. My mind travels in several directions when I finally pinpoint the bar. London. Cocktails. Hunter.

Fuck.

How did I get home? Well, at least I made it home. I open my eyes and the room registers.

No. No. No. This is not my home and it's not Dan's, which brings me a fleeting sense of relief. Briefly. Where the hell am I? This isn't London's guest room, either.

I'm wearing a large black T-shirt. It's a male shirt. Oh my God. I whip my head to my side and it screams in protest. At least there is no man in bed beside me.

The contents of my stomach call for attention. I feel around the side table and turn on the lamp.

Whoever kidnapped me left a glass of water and aspirin for me, but I don't think I can take them. The violent swirl in my stomach propels me out of bed.

Two doors.

One is ajar.

I dash toward it and thank God I reach the toilet before I retch. Fuck. I swear like a sailor while I splash water over my face. It accomplishes little, mostly just worsening the state of yesterday's makeup.

After I return to sit on the bed, I take the aspirin. Drinking feels good. In my mouth. My stomach, however, protests again.

The room breathes with understated luxury. As my brain decides to make its reappearance, I start piecing together the events of last night.

London ordered us three drinks each.

Hunter showed up.

London kissed his friend Ash.

Hunter said he was glad I never called.

I went to get drinks.

His scorching touch on my skin.

I hugged him? He carried me?

No. No. No.

I hurry to open the other door, my head throbbing, my heart hammering, my dignity in flames. My bare feet step from the plush carpet onto the wooden floor of a foyer or a hallway. A huge vase on a round table reigns in the middle. Everything is bright white, with a few light brown accents.

I hear a door click and my eyes lock with Hunter's. My dignity floats to my feet in ashes.

"Good morning." He smiles a smile that should be banned for safety reasons, because now my underwear is aflame as well. "London's assistant got this for you to wear."

I comb my brain for words. Several are coming to mind, but the only sentence they seem to form is *what the fuck*. So I go with that.

"What the fuck..." It's half question, half an open-ended statement.

Hunter ambles toward me and hands me the clothes bag.

"Did I sleep here?" I frown. More at myself than

him because thank you very much, dear brain, for stating the obvious.

"Clearly." The amused expression on his face should piss me off, but I have other worries right now.

"Why?"

"You were in no state to go home. It was too late for me to take you back to Brooklyn and London was otherwise engaged, so she suggested you stay here and she'd organize clean clothes for you. Apparently she has the keys to your place."

Too much information. Too many sentences, but I try to grasp the gist of the situation. "Where are we?"

"My place."

"Brooklyn Heights?" As soon as I blurt the words out, I realize the mistake.

Hunter jerks his head back and studies me. "Upper East Side."

"Oh." I don't say more, partially relieved he didn't demand an explanation of why I assumed he lives in Brooklyn and partially because my brain is broken. And not only because of my fucked-up behavior last night.

I got drunk and blacked out. What is wrong with me? I'm a teacher. I can't get drunk in the middle of the week and sleep at my student's house. This is bad.

I grab the bag from him and run back to the bedroom.

"How do you take your coffee?" Hunter's casual voice reaches me before I close the door.

I lean against it. Okay. I can get dressed and leave here without being seen. Hopefully Caroline is at her mother's. Yeah, probably that's the case. They must be divorced. He wouldn't bring me over. And he wouldn't be out at a bar if Caro was here. Unless he has a babysitter.

Opening the clothes bag, I curse London. But then I look inside a small plastic pouch that hangs on the hanger with my dress and I have to admit she did take care of me. There is clean underwear—I will never look her assistant in the eye again—and brand-new toiletries.

Yesterday's dress is on a chair in the corner, and my handbag sits on the floor beside it. I find my phone. One missed message from Dan. Okay, that's not that bad. I need to be at work in one hour. That's manageable too.

I stuff my things into the clothes bag and hope I can smuggle it into my locker before running into anyone.

The sun is warming up the Manhattan skyline and I pause for a moment to admire the view of Central Park. Wow. Hunter has done well for himself. Then I remember where the money came from and I deflate.

In clean clothes and with my face washed, I feel

reasonably normal. The only thing left is the walk of shame. It's ironic. I slept with Hunter once before and nothing happened between us, and now I've slept at his place and again nothing happened. Yet I'm ashamed.

I should be. My brain serves me snapshots of last night and I groan. I don't remember everything, but I was touchy. And hopefully not chatty as well.

As I leave the room, hoping I can just sneak out, my fortune turns even bleaker as I run into a woman who gasps and jumps, taken aback. She has gray hair cut into a stylish bob and Hunter's eyes. She must be a relative. His mother, probably. So much worse than a random babysitter.

Wait? Does he live with his mother? Or was she here to watch Caroline? Before I manage to greet the woman, Caroline runs out of another doorway and stops in her tracks. She widens her eyes and gapes like a fish out of water.

"Mrs. Lowe?"

The woman steps back like my name physically attacked her. Hunter appears at the back of the long hallway. "Good morning, Caro. Mrs. Lowe came to walk you to school. It's a special treat for new students."

Okay, I can work with that. "Surprise. I hope you'll accept a muffin for breakfast on the way to school."

Thank God I've rediscovered the powers of sentence formulation.

"Really?" Caroline looks at the woman and then at her dad, grinning. She even bounces, delighted as if it was a Christmas morning.

Something good is coming out of this awkward situation. I might turn this into a tradition for all new students. I bask in her joy, and for a moment I forget about my predicament here.

The woman clears her throat. "I'm Caroline's grandma. Freda Stuart."

"Sydney Lowe. Nice to meet you." *Please. Ground. Swallow. Me.*

"Get ready, pumpkin, so you can get the treat from Mrs. Lowe and won't be late for school."

"Don't call me pumpkin," Caroline says to her father and turns to me. "Will you wait for me, Mrs. Lowe?"

"Of course." I exhale a long breath as she returns to her room. Her grandma gives me a skeptical look, mumbles something about helping Caro and leaves.

Thank you, I mouth and Hunter winks. "Come and get your coffee."

I follow him, walking as though the floors were wired with explosives. I don't want to be alone with him. In his kitchen. And why is he so rich?

He's acting friendly. What did I tell him last night? The internal groaning roars in my hungover mind.

The modern kitchen is large, with sleek, beige cabinets and a rectangle island with a range. A breakfast table by the window faces the same side as the guest bedroom.

My days would be better if they started here. It's beautiful. Maybe money can sometimes buy happiness after all.

"I hope I didn't traumatize you last night." I take a sip of the coffee he handed me.

He chuckles. "Only a little."

"In my defense, I had a really stressful day, and I didn't expect my release session with London to be intercepted by anyone."

"I hope I'm more than anyone." His voice infiltrates my pores with a soft feeling. I swallow without taking a sip. The energy zaps between us as Hunter steps closer.

"Thank you for taking care of me. I'll kill London for letting you do that, but that's beside the point. I'm mortified by this. It's so unprofessional."

"Yeah, you mentioned that about a hundred times last night." He smirks and I groan, dropping my head. I'll be staring at the floor from now on in his presence. It's the only way to prevent death by humiliation.

"Don't worry. I'm glad I could help." He smells so

good. "You were delightful company once you stopped glaring at me."

He is too close. How did he get this close? Taking the cup from my hands, he puts it on the counter behind me, leaving his hand there. He moves the other arm to the other side of me, bracketing me between his huge muscles as he leans forward.

Our eyes lock and I'm struck with a sudden lack of oxygen, a wave of heat and an indecent dose of desire. Hunter looks at my mouth and I can't help but lick my bottom lip.

His warmth mixed with his distinct masculine scent wraps around me like a cashmere blanket. I want to lean into that sensation, but this is so wrong.

He is who he is. He said he was glad I didn't call. He is who he is. I'm his daughter's teacher. He is who he is.

My frantic thoughts abruptly halt when he lifts his hand and outlines my bottom lip with his thumb. He hasn't even lowered his mouth to mine and the experience is already as strong as his kiss three years ago.

I'm helpless and wound up. His essence spreads through my veins, leaving lingering warmth. It's an aphrodisiac. No wonder I'm defenseless. His gray eyes peer through me with an intensity scorching and chilling at the same time.

Confusion and yearning tug at the edges of my

mind. I want him to kiss me. I don't want the conse-quences. I want a chance with him. But then I don't do commitments, and Hunter is not interested anyway.

"I'm ready," Caro calls from the hallway before she bursts in. Hunter leaps away and smoothly scoops her up into his arms. He twirls her while she giggles and protests half-heartedly.

He's doing it as much for my benefit—to let me recover—as for theirs. I push aside the conflicting emotions and admire the bonding moment between father and daughter. I can have a lot of unresolved feel-ings about the man, but seeing him like this spreads like warm honey across my chest.

"Let's go then, ladies." Hunter puts Caro down and bows to both of us.

His mom watches me with an unimpressed expres-sion as we leave the apartment. Walk of shame, after all. And I deserve it.

Caro practically bounces in front of us. We stop at a coffee shop and I get breakfast for everyone. We carry our brown bags, but Caro immediately attacks hers, happily skipping along the way.

"Yesterday she dragged her feet and wanted to return home several times, and look at her now," Hunter says.

"First day of school is difficult for many kids." I try to sound normal, but nothing about this morning is normal. Yet walking with these two feels so natural, like we've done this trip many times before. It's disconcerting.

"Yes." He sounds deflated, sad.

Shit. There wasn't much in Caroline's file and I just assumed she transferred for logistical reasons, because the family moved or perhaps academic reasons, to be in a better school. Now I'm not so sure. I remember her wide eyes and the shyness that bordered on fear yesterday.

"Was there a particular reason she changed schools?"

Hunter sighs and scratches his nape. "I failed her."

The statement is charged with so much pain, I stop. He looks upward, gathering strength.

"We're going to be late," Caro calls from an intersection.

"Do you want to talk about it after school today?" My plan to avoid Hunter is reversing faster than I can navigate.

I don't want to see him after school. I don't want to get into a situation like this morning. Or last night—I groan inwardly at the thought. But if there is something I need to know about Caroline, to help her transition, I have to talk to him.

He thinks for a moment, not jumping at the opportunity. I don't know if he struggles with the same objections as me or just doesn't want to talk about whatever it is he considers his failure.

"Okay," he says at last. "I'm picking her up today. Maybe we can show you our ice cream route." He glides away to catch up with Caro.

The man glides for real. He moves like a graceful predator. Powerful and lithe. And how did an after-school parent-teacher meeting turn into an ice cream outing with them?

I thought he wasn't interested. He said he was glad I never called. And now, after the almost kiss in the kitchen, he is acting... I don't know how, but definitely putting me into an impossible situation.

I'm his daughter's teacher. Even if he's not married now, he was at the time of our first meeting, and still he asked me out. That's not a pattern I can ever accept. I groan again. It seems the sound of the day. I can't think with this hangover. I'll be happy if I somehow live through the day.

"Mrs. Lowe, hurry up," Caroline urges me and I catch up with them, walking alongside her, with Hunter holding her hand on the other side. Our eyes meet and I'm instantly teleported back to his kitchen. He's devouring me with his eyes. Why? What encouraged him to act like this? It's very different from last night. The portion I remember.

Did I say something to give him any ideas? Shit. I

look away as someone bumps into me. We're almost at school. Whatever he thinks is possible between us, my temporary paralysis in his kitchen probably sent him the wrong signal.

"Mrs. Lowe, would you like a copy of my magazine?" Caroline snaps me out of my freak-out.

"You have a magazine?" I meet her beautiful eyes. They are large and brown, not like her father's at all, but they are rimmed with thick, long lashes just like Hunter's.

"Yes, I have an issue every month, summarizing all that happened. I mean the not boring stuff. Mommy suggested it," she says with pride.

Of course. She has a mom. And where is she? "I'd love a copy. Thank you, Caroline."

"You're welcome. I believe you'll read it. Uncle Ash throws it out, I'm sure. His understanding of my news is understating." She rolls her eyes and I don't hold back my chuckle.

"Underwhelming, Caro," Hunter corrects her. "A lot of Uncle Ash is underwhelming, but he has a good heart."

"I don't think he has one. The other day he yelled at a pigeon who pooped on his jacket. The poor bird can't choose where its poops fall."

We both laugh at her stance as she shakes her head and spreads her little arms in dismay. But also because

I've only met Ash once, but I can picture him yelling at birds.

"I'll meet you in the classroom, Caro. Can I call you Caro?"

"Of course, all important people call me that." She turns and hops up the stairs. Her deeming me important spreads a pleasant fuzz around me and scares me at the same time. This is what I've been avoiding as a sub teacher. I don't want to be someone's important person. It only leads to a brutal heartache.

"I'll see you this afternoon," Hunter whispers, and it definitely doesn't sound like a formal school meeting. I need to stop it now, but he wants to open up about something he clearly considers his failure in regards to Caro. I can't ignore that.

"Have a nice day." It's all I say before I walk away, trying hard not to run. Yesterday was a disaster and today is not shaping up any better. A ball of confusion and guilt rolls slowly around my stomach, adding to my alcohol-induced nausea.

And it only gets worse when I spot Dan who is glaring in Hunter's direction.

Chapter Thirteen

Sydney

I knew something was amiss as soon as Caro's large brown eyes widened and her shoulders shot up in tension. Reading in front of the class could intimidate many kids, let alone someone who didn't yet have friends or any history here.

But her reaction when I asked her to pick up where we left off in the book was more than the usual shyness or stage fright.

She swallowed hard, her eyes pleading.

"Or actually, I just realized it's almost recess, so let's talk about your homework." While the entire class groaned, Caro's lips quivered with a smile. She exhaled and closed her eyes briefly.

That's why I asked her to stay behind when the other girls ran out to enjoy the playground.

"What do you mean you can't read?" I sit beside her at her desk to ensure she feels safe.

"It's too hard. I can't learn it. I think I might be stupid." She shrugs, stretching the hem of her skirt with her fingers.

"Caro, look at me, please." I teeter between authority and kindness. She lets out the saddest sigh and turns her head, chocolate brown eyes full of hurt. "You're not stupid. I know I only met you yesterday and I don't know a lot about you yet, but one thing is clear. You're very bright."

She shrugs again, resigned. Where is the excited girl from this morning? Her self-confidence completely disappears in an academic setting. Yesterday I assumed it was simply the new school/first day behavior. Today, I'm not so sure.

"Can I go outside now?" she asks as though I'm holding her captive. To punish her. To torture her.

"Of course, you get the break like everyone else. I'll talk to your dad and we can find a few minutes after school to see why the letters on the page don't change into words in your head. Okay?" I stand up and she nods and scurries away, her lack of comfort with this conversation obvious.

"And for this week, you're excused from reading in front of the class," I add as she reaches for the door.

She whips around, the tension in her shoulders easing up visibly. "Thank you." She dashes out with a smile. First one I've seen within these walls.

I don't have recess duty this week and decide to stay in the room and avoid the teachers' lounge. I don't want to run into Dan. I'm not ready to face him and discuss our breakup. Hopefully he doesn't want to discuss it. Frankly, I'd prefer if he pretended we have no history.

I close my eyes to relax, but my mind keeps wandering back to last night—or rather this morning in Hunter's kitchen.

I flop into my chair, lower my head into my hands and breathe through a wave of nausea. I can't deal with my life because my massive hangover is draining all my energy.

The bell rings and the squeals, laughter, and hundreds of footsteps fill the corridor outside the classroom. Recess is over. Shit.

Somehow I survive the rest of the day, providing less than stellar education to my pupils. Not that they complained about all the crafting and games. Second day with my new class and I'm already falling behind.

The beauty of substitute teaching was that I didn't need to care or feel attached to the overall result. Now

I feel like I'm failing these girls, giving them fifty percent instead of the hundred and fifty I usually strive for.

And I only have myself to blame. Who gets drunk on a Monday night?

As soon as I dismiss the class, I pick up my things and hope to get out of the building without being intercepted by anyone. I'll talk with Hunter briefly about Caroline and politely decline the ice cream date. Not a date. The outing.

I pull my bag from the drawer, and when I look up, I yelp. Dan leans against the door frame.

"You startled me." I exhale with my hand on my chest, as if that could slow down my heart rate while it attempts an escape through my throat.

"Sorry." Dan steps in and closes the door behind him. So much for avoiding the conversation.

He walks to me and stops in front of the board, tugging at his jacket. He isn't dressed up like yesterday, instead wearing a button-down shirt and a blazer with his jeans. Still very handsome, but not as relaxed as yesterday. Dark shadows show under his glasses.

"Where were you last night?" He sounds cold and accusatory.

"What?" I snap, my voice coming out as a raspy squeal, courtesy of my dry, hungover mouth. And two emotions that fight for attention—guilt and indignation.

"I was distressed by the way the events unraveled yesterday. I went over to talk to you."

I raise my eyebrows and he adds, "I needed to talk to you. To apologize. To patch things up, Sydney."

"I went out with London." Guilt clutches at my stomach. Since this morning, I've had a hard time focusing, thinking, maintaining basic human functions. And my misery has just expanded tenfold.

I don't want to lie to Dan, but I can't imagine telling him the complete truth would be taken lightly, even though we're no longer together. I slept at another man's house. A parent.

"Are you okay?" Dan frowns. Some of my conflicting emotions must show on my face.

No, I'm not. I'm tired, with a huge hangover and unresolved attraction to the father of my student.

"I have a headache," I say instead. Technically true. I wish he would go away so I can think. My heart and other voices are screaming in my head, demanding we abort mission.

When I stormed out of the park yesterday, I was upset. Not about Dan's behavior, but at letting our relationship derail this much without me addressing it sooner. If I'm honest, this thing with Dan has never been more than a convenient distraction.

Does that make me a bad person? I don't know. I

truly believed we were on the same page, that he wasn't looking for anything long-term either.

Perhaps Lo is right that I was never open enough with Dan to clarify my position. I guess I never truly cared enough. It's not like he's ever told me he loved me. I would have pulled back right then.

Yet guilt weaves through me as I look at him. And it's not only related to this morning's almost-kiss with Hunter. I'm half surprised and half relieved our breakup impacted me very little.

"Sorry to hear that." Dan plays with the eraser, then dusts his hands and puts them into his pockets. "I'm sorry about everything. I can see now how I got it all wrong. I just kept surprising you with these big life decisions. I made assumptions and rolled all over you with the moving-in-together suggestion at the worst moment ever. I thought I was protecting you from further stress on your first day. Sorry. I should have done it all very differently."

He sees my point. He gets it. I'm relieved I don't have to explain and argue. Though a big part of me questions why his apology doesn't spark happiness. Dread claws at me because Dan's words don't seem to lead to the destination I want. My goal is to remain friends. Or at least reasonably getting-along coworkers.

Before I can react, he continues. "I got it all wrong and I want to correct it. I don't want to fight anymore. I want to give you what you deserve, Sydney." He pulls a black box from his pocket and panic immediately rises inside me, expanding so quickly that I instinctively step back.

Clutching my purse to my chest, I search for a response. I want to say something. Stop him. Rewind time. Anything. But I'm frozen. I'm in the middle of a nightmare and I can't wake from it because I'm not actually asleep. I have to live through it.

"I love you, Sydney."

Involuntarily I glance at the door, yearning to run out. To escape this impossible situation. I've been with this man for almost a year and he knows nothing about me. How have I never seen how self-absorbed he is?

"This would have been the correct order of discussing things. I'm sorry I left you in doubt. There is nothing else I want more than to spend the rest of my life with you. I'm pragmatic, so I'm not going for a ridiculously elaborate proposal, but I think this is the natural next step for us." He opens the box.

A large diamond sits in a nest of tiny pink stones surrounding the solitaire. It's a pretty ring. Large, with an intricate design. Nothing about it matches my taste or personality. It's not what I would want even if I *did* want a ring. It's something you'd buy with a budget you'd set aside prior to entering the store. Practical. Like Dan. I hate pink. I always have.

"Dan, I will never get married. Never. I told you before." My voice is level, but there is nothing balanced inside me. Just a minute ago, I thought he understood where I was coming from. That we were on the same page. We're not even in the same fucking book.

"Yes, but that was when we met. We have a good thing going on here. I love you, Sydney. People say things in grief, but then they change their mind." He reaches out a hand, but I recoil.

The determination in his eyes shocks me. Aside from the fact that he's proposing after I broke up with him, he's completely dismissed my feelings toward marriage. He knew from the beginning. I might have not formulated my feelings about commitment overall, but I told him there were no more vows for me. I've been there, done that. Still licking the wounds.

"I'm not fucking changing my mind. Not now. Not ever. It's one of my core beliefs. I don't believe in marriage. Period. And now you steamroll me with your poor choices all in one day and then think you can fix it with a ring?"

Dan sighs, but he doesn't seem put off by my reaction. "Okay, I'll do it the proper way." He sinks down to one knee.

I blink a few times, but there he is, staring at me with expectation. And confidence. There isn't a trace of the nervousness he carried when he entered the room. At some point in our conversation, he started believing he was doing the right thing.

Somewhere down the line of our relationship, I thought I began to like this man. To be honest, I liked his reliability. His predictability. The companionship after being lonely for way too long. But have I ever truly liked *him?*

I swore off the institution of marriage after Jeremy. But this is no longer about a marriage license. This is much deeper. Much scarier. More painful. How did we end up here?

"Dan, stand up right now. I'm not marrying you. Or anyone else. And how presumptuous to assume that after I broke up with you after your moving-in proposal that an engagement is the solution. What happened yesterday deeply shook my faith in this relationship, and you come and do one thing that I flat-out told you I'm not interested in."

Color drains from his cheeks, but I don't stop. "And here, of all places? Jesus, get up before someone sees you."

And with my magical powers of untimely manifestation, the door clicks. I whip my head around and meet Hunter's eyes.

Chapter Fourteen

Hunter

It's been a week since I barged in on Sydney's proposal. The feelings are as raw as if it happened two minutes ago.

I stir my oatmeal and stare at the weather forecast on my phone. Not that I'd notice if it rained frogs. Or a tornado swept through New York. I've been absent-minded for a week now.

My initial shock immediately turned into murderous thoughts. I can't erase the image of Sydney's face from my mind. She looked at me like a deer in the headlights, shocked someone had interrupted the proposal.

The reasonable thing would have been to congratulate her, but apparently I'm way past being reasonable when it comes to the woman. So I've been ignoring her.

The more I try to erase her from my mind, the more she lingers. I stopped my housekeeper from changing the sheets in the guest bedroom and I kept the T-shirt she wore the night after the first school day unwashed.

It's unacceptable behavior, but my obsession is far from allowing any logic. Three years ago, when she didn't call, I fed the fantasy of her for way too long. I won't make the same mistake again. So many times I wanted to call London and get Sydney's number, but I respected her decision. I can be strong again.

"Caroline is outside." The words came out of her like she was speaking for the first time, her vocal cords surprised by the exercise. I glanced at her fucking fiancé before I slammed that door behind me and I ran. Thirty seconds of my life I wish I could bleach out of my memory.

She's in a relationship? Fuck me. Why I'm so upset I don't know. It's not like there was something between us. It's all been just my imagination.

The almost-kiss from the other morning after the woman slept in my house has been replaying in my head with the same frequency as our first kiss has been for years now.

The reel is burned into the edges of my conscious-
ness, regardless of what I've been doing.

This is ridiculous, and I've concluded it's the result
of expectations. Nothing has ever happened between
us, so it must be the tease and the anticipation of the
time we've spent together flooding me with thoughts
that are not warranted or normal.

Now my conclusion might be correct, but it does
shit for me. I still think about Sydney, and I oscillate
between disappointment, anger and longing.

I need to fuck someone soon, before lusting after
this woman is the death of me. That must be it. I
haven't been with anyone for too long. I misinterpreted
Sydney's drunken words and cuddly behavior. I'm out
of practice because I've been too focused on Caro and
the business. I haven't been on a date for years.

"Are you listening?" Mom's voice startles me and I
drop my phone into my breakfast bowl.

"Shit." I fish it out and walk over to the island to
wipe it clean with a paper towel. "Sorry. What were
you saying?"

"You need to pick up Caro this afternoon."

I stiffen. I've been avoiding the school drop-offs
and pick-ups for a week now and I'm not interested in
resuming them. Ever. Very mature. "Why?"

"For one, I have a doctor's appointment. Besides,
I've been doing it since the third day of school. Darling,

you know I'll help you any time. I love my granddaughter, but I can't be a full-time parent to her. She needs you. What's going on?"

"Don't be so dramatic. I've been too busy lately, that's all. I'm here for dinners and goodnight stories. Just the school runs have been difficult."

Shit. I've been using my mother because I'm a coward.

I dump my uneaten breakfast in the sink and rinse the bowl. "Of course I'll pick her up today. And why don't you stay at your place and get a break. I'll walk her to school again in the morning." I wipe my hands with the hand towel, gripping and yanking it to relieve some of my frustration. *Get it together, asshole.*

"Okay, I'll stay home. I want to be here for you and Caro as much as possible, but I'm getting too old for this." She sighs. "Have you spoken with Mrs. Lowe?"

"Why would I?" I retort, sounding like a teenager caught playing hooky at school. Too fast. Too guilty. Too fucking immature. The noose of resentment tightens around my throat.

My mom raises her eyebrow and amusement flickers around her face as the tiny lines around her eyes deepen. "Because she asked to speak to you about Caro's problems with reading. Last week. The day after she so kindly came to walk Caro to school." The mocking tone is what I probably deserve.

"Right. I forgot. I'll talk to her today." I practically run out of the room, leaving my self-respect and my mom behind.

And I almost ram Caro. "Hey, pumpkin, ready for school?"

"I'm not sure about some squash, Dad, but I'm ready." She rolls her eyes at me.

"Let's go then, darling." My mom walks out of the kitchen and they both leave.

I scratch my nape, exhaling. I'm an idiot. Fucking idiot. In my obsession over Sydney, I've abused my mother's time and neglected Caro's issues. Idiot and asshole.

I take a cold shower, trying to think about work, but the purpose eludes me. I haven't slept well in a week, and even a cold shower isn't enough to re-engage me. As I walk into my closet, my phone rings.

"Hey," I growl.

"Where the hell are you?" Ash sounds more than stressed. "They'll be here in ten minutes."

They? I scramble to find the part of my brain that is not Sydney-fucked and remember which important meeting I'm about to miss.

"I had a situation at home, but I'm on my way." Add business neglect to the list of my recent achievements.

"Hurry. I'll stall them, but get here pronto." The

edge in Ash's voice sets off all sorts of alarms in my mind.

I've always been the one on top of things, so what does it say that he's now more dedicated to *my* fucking business? I need to get laid and rid myself of Sydney's allure once and for all.

I get dressed in record time, grab my keys from the console table by the door and dash out.

A Fortune 500 company residing next door to our gym contacted us about their fitness program. They are interested in offering membership to their employees as a benefit, which could be an amazing opportunity to triple our numbers in one day. They are coming to tour the facility and discuss the terms in seven minutes.

At least the gym is only a fifteen-minute walk. I run the entire way. It helps me clear my head. Somewhat.

I burst into the gym. I haven't been working out as religiously as I used to, but I haven't even broken a sweat. At least there's something I can be proud of.

To my surprise, I manage to arrive before the potential client and I stay focused for an entire half hour. The meeting goes beyond our expectations.

"We might need another location soon." Ash high-fives me as soon as they leave.

"Let's not get ahead of ourselves." I wave at a few regulars lifting weights on my way to the office.

"What's up with you, dude? You've been distracted since that night with London and Sydney. What happened?" He plops onto the sofa by the door and swings his legs up, settling in.

"Nothing happened, and don't get too comfortable. I'm sure you have work to do." But I'm the one who has work to do. I've been pushing papers around and avoiding emails for a week.

He whistles. "So it's what hasn't happened that is the problem—"

"Oh, it's what happened. Like her getting engaged the following day?" I snap. Why did I just say that? The last thing I need is Ash knowing what an idiot I am. I won't hear the end of it.

"What? No way. The chemistry between the two of you was so palpable, the bar was under a serious fire hazard last Monday."

So I'm not imagining it. "I walked in on him proposing, so I guess your chemistry radar is broken."

"That makes no sense. London didn't mention anything." His eyes go wide and he jerks up on the couch, suddenly very interested in a magazine on the coffee table. He adjusts his seat and rolls the magazine up.

"When would she not mention something?" My best friend starting something with Sydney's sister is only going to fuck things up further.

"We hooked up again this weekend, but it's nothing. Back to you. I can't believe Syd is engaged, though. How do you feel about it? Besides the foul mood and general grumpiness. Do you want to go out tonight? Let's find ourselves some willing but completely no-strings-attached pussy. That always helps."

"You might be onto something. I need to snap out of this. I can't tonight though. And get out of my office, I have work to do. And so do you." I glower.

Ash rolls his eyes and saunters toward the door. "I'm going to check on Tribeca. Enjoy your brooding." He closes the door before I can throw a stapler at him.

I haven't been brooding. It's not like I have feelings —other than attraction—for Sydney. I need to snap out of my daydreaming. Work should fix everything.

I attack the pile of emails to respond to, paperwork to review, orders to process, payroll to approve, financials to reassess.

When my cell phone rings, I realize it is way past lunch. Good. Work is a decent distraction from Caro's teacher. I'm not even going to say her name again.

I grab my phone. It's the school. My stomach tightens. It's never good when the school calls. Worry coils around my intestines.

"Hunter Stuart," I practically snap into the phone.

"Oh, hi, it's Sydney." So much for deleting her name from my mind. "I'm waiting here with Caro, but her grandmother hasn't come to pick her up and she's not answering her phone."

Fuuuuuuuck.

"I'll be there in ten minutes. Can you stay with her?"

"Of course. It's raining. We'll be in the classroom."

"Thank you."

I've completely lost track of time. I dash out of the gym and for the second time today I run like a lunatic for several blocks. By the time I reach the school, I'm drenched. I take the steps to the entrance three at a time.

I scrub my hair to stop the water from running down my face. It achieves nothing, so I enter the building sopping wet, immediately enveloped by silence. I wipe my shoes on the doormat and head down the hallway.

Singing practice is not going too well behind one door, but otherwise the place seems deserted. Every step squeaks and echoes through the corridor. I slow down, hoping to temper the sound and remain unseen. As if gliding through the place unobserved can erase my lateness.

Another set of footsteps creaks on the staircase and I look up, meeting the gaze of the man who knelt in front of Sydney last week. So her fiancé is her colleague. I scan his face and realize I've seen his picture recently. Where?

"You are dripping all over the floors," he says when he reaches me.

Don't fuck with me, asshole. "That's what happens when it rains."

I continue walking because the animosity sweeping through me at the sight of him is unreasonable. I can't remember the last time I completely lost command of my emotions. Not for years, surely. A few hours with Sydney and my self-control is nonexistent.

"What are you doing here anyway?" he dares to ask.

I whip around. "Who are you?"

"Principal Dan Ravinski. And you?" He doesn't approach me to shake hands—he glares at me, exuding authority I suppose. And failing. But now I know where I've seen his face. The school sent out an email announcing his hiring.

"I'm a parent picking up my daughter. If you'll excuse me, I'm running late already." I start walking again, the sound of my soles deafening. After a beat, the creak of his shoes recedes. Smart decision, asshole.

The door of Caro's class is ajar and I hear her soft voice. I stop and realize she is telling a story, but she is struggling to get the words out. I peek through the opening.

Sydney sits beside Caro. Every adult who sits at those kid's desks looks ridiculous, like a giant in a dwarf's house. No one can retain their dignity when siting on those Lilliput chairs.

Somehow, Sydney appears gracious. She is wearing a red top with a V-neckline and my eyes travel down her cleavage. Her hair is up in a messy bun, exposing her neck. I can't decide where I want to sink my teeth first. The swell of her breast or her clavicle.

Snap out of it, asshole.

I will my eyes back to Caro. She is not telling a story, she is reading it. My stomach tightens. To my surprise, while she seems to fight with the page, her posture is fairly relaxed. She finishes a sentence and looks at Sydney.

"Well done, Caro. You've made such good progress already. Don't read anymore today. Tomorrow afternoon you can read with your dad or grandma again. Let your reading brain rest a little." She winks and Caro beams.

She notices me then. "Dad, did you hear? Mrs. Lowe says I made progress."

Seeing her this pleased with anything school-related is such a shock that I have to blink a few times. "I heard you reading, sweetheart. I'm so proud of you. Mrs. Lowe is an excellent teacher."

I avoid Sydney's eyes, because part of me wishes I

didn't find good qualities in her. So what, she is good at her job. And she's helping Caro. Fuck, if that's not adding to her attractiveness.

Caro comes over to hug me but stops short. "Did you forget the umbrella?" She puts her hands on her hips and cocks her head. Her typical I-can't-believe-how-dense-you-are gesture is adorable and annoying at the same time.

"I've been wanting to talk to you about Caro's reading," Sydney says. She lifts something from Caro's book. It's a piece of cardboard with a tiny rectangular cutout. "When Caro covers the rest of the page, she can focus better on each individual word, which helps her read it. It's a simple aid, but it works for now. When you have a moment, I'd like to understand how her previous school addressed her learning needs."

Sydney doesn't say learning issues or disabilities, she simply calls them needs. It rolls around my chest with surprising warmth.

"Caro, go to use the bathroom before we leave. I'll talk to your teacher while I wait." I kiss the top of her head.

"Can we go to visit Mommy?" she says, surprising me. "I'd like to read for her."

"We'll go another day. It's raining today."

She nods and leaves the room.

"Her learning needs were addressed with pressure

and ridicule." I avoid Sydney's gaze and stare out the window. "She was under constant stress, and then the little fuckers in her class made fun of her." It's hard to explain how badly we failed our little girl and the memory of it coils around my nerves, angering me all over again.

Sydney sighs, then turns to look in the same direction I am. We're silent for a moment before I chance a look at her. Her forehead is ridden with lines, as if considering what she wants to say next.

"I'm sorry to hear that. She's pretty much lost the first two years of reading level and she has a lot of catching up to do." Her words hit me with devastating precision, though she doesn't sound accusatory. Her tone is soothing, her voice warm. "We'll definitely help her with writing and reading, that's not an issue. It's her self-confidence and self-worth that need work. She told me she thinks she's stupid."

I lower my head and rub my nape. "Thank you for helping her, and for treating it as a fixable problem." Not only did I realize way too late that Caro needed help, now I've avoided the problem for a week because I can't keep my priorities straight. "What can I do?"

"Read with her daily and praise her for her progress. Has she been tested for dyslexia?"

Sydney remains standing behind Caro's little desk,

probably ensuring there's distance between us. Or I'm making shit up.

"No. The first year in school she memorized all the words they were reading and instead of reading she recited. Her last teacher discovered Caro was practically illiterate only in the second grade, but it was explained by either her laziness or the situation at home."

Sydney winces and chews on her lip for a moment. "I'm sorry to ask you this, but the contact information in her file is only yours and her grandma's. Are you divorced?"

"No, no. Caro's mother died last year." I look toward the door to make sure Caro can't hear us. It's ridiculous, but part of me wants to shield her from that brutal reality even though she has to live it every day.

"I'm so sorry. And a bit relieved..." Sydney slaps a hand over her mouth, her eyes wide with horror. "That came out really wrong. It's just when you refused to visit her mom earlier due to rain, I thought you were being a real asshole."

I chuckle. "Fair enough. Though I try to limit our visits to the cemetery. It's a weird balance, but Caro's therapist suggested she needs to decrease her frequent visits in order to move on with her life, not remain stuck mourning her mother. Last year we were at the cemetery three to four times a week."

Sydney walks around the little desk toward me, but stops, her eyes bouncing around like she's trying to decide what to say next.

"Congratulations on your engagement," I blurt.

She snorts. "Is that why you've been avoiding the school?"

Suddenly, the room feels smaller. The air zaps with sensual energy. I become hyper-aware of my breathing, of Sydney's shallow pants, of the singing somewhere down the hall and the silence between us.

She holds my gaze, challenging me.

"Yes," I admit, the short word coming out like a gurgle.

She whips her hand to her face, her fist closed, her ring finger outstretched. It kind of looks like she is flipping me off with the wrong finger and I'd deserve the gesture. The lack of the ring pleases me way more than it should.

I step closer to her. I want to tell her I'm glad she's not engaged, but I don't want to sound like an asshole. Even if she said no to the principal, they might still be together. And they must have been together when she didn't try to stop the almost-kiss in my kitchen. Thank God Caro interrupted us that morning.

Suddenly we're too close, our bodies mere inches from each other. Sydney's scent of a citrussy rainforest reaches my nose and spreads through me like a potent drug. I tuck a loose strand of hair behind her ear.

My eyes fall down to her luscious lips. She swallows hard with a shudder. Her eyes flicker with desire. It's as strong as mine, I'm sure of it. The moment is so charged that I might explode with frustration if I don't follow through.

I want to kiss this woman so badly, I stop thinking about where we are, who we are and all the potential complications.

"I'm sorry you lost your wife," Sydney whispers and I jerk out of my state. What?

"My wife?" I blink a few times.

"Caro's mother." She frowns, probably assessing my mental faculties.

"Caro isn't my daughter."

Every time I've admitted that to a woman—there haven't been that many—they are pleased. Like it's a burden lifted. Mind you, I haven't seen many women in that sense since I adopted Caro, but Sydney's reaction is totally different. One of horror. She's shocked.

"She's my sister's daughter. She started calling me Dad after Julia died and frankly I'm her dad in every senses of the word. Her biological father bolted before she was born."

Sydney steps back like my words hit her physically. She puts both hands over her mouth. It's a sad story, but her reaction seems extreme. Or she really is emotional and loves Caro already enough to care this much.

"Can we go now?" Caro says as she comes back in the door.

"I'm coming, sweetheart." I call after her and turn back to Sydney. "I'm sorry this is so distressing to you."

She gasps with horror. "You have never been married?"

Chapter Fifteen

Sydney

"Why would someone propose in a classroom after school? That is the world's worst proposal." Lo takes a sip of her champagne. "Stupid for a headmaster, isn't he?"

I close my eyes so the esthetician—a stunning, model-like blond—can lower slices of cucumbers to my lids. It's Saturday and my funk over the past two weeks convinced me to accept Paris's invitation for a day of pampering.

Not that I can afford The Ritz-Carlton spa, but I desperately need to relax and London badgered me into letting her pay. She joined us because she's pissed about something in her life, which is more or less her usual attitude.

"I really believe he was hoping for a logical, adult conversation to confirm what we both planned, but never discussed."

"What a romantic," London snorts.

"Don't be mean," Paris chimes in from my other side. She and London are twins, but I've always been closer to Lo. While they are identical in looks, their personalities are nothing alike.

Paris is gentle and comes across as a bit naïve—probably a mask—whereas Lo is tough and pragmatic and often angry at the world.

The blond supermodel gently rubs a cooling concoction into my pores, and though she's only touching my face I feel it deep in my soul. When was the last time I let someone take care of me? Or rather, when was the last time I let myself accept the care? I've been lonely for so long that a stupid facial brings tears to my eyes.

"I don't want a romantic proposal. I don't want a proposal. Period. What I want is Dan not being my boss, so I don't have to see him, and Hunter not being in my life." I groan, partially distressed by my situation and partially savoring the magic fingers on my cheeks.

"Is that really what you want?" Paris asks.

The question hangs there, suspended in the flower-infused air with its poisonous fingers crawling up my skin. I don't want to want what I want. I shouldn't. Damn Hunter with his muscles, smile and charming conversation skills. Damn him with his kissing talent and powers of arousing proximity.

"Let me enjoy this facial," I grumble.

But I can't relax. Dan remains my boss and I can do without his glowering. He's ignored me since the proposal, but it feels like the calm before the storm. The man was hurt by my rejection.

Chocolates and flowers have appeared at my desk a few times, but he hasn't tried to discuss our relationship. One that doesn't exist anymore. Though after he thought marriage was what I wanted when I broke up with him, I worry he might not have understood we really are through.

I'm done with Dan, that's for sure. Which leaves me with another man in my life. Jesus. He isn't even in my life. Not for real. Why am I such a mess around Hunter?

I've avoided him successfully for the past few days, but that doesn't mean I haven't thought about him. He hasn't left my mind for a second as much as I try. I've contemplated what could have been, had I not followed him after our date. If I hadn't made assumptions about him.

He invades my dreams. He reigns over my waking hours. My infatuation with him is ridiculous. Shit. This spa treatment is not relaxing me.

After I realized he's never been married, I made some lame excuse and hurried away, leaving him there dumbfounded. On top of everything else I've learned about the man since the first day of school, I can only conclude I've been really narrow-minded in my view of him.

I hate myself for that. I have a tendency to think the worst in general—courtesy of my late husband—but to preemptively judge someone? Not give him the benefit of the doubt? I'm so disappointed in myself.

"What's going on with you two?" I ask when we're sipping green tea in the lounge after our facials and massages.

I stare into the flickering blaze of the faux fireplace, the orange and yellow flames failing to warm me inside.

"I decided to do something daring in my life," Paris announces, her eyes closed, her blond locks splayed across the white pillow behind her.

While my sisters took advantage of their identical looks when they were in school, nowadays Paris rarely looks like Lo. She has been changing hair color almost as often as her underwear.

She's very shielded and careful in her life, and

something daring in her books might mean not recycle one plastic bag.

"No fucking way." Lo laughs. "Like what?"

"I wrote down a bucket list of items I dare myself to try. The first one was to get someone else's coffee at Starbucks."

I sink into my bed and chuckle. "What do you mean? You stole someone's coffee?"

"Well, I waited till they called someone's name and then I smiled, said I volunteer and took it."

"What?" Lo and I ask at the same time.

"First item on my bucket list. Done. I can move on." Paris huffs.

"Didn't they protest?" London asks.

Paris's cheeks turn crimson. "I kind of rushed out, but nobody followed me. The adrenaline was real though."

London lifts onto her elbows. "Did you enjoy the drink?"

Paris turns to look at me, biting her lip, and then she throws up her arms in exasperation. "I gave it to a homeless person because I felt bad."

Lo and I barely stifle a laugh.

"If you want more adventure in your life, I'll take you on one of my trips." Lo shakes her head.

Paris covers her face and groans, and I can't help but giggle. "What else is on your list?" I ask.

She starts counting on her fingers. "Sky-diving, learn to speak Portuguese, travel to Italy on a small budget, one-night stand—"

"Careful with that one. I had a friend with benefits who believed we were heading toward happily ever after. It seems like the Lowe sisters are sending confusing signals." I roll my eyes.

Paris crosses her arms across her chest and pouts.

"Not me." Lo sighs. "My signals are all straightforward. Fun only. Speaking of which, I went to a swingers' party," she whispers, and we both whip our heads in her direction. She shrugs, her eyes sparkling with mischief.

"What?" I sit up straighter.

"With whom?" Paris rolls to her side and puts her hand under her cheek, as if ready for a bedtime story.

"Alone. Women can go alone. Only men need a partner to get in." London shakes her head, annoyed by our lack of awareness.

"I thought you had a thing with Ash?" I swing my legs over the edge of my bed and lean closer, resting my elbows on my thighs.

Paris climbs across to sit next to me, almost knocking over the small side table between our beds.

"Who is Ash?" She scoots closer. We huddle together like we used to years ago when we shared a room.

London rolls her eyes. "Focus. I want to tell you about the party."

I chuckle, and a bit of the tension from my shoulders disappears with the laughter. Hanging out with my two carefree sisters is a good idea, after all. "Okay, but please remember this is not a private space."

To make my point, I look over my shoulder. Our reclining chairs are turned toward the fire with our backs to the lounge. We have more privacy than other guests since we snatched these spots.

Just the same, we garner attention from other guests with Paris's confession and the ruckus she caused by jumping beds. Her clumsiness has always been a source of entertainment for the family.

A group of women is chatting in the corner and a couple seems to sleep behind us. Whispers and soft laughter hum across the room, so hopefully London will keep the volume down.

"So there were these two couples and they switched partners. One is screwing the other woman in the corner against the wall and the other two are on the couch. This gorgeous banker is eating me out on a sofa beside them."

I don't know if I should laugh or run. Actually, for the first time in my life I feel a pang of jealousy for London. I have never envied her wealth, her men, her social status. None of it. She pours herself into many causes and helps so many people that I often don't even think about all this other stuff.

Right now I yearn for her free personality, her ability to enjoy life without fear or anxiety. Despite the trauma she went through as a young adult with her first love, despite her hard work to raise money for leukemia research, the expectations and burdens that come from her fairly public persona, London chooses fun. Recklessly. Unapologetically.

"The woman on the couch orgasmed and it was loud and looong. I mean she kept going and going. I was jealous. Like come on, bitch, my turn now. Suddenly, a thud and a yelp ripple through the room. The asshole in the corner drops the woman and crosses the place, all red with fury. He pulls the dude off his wife and starts yelling at her that she's never come this hard with him and has she been faking her orgasms all their marriage. It was epic."

"Oh, my God. How did it end?" Paris plasters a hand over her mouth, her eyes gleaming.

"The party fell apart, security was called, and needless to say the poor wife was the only one with an orgasm that night." London shrugs and plops back into her recliner.

"And a memorable one." My shoulders heave with silent laughter.

"Cheers to that. I wish I had snatched that man at the beginning." Lo winks.

We sit in silence for a moment to stifle the giggles.

"So what about you and Ash?" I don't know why I ask, because the topic is dangerously close to the other topic I'm trying to avoid.

"We're somewhere between casual and over. I can break it off if it bothers you."

"Who is Ash?" Paris throws her arms up in frustration.

"No. Why would it bother me?" Why am I lying? "Okay, it bothers me a bit because if you get more serious... you know."

"I can guarantee I'm not getting serious. With him or anyone else. He's fun in the sack, but he's too focused on money and success." She gives me an unimpressed look and turns to Paris. "Ash is Hunter's friend."

"Do you *want* to get together with Hunter?" Paris asks.

"Our attraction is purely physical. I don't know if I can go there. And with me being his daughter's teacher, we can't be together. It's just too complicated."

I reach for a handful of nuts on the coffee table between us, not really wanting them. Anything to occupy my hands.

London huffs. "And don't forget you didn't really like what he was doing, or perhaps still does."

Her words remind me I might have lost my sanity and my appetite. I drop the handful back into the small bowl.

"He doesn't. He told me when we were at the bar. He also said he's glad I'd never called him back then." I take a sip of my tea, the warm liquid soothing my stomach.

Even if there wasn't the weird history between me and Hunter, I don't want to be attracted to a parent. I've just leaned into taking my job more seriously again and I don't want to jeopardize that, especially with Dan already an issue.

"That might mean all sorts of things. Based on your recent interactions, the sparkles are bouncing between you, so for once listen to your gut and not your brain." London takes an apple and polishes it on the sleeve of her soft robe.

"Sparkles are not enough. Look at me and Dan."

Paris, who has never met Dan, raises her eyebrows and Lo snorts. "There were never sparks between the two of you. Dan was safe and reliable. He was a good backup plan while you waited for something more exciting to come along."

I stare at her, horrified. My shock comes from two

places, though. I can't believe she would say something like that, to diminish someone this way. But more concerning is that she might—just might—have touched the truth.

Somewhere deep down, I've always known he was a substitute boyfriend. That realization shakes me with seismic force.

"I'm a horrible person." I put the mug down and cover my eyes with my forearm.

London reaches across to squeeze my shoulder. "You're not. You didn't date him, waiting for this to happen. It's just happened this way. Let's focus on Hunter, though. Why are you fighting the attraction so much? You're making all these assumptions about him. Just talk to him, explore where it could go."

"How would I explain why I never called? I can't tell him that I followed him. I completely misjudged the situation. What's wrong with me? First Jeremy, then Dan, and with Hunter... Jesus, I don't even know how to reconcile my assumptions there."

"There is nothing wrong with you. Since Jeremy you've been living your life safely, which is under-standable. That's why you attracted a man who was looking for the same—safety. But when a man who is anything but came into your life, it knocked you off-balance." London takes a bite of her apple.

"There is nothing wrong with safety." The soft

robe turns into a furnace suddenly as the idea of the *non-safe* man pools in my core. I grab a magazine to fan myself.

"True," Paris says. "If you don't mind missing out on things that require risk. Things that come with wonderful surprises, satisfying rewards, unforgettable memories." She puts her hand around my shoulder.

"Like stealing a coffee," Lo deadpans and Paris groans. "But while not speaking from experience, Paris is right."

I wipe a tear away, trying to find words and solace in the flames before me. I want to defend the way I've been living, but it has never been my primary choice. Defaulting to safe choices let me avoid experiencing the heartbreak and disappointment of my marriage again.

There is a difference between happiness and contentment. I've been content, but have I been truly happy with my life?

"You're used to your boring way of life." Lo picks up on my internal turmoil. "It's hard to see the forest for the trees, but I remember the fun Sydney. And maybe you're not as crazy as me, but you used to be adventurous. Full of life. Maybe that's what Hunter inspires. Maybe that's why his lifestyle—former lifestyle—provokes something in you, and it makes you feel more alive."

"I don't think Sydney should break her hermit ways for a man. You should go back to your entrepreneurial plans. Take risks within your control and allow yourself to fully rediscover your self-confidence." Paris pats my hand.

I used to be full of life. I had plans. I was going to start my own school, focused on alternative teaching methods to cater to kids with different learning needs. I used to spend my weekends hiking, traveling. I volunteered at a library reading program.

Before Jeremy died, I had a life. That life was put to an abrupt end. Everyone's always believed his secret gambling was what broke me. But that's because I've told no one about the real extent of his betrayal. The resentment it seeded inside me that grew into a full-blown garden of mistrust and apprehension.

Hunter sparked something in me. Desire. I haven't longed for anything because I couldn't afford it. I haven't longed for anyone because getting attached meant exposing myself to losing someone. Maybe Paris has uncovered an important piece of the puzzle. I need to find my self-confidence first.

I try to enjoy the spa day, but I'm more wound up than I was before we came. I want to tell my sisters the whole truth about Jeremy's past, but I'm so ashamed of my years-long ignorance during my marriage that I can't bring myself to do it.

We leave the spa and sadness descends on me as we cross the lobby. This is where I met Hunter under the wildest circumstances. And this is where I decide that some things in life we just have to let go of, regardless of how much we want them to work out.

Chapter Sixteen

Hunter

When I got the call, I bolted. I abandoned Delaney, leaving our meeting without saying goodbye. I scared the receptionist and two clients at the front desk as I toppled over a leaflet stand, and cursed as I headed toward the exit.

My mind raced in a million directions, even as it remained frozen in one place. A place decorated with darkness, dread and fear. I wanted to move from there, but the call from Sydney imprisoned me in anxiety. So I ran.

Forgoing the elevator, I rushed down the stairs. Outside, I pushed through flowing pedestrian traffic that felt like a brick wall. I sprinted through Central

Park, narrowly avoiding several collisions with idiot tourists.

I didn't stop or slow down, but the twenty minutes it took me to get to the museum felt like a lifetime of torture.

"What happened?" My voice snaps like whip.

Silence descends on the foyer, and even the eight- and nine-year-olds in the corner shut up so promptly that I can hear my heart thundering. Everyone else probably does as well.

I yank my gaze away from the children because I don't want to scare them. At the same time, I don't care.

My eyes land on Sydney, standing in a circle with two other adults and a uniformed guard. The concern on her face punches me in the gut.

She should be fucking concerned.

Yet a small part of me chimes in through the screams of fear and tells me I want to comfort her. Fuck that.

She steps forward. Pain and worry in her eyes mirror the ocean of anguish that's swallowing me. "Why is nobody doing anything?" I push through my teeth.

"We've looked everywhere in the building. We counted all the children before we entered the museum. A security team continues searching." Her voice shakes, her eyes plead. I don't want her to feel like this. What? Goddammit. I have other priorities now.

"Are you sure she didn't slip out?" I pray I am wrong.

Sydney's breath hitches. "Would she do that? Why? Where would she go?" She keeps shaking her head, as if she wants to push the idea out before it blooms into a clear probability.

I rake my hands through my hair and turn. I can't look at her. She is responsible for Caro and now my daughter is gone. Lost. In the middle of this humongous city. My stomach churns and I bolt for the door.

The cool, early October air fills my nostrils, but doesn't reach my lungs. I pace the landing, jog down the few stairs and back up. Physical activity has always provided me with clarity. As I trot up for what might be the tenth time, I more sense than see a figure at the entrance.

I don't have to look to know who it is. I don't want to look because part of me holds Sydney responsible for Caro's disappearance.

I bounce back down. *Think. Think.* Where would she be?

"Hunter." It's barely a whisper that leaves her mouth, but it dusts my skin like an electric current. I stop and find her eyes. I want Sydney to disappear instead of Caro, and at the same time I want her to stand by me in this difficult, fucked up moment.

"If something happens to her..." I grit out the words, unable to finish. It's a tangled, panicked threat. I aim a vicious frown at Sydney, but she withstands it with dignity.

While her face shows all sorts of emotions—none of them positive—on the outside she remains calm. I don't know if I'm grateful or resentful of that.

"The security team is positive she is not inside. They're reviewing CCTV footage to confirm she left the building. We've called the police. Two colleagues are coming from the school to take the kids away, but I'll stay here and help look for her. Can you think of any place she'd go to?"

I shake my head and pinch the base of my nose, trying to calm my racing—and fucking unhelpful —thoughts.

Think, asshole. She needs you at the top of your game, not a pile of useless trash.

"She entered the building with us, so she must have sneaked out. Where would she go? Home? Your work? What about the ice cream place you go to? Is there anything around here that might intrigue her?"

I inhale a long, calming breath. It doesn't calm me, but the oxygen in my brain does some good and the fog lifts slightly. I rushed here on autopilot and I finally take my surroundings in.

We're standing in front of the American Museum of Natural History. Would she have gone to Central Park to find the ice cream truck? She has no money. Would she head south to get to 74th St. and the gym?

Why? She seemed to like the new school and Sydney as her teacher. She hasn't complained about the other children. Have they been giving her a hard time?

"Have they searched the grounds?" It's an idiotic question because of course they have, but asking gives me a false sense of control as my own helplessness keeps stabbing my insides.

Sydney nods and I groan.

"Has she ever been here?" she prompts again. Her questions are more helpful than mine, but I don't fucking have answers. Panic strangles me.

"To the museum?" Sydney continues, not showing any frustration from my lack of answers. "The police could help us search Central Park. You go there often, don't you?"

"We've been here once, but I don't think there is anything here. And she wouldn't go to the park by herself." *Would she?*

"Does she have any friends living around here?"

With each question, another wave of desperation splashes over me.

"No. And she wouldn't just run away. She must be somewhere here. How do you lose a child?" The moment I say it I regret it, even though it's not a completely outlandish thing to ask. To accuse.

Sydney flinches and swallows.

"There is nothing around here, no memories she would like to revisit?" She struggles to keep her voice even as tears pool around her eyes.

Traffic roars on Columbus Avenue, ratcheting my desperation and fear to a new level. How do you find a child here? What if something happened to her? What if—?

Don't go there. Don't go there, asshole.

"Hunter, I'm really sorry. Really sorry." She puts her hand on my biceps and I want to recoil, but the warmth and empathy seep from her touch through my sweatshirt, crawling into the dark crevices of my heart.

Sydney shoves a phone under my nose. "You can be mad at me later. First, let's find her." I look at the map on the screen and then at Sydney, frowning. "Zoom in and look around. Maybe there is a bakery, or a book or toy store she likes."

It takes me several moments before I truly force my brain to focus on the web of streets on the screen. Part of me fights the idea. I can't locate Caro on a fucking map. Where the hell are the police?

I'm about to turn off the screen when my eyes land on a familiar name.

"I think I know where she might be." I run toward the intersection, cursing as the lights turn red. Sydney follows while she talks on the phone, explaining to someone we're leaving the premises.

Sirens blare and screech to a halt behind us, the kaleidoscope of blue and red lights flickering through the air. I can talk to the police later. Right now, I'm propelled by new determination. My mission might be futile, but action is much better than helplessness.

Sydney stays one step behind me. She doesn't talk. Doesn't question our destination. She simply keeps by my side. A silent, confident pillar of support. Even in her heels, she somehow keeps up with my much longer gait.

It takes us less than ten minutes to reach the Tecumseh Playground on Amsterdam. Caroline used to spend time here with her mom and she's been bugging me to come again. I didn't find time. Please let her be there.

"Caroline," I call.

A group of young women laughs and chats in the corner.

A lone woman reads a magazine on a bench.

Kids are climbing, sliding, roaming everywhere.

"Caroline," I yell again as I bounce between the children and parents like a lunatic. I'm out of my mind, so yeah, people, crazy person on the loose. I glare at one mother who scoots her little boy behind her.

The young women disperse to shield their proteges. A little girl looks at me wide-eyed and starts crying.

It's a small playground with a wood-and-ropes jungle gym, monkey bars, slides and swings. Caro is too big for it now, but I understand the sentiment of revisiting it. It hits me with a devastating intensity. I've been so focused on encouraging her to live forward and not get stuck in the past that I've completely ignored her need for grief or memories.

"I don't think she is here, Hunter."

I startle and spin around. I forgot Sydney was with me. I must look like an idiot who lost his ability to process words—and I probably did—because she repeats, "I don't think she is here."

The vise around my chest tightens, the fear creeping through my bloodstream. Sydney reaches and rubs my arm, but I step aside and rake my hair with my fingers, grabbing a fistful. I kick a pebble and run out through the little gate.

The street is unforgiving, bustling, fucking dangerous for a little girl. It must be loud as well, but I can't hear anything through the thunderous pulse in my ears.

Never have I hated this city before.

A melody chimes beside me and Sydney answers her phone. My legs lead me back toward the museum, even though I know Caro isn't there.

"Thank God. Thank you. We'll be right there."

Sydney's relief hits me like a tsunami and I almost stumble. My eyes prickle as I look at her.

"They found her."

Sydney

We rush into the police station, Hunter likely unable to communicate rationally yet. I jump in front of him to talk to the officer at the front desk. His energy is threatening enough to get himself arrested before we get to Caro.

"Just a moment." The young officer with the reddest lipstick I've ever seen picks up the phone.

Hunter is so close behind me, his breath steams my nape. His every ragged breath pulses in sync with mine. I can't look at him. I don't want to see the hate in his eyes. I lost his daughter.

I lost a child in my care. Losing any child would

have been horrible, but his daughter? The universe hates me.

We haven't spoken in two weeks, and I've imagined our next encounter a thousand times. After I decided I wouldn't give in to this attraction, but rather focus on rebuilding my ability to move forward with my life, Hunter remained the key player in my fantasies.

Getting together with him is not a good idea, but that hasn't stopped me from dreaming about him. In my wildest dreams, I never imagined we'd next meet over something this unforgivable.

"Daddyyyyy—" Caro runs to him. He envelops her in his bear arms, his eyes welling up. A tear rolls down my cheek. It's a relief, but also something else. I'm touched by the scene in front of me.

This man. This single dad. Life threw shit his way. Unlike me, he stood up and embraced the challenges. I refuse to get attached, but he has no choice. He has this little girl.

A girl I lost.

Hunter pulls back, his hands holding Caro's shoulders while he examines her, as if not believing she's really here. Unharmed.

"I'm sorry," Caro whispers. "I thought I could sneak out to the playground where Mommy used to take me and be back before anyone noticed, but the streets were too confusing and I got lost. Are you mad?"

Hunter lets out a long breath and bows his head. Looking up again, he scoops Caro into another embrace and stands up with her. She isn't a baby anymore, but in his brawny arms she looks tiny.

"I'm just happy nothing happened to you. You gave me and Mrs. Lowe quite a scare. You can't walk out into the street by yourself without telling someone." He buries her head into the crook of his neck and strokes her hair.

She hooks her arms around his neck, and I catch myself wishing I was a part of their reunion. That I was privy to the connection and affection they share. It's a ridiculous notion. If anything, today's failure removed that option permanently.

How could you lose a child?

Hunter's words from earlier play on repeat in my head, brewing more guilt inside me. My pessimist's mind conjured so many horrible scenarios today, I can't shake off the dread.

While Caro is safe and sound after a patrol officer discovered her, I can't help but ask *what if*. The unhelpful but very persistent question injects self-loathing into my veins.

"You're smothering me," Caro mumbles.

Hunter chuckles and puts her down.

"Mrs. Lowe will stay with you while I take care of the paperwork, sweetheart."

Caro turns to me with a smile, but Hunter doesn't as much as look my way. He turns to speak to the officer who came over with Caroline.

"Do I have to go back to school today?" Caro yawns and leans against me. I wrap my arm around her.

"I think the school day is over." If only my priorities could be organized in the careless way of children. So much freedom.

"But I forgot my blankie there. I think it's lost. Mommy gave it to me to protect me. To remember her."

I've noticed she has a small silk handkerchief she'll ball up in her palms during class. I thought it was just a fidget device. It's so much more for her. "It will wait for you there."

"What if I lost it? I can't sleep without it. What if it's gone? Mommy can't give me another one." Her lips tremble.

I stroke her hair. "I'll go look for it, okay? I'm sure it will turn up."

She sighs, her shoulders relaxing. I lost the child—I can at least retrieve her blankie. Especially since it's her coping tool.

"I'm sorry, Mrs. Lowe. I didn't mean to scare you," she whispers, and my chest constricts.

I'm a teacher. Of course, I like children. But this little girl is growing on me with her raw honesty and maturity beyond her years. A survival mechanism in a world without a mother, a strength she shouldn't have needed this early in life.

"I know, Caroline. Next time you want to visit a playground to remember your mom, tell your dad or your granny."

She turns to me, frowning. "I've been telling him, but he never has time."

Empathy swamps me and I want to wrap her in it. Part of me wants to blame Hunter for limiting his time with her, but I know he's gone above and beyond for this little girl.

"Your dad is very busy." I wish there was an easy way to explain without sounding like I'm making excuses for him. "He cares about you a lot, but sometimes you need to be patient."

Squinting, she nods, assessing the merit of my words. "I miss my Mommy and I don't want to forget her."

Her words punch me in the stomach and push a large lump up my throat. I thought I was a master of grief, but Jeremy left my life with a bitter aftertaste. This little girl is forced to grow up without the most important person in her life. We can all offer compassion to her constantly, but we'll never fully understand her struggle.

"You'll never forget your mom. You might not clearly see her face or hear her voice, but she is the most important treasure in your heart, and your heart knows how to guard that treasure."

She snuggles against me. I look up and jump a little when I find Hunter standing closer than I expected. How long has he been observing us?

His eyes are stormy as he scans me. Heat builds up in my cheeks, but it's nothing compared to the flames licking at my core. His gaze is both promise and threat. I'm not sure if he is angry or aroused. Something that feels like a mixture of lust and fear crawls up my spine.

A computer keyboard rattles somewhere, footsteps shuffle around. Activity is happening in the background, but all my senses are fixed on the man standing in front of me.

The thunderous energy he emanates swallows me, eating away at my resolution to resist him. He furrows his brow, his hooded eyes aiming with precision. He's about to pounce. I'm sure of that. The question is if he leaps to kill or to thrill.

Chapter Seventeen

Hunter

Sydney's voice, soft and soothing, drips over me like honey as she reads the bedtime story. From the doorway I see Caro fighting sleep, her eyes drooping. The picture tugs at my heart.

I've never brought a woman to our home before. All my relationships since Julia got sick were either professional or too casual. And the few dates—hook-ups really—I've had since becoming a full-time dad never got far enough to even contemplate Caro's introduction.

The picture in front of me feels natural.

Sydney found the blankie, but got held up dealing with school paperwork in the aftermath of Caro's disappearance. By the time she came over we were getting ready for dinner, and Caroline insisted Mrs. Lowe join us. And in her charmingly manipulative way, somehow tasked Sydney with a bedtime story as well.

Not that I mind. I'm not even sure why I'm standing here watching them, because what I really need is a glass of whiskey. Or two. The nervous energy continues buzzing through my bloodstream and I need to release it badly, but I can't leave Caro here and go to the gym.

I feel like I'm about to jump out of my skin though. There is no way I'll be able to fall asleep tonight. I haven't even checked Ash's voice mails or texts because I can't deal with that shit now. Although having bolted from the meeting this afternoon, I should at least send an explanation to Delaney.

When Sydney closes the book and kisses Caro's forehead, my heart pulses faster, spreading even more honey through my system. Life is so fucking unfair. What do *I* have to give to this little girl? I can never replace her loss.

I couldn't even take her to a fucking playground. Drumming my fingers on my thighs, I fight the nervous energy that creeps up a notch, mocking me with its ugly snarl. Failure. That's what I am.

I push off the door frame as Sydney passes through, then I close the door gently. Without thinking, I channel the built-up tension into inappropriate action. I spin Sydney around and push her against the wall. She utters a soft gasp as I raise her hands above her head and capture her mouth.

She stiffens beneath me at first, but then she welcomes my invasion. This kiss is not a soft discovery like our first one, years ago. It's punishing and desperate, swirling with all the worry, desperation and helplessness of the past hours.

She tastes like apples and cinnamon—from our impromptu dessert earlier—and suddenly I'm addicted to that flavor. I groan in response to her soft moan and grind my hips against her, seeking the release I don't deserve.

We shouldn't be doing this. I should stop, but I'm past reason. Everything else has ceased to exist. It's just me with my reckless need to process the horror of today. And this woman who keeps escaping me— which might be smart—and teasing me at the same time without even knowing it.

Sydney wiggles her hips, maybe to push me away or nestle me closer, but her mouth seems eager to keep going. I'm so absorbed with the essence of her and my own adrenaline that I let myself drown in the connection.

Her body is soft against my taut muscles. She fits

perfectly against me. She feels too good. Too dangerous. Too forbidden.

Caro whimpers behind the door and the soft sound splashes over me like cold water. I jerk away so fast, Sydney stumbles. My heart bruises my ribcage in its violent thunder. I scrape my fingers through my hair, trying to compose myself. What the fuck am I doing?

I open the door and peek in, but Caro is fast asleep. Closing it again, I lower my forehead to the wooden surface, wishing it was a block of ice. I can't look at Sydney. I don't regret the kiss, but I regret the circumstances. I took it because I needed an outlet. But I had no right to do it. Not here, a wall away from Caro. With her teacher, nonetheless.

"I'm sorry. I shouldn't have done that." My voice cracks through the lump in my throat. I turn and walk to the living room, leaving her standing in the shadows of the hallway. Asshole. I drop to the sofa and close my eyes, tilting my head against the backrest.

"Good night, Hunter." Sydney's voice reaches me from the far side of the room.

"I'm the worst father ever." I don't know why I choose this moment to voice my biggest fear. I don't open my eyes. I can't look at Sydney, because I don't want to see the agreement in her eyes. Or the apprehension after I practically attacked her in front of Caro's room.

"Don't be too hard on yourself. Caro adores you and you're providing her with the best life. You love her and you show it to her all the time. It's the most important gift you can give her... to grow up in a supportive, loving environment."

Sydney's words sink in slowly and deliciously, but I don't let myself bask in them. She's only trying to make me feel better.

"Is that enough?" I challenge, rubbing my face. "I've been working so hard. I didn't even take her to that stupid playground. I didn't realize how important it was to her. I have to ask my mother to help several times a week. I don't have time to take her on vacation. I haven't signed her up for any after-school classes because I don't want to be bogged down by her schedule—"

"You accepted her without hesitation after her mother died. You pulled her out of the school where she was suffering, and you did everything you could to help her feel safe again when interacting with other kids. And, let me repeat, you love her. And you let her be who she is and support her. So many parents turn their kids into projects to fulfill their own dreams. Just the fact you feel like the worst parent ever is confirmation you're not. The worst parents never contemplate their own failure."

I finally look at her. Part of me finds her words

soothing, but another part stubbornly believes she is just saying what I want to hear. "Thank you. For everything today. I really appreciate that you brought the blankie and stayed longer. Not that Caro gave you much choice." I utter a dry laugh.

"The least I could do after losing her." A shadow passes across Sydney's features and she winces.

I've been so absorbed with my fear and guilt that I ignored how much the whole situation must have impacted Sydney. Frankly, mere hours ago, I was blaming her myself. It stemmed from fear and panic, but I've been too self-absorbed to see that she was suffering also.

I stand up and walk to her, but not too close, to prevent myself from pouncing on her again. I'm still sporting a semi in my pants. Though to be honest, I could stand on the other side of the room, the other side of the city or the world, and feel an undeniable pull.

"Don't blame yourself." I exhale deeply for the zillionth time since I received the call about my missing child. Not even fucking breathing comes easy anymore. "Caro sneaked out. In the end, we got lucky, and she was unharmed. I'm sorry I was harsh with you before. I don't blame you."

Sydney nods. She opens her mouth and closes it, licks her lips and repeats the gesture without speaking the actual words clearly waging a war inside her. Finally, she settles on a simple, "I'm sorry about today."

Not simple at all. The words hang there with their ambiguous meaning. Is she referring to the kiss as well? I blame myself for losing my shit, but it's not like she wasn't an eager participant. I don't know how to dance around her for the next several school years because every time I see her, a stupid, sappy movie plays in my head.

The script has been similar for years now. Sydney tucking hair behind her ear and blushing, unsure how to approach our first meeting. Sydney laughing at something I said. Her eyes widening with surprise when she learned we share a love of dark Scandinavian crime thrillers. Her sighs when I massaged her feet. Her heartbeat against my ribcage in the hotel's elevator. Leaning against me when she got drunk. Confessing she searched for my scent. Snuggling into me as we walked home. Reading with Caro in the classroom. Reading to Caro just now.

"I'm not sorry about the kiss earlier. I'm not sorry about any of our kisses, or the almost kisses. I'm sorry about the circumstances." My hands are useless appendages I don't quite know what to do with, so I keep fisting them in the rhythm of my speech. "I regret I blamed you for getting engaged, and I'm sorry you're my daughter's teacher. I'm sorry you never called three years ago—"

"You said you were glad I never called." She frowns and wriggles her hands in front of her. "At the bar. Your words hurt me."

"Not as much as you not calling me." I might as well be honest with her now. Our relationship has been nothing but missed opportunities, missed conversations, missed timing. There shouldn't be much to lose at this point, but the thought is like a nautical knot around my stomach because I feel like I'm losing again.

She widens her eyes and shakes her head vigorously. "Why did you say it then?"

"I thought it would lift the awkwardness, but also… I'm glad you didn't call me because I didn't deserve you then." Needing the physical restraint, I put my hands in my pockets.

She doesn't react to my words. Not in her expression, but I notice how her breasts heave faster. Regardless of how we feel in each other's company, we need to be realistic. "And now the situation is too complicated."

We stare at each other in silence for a century, each second riddled by what could or should be. "I told you I'm not engaged."

She suggested that last time, but we didn't get a chance to discuss her relationship status. We might have more obstacles to overcome, but I latch on to that confirmation like it's the first drop of water after years of drought. "You're not dating the principal?"

"No. But I'm still Caro's teacher—"

"And I'm still a former escort. You used to have an issue with that, which I understand."

"I made many assumptions three years ago. Assumptions that led to a misunderstanding. I thought you were married. I decided you were just doing your job, even though everything about that night felt too real, too good, too authentic. Also not enough."

What her words do to me... Jesus. "In that case, I'd very much like a redo of that date."

She swallows a few times and then steps forward tentatively. I mirror her move and we meet halfway. I don't know if my intentions result from today's stress or from the insatiable need to discover what we could be.

"I'd like that." The tremor in her voice is almost imperceptible, but it sends a jolt of desire down my spine.

I cup the back of her neck and crush my lips against hers. It's savage again, but not because I need to let loose after a shitty day. All the pent-up tension, the pages of unspoken words between us since that first night, everything melts into this kiss.

Sydney wraps her arms around my shoulders, and as I dip her head backward, adjusting the angle, she digs her nails into my skin, holding onto me. Her lips taste even better as we both dive into the kiss with all we can take and give.

Her tongue is more confident and her almost inaudible moans reverberate through me like sirens calling, seducing me. I want to bend her over and finally have her in every possible position I've imagined.

At the same time, I want to savor this kiss and take it slowly, to relish every moment, to seek a languid restitution for all the denial and delay.

"I should probably look up the school policy." She is breathless as I leave her lips and trail down, kissing her jaw, her neckline, the crook of her shoulder.

"Too late for that, Mrs. Lowe, we're doing this. Fuck the rules." I dust her earlobe with my words, savoring the shiver my whisper sends down her body.

"I'm already in trouble—not only have I lost a student, but I broke up with the principal." The way she clings to me is wanton and somehow innocent at the same time.

I squeeze her ass, delighted at how well it fits in my hands, and bite her shoulder. "Don't talk about another man when you're with me."

"So we're going to deal with everything by denial?" She struggles to sound strict and serious as her breath hitches when my tongue traces the neckline of her dress. It's a simple cotton dress that hugs her curves like a second skin, and it takes all my restraint not to rip it off.

"Works for me, Mrs. Lowe. Right now, I'd like to discuss more important things we need to address first." I lock my eyes with hers and watch every muscle on her beautiful face as I cup the curve of her breast. A soft whimper escapes her when I brush my thumb over the hard peak of her nipple.

She swallows and licks her lips. "I'm not sure if this is a good time for such a discussion. For any discussion."

I lower my forehead to hers, keeping my hand on that intriguing curve. Each part of her fits so well with mine. "You're right. Less talking, more doing. Just to run over the agenda, though. I'd like to see if you're as wet for me as your nipples are hard."

Her eyes widen with a mixture of shock and arousal.

"And then, sweetheart, as soon as my hand confirms how you really feel about me, I'm going to shove your panties to the side and thoroughly explore those swollen lips."

She bites her lower lip, clinging to me as her knees weaken under the influence of my words. I grab her tighter around the waist and dip to reach for the hem of her dress to demonstrate my idea.

"Would you like that, Mrs. Lowe?"

She nods and her moan breaks through the charged air in the room as I drag my hand up her thigh. Her skin is like silk against my rough fingers. I trace over the delicate fabric of her underwear, and Sydney sags into my arm with another moan.

"Jesus, sweetheart, you really are soaked for me," I drawl. "Would you like to hear what else we should not discuss?"

Her head falls back as I draw circles with my finger over her clit. "Yes," she rasps.

"I'd like to take you back to The Ritz-Carlton and test every surface of that suite just like I should have back then. I'd fuck you so thoroughly you would need to take time off, Mrs. Lowe. I would make up for our lost time and give you an orgasm for each month you didn't call me."

I increase the pressure of my finger and Sydney whimpers.

"It sounds like a threat," she whispers.

"Oh, it's a threat, sweetheart. And it's a vow."

Chapter Eighteen

Sydney

"You're putting me on probation?" I shake my head as if the words might make more sense once rattled.

"Look, Sydney, I can't play favorites, and what happened at the museum was negligence. It doesn't reflect well on the school. You lost a child." Dan takes off his glasses and starts polishing them with the tip of his tie. A blue tie with tiny yellow patterns I bought him as a good-luck tie when he started interviewing for this job.

"Of course you shouldn't play favorites, but would you close a case with another teacher without investigation? How have you drawn your conclusion, Dan?" I'm not sure why I'm fighting him, because I was responsible for Caro and she went missing. It was my fault. I've had nightmares about it for the past three days.

The nightmares have been taking turns with spicy dreams since the night at Hunter's when things got heated, and then Caroline cried out and both of us snapped out of our delusional fantasy. It was reckless. We were both reacting to the traumatic experience of the day.

We will find out soon how real it was because we are going out tonight. On an actual date.

"You lost one of your students, Sydney, and I don't think an investigation would reveal anything pertinent."

"Okay." Part of me is certain this is his retaliation for breaking things off with him, but it will do me no good to point out his methods are unethical. At least now I know I need to be very careful in the future, because my actions won't be judged fairly. This includes publicizing my relationship with Hunter. If there is one.

We'd have to keep things secret for Caro's benefit for the time being anyway.

"Okay?" He studies me with a frown. His face is laced with questions, possibly even disappointed that I'm not begging him.

"I don't think your decision is fair, but I'm

accepting it. What else do you want me to say?" I shrug and stand up. His office is filled with the light streaming through the three floor-to-ceiling windows, but no amount of sunshine can make this conversation warm.

He stands up as well and walks around his desk. Before I can reach his door, he curls his hand around my biceps. "Wait, Syd."

"Dan, please." I don't even know what my plea is.

"I miss you," he says. "I shouldn't have proposed and spooked you. I don't need you to marry me. I don't need you to move in with me, but I don't have time or energy to date and look for someone else, and we were good together."

My sisters were right—Dan was safety and comfort. He helped me fight my loneliness, and clearly I was the same for him. He is handsome and intelligent, but he can't be bothered to look for a partner?

I study the hairline wooden ridges of his door for a moment before I face him, yanking my arm away from him. "Dan, are you suggesting we get back together because it's convenient and easier than looking for someone else? Do you really think that's a proposition that would win me over?"

"Come on, Syd, you never wanted the romantic gestures and all that sweet stuff. That's what I liked about you. You were very practical in our arrangement."

"Our arrangement, Dan, was an upgraded version of friends with benefits. You voided that arrangement when you asked me to move in with you and then tried to smooth it over by proposing. It's not about my residence or the engagement ring. It's about both of us wanting something else from a relationship."

I shouldn't even be indulging him in this conversation. A part of me hopes he'll get closure. A part of me wants us to get past the awkwardness and his hurt feelings. Jesus, part of me regrets I ever engaged in anything with him in the first place.

"I want for things to be back as they were," he huffs.

"Until you decide to move to the next stage without talking to me to know if we're on the same page? For fuck's sake, Dan, the fact we were not even remotely aligned is a clear sign we shouldn't continue."

"I thought you wanted—"

"Exactly, you *thought*, and you thought wrong."

"Syd, don't tell me you don't at least miss the sex."

Who is this person? Begging me for a second chance is so off-putting. I shudder. Pity mixes with consternation at the pit of my stomach.

I shake my head for the second time since I've entered this office. Again, it doesn't rearrange reality for me. "This is a place of work, Dan. You're my boss. Let's just keep things professional."

I leave so fast, I trip and bump into Melissa's desk. "Sorry." Heat spreads from my neck to my ears, burning me with indignation and exasperation.

Screw him. He wants to get back together because he is lazy and doesn't have time to look for another lay. Jesus.

I grab my things and walk out of the school, trying to shake off the aftertaste of that conversation. I pull out my phone and call Hunter.

"Hello, Mrs. Lowe, are you impatient for our date tonight?" His silky voice brushes over my skin with soft coolness, sprouting goosebumps.

"I could be calling about Caro," I point out.

"Caroline is safe and sound with my mom, and I'd prefer not to have a heart attack every time you call me. Also, it's after hours. If you're calling to ask how to dress tonight, don't worry." He lowers his voice to a dangerously sensuous rumble. "I don't plan on keeping you dressed for long."

"That's presumptuous, Mr. Stuart." A smile stretches across my face.

"I don't assume, I plan, sweetheart. Wear whatever you want... Perhaps something you won't miss once I rip it off."

Jesus. "You're such a romantic."

"At your services, Mrs. Lowe."

If I continue smiling like this, I might crack my jaw. "You're distracting me with your promises. I almost forgot why I called—"

"To hear my devastatingly sexy voice, of course."

"Where have you been hiding that ego until now? I don't think there is a storage facility large enough in NYC." I try to sound stern, but my voice is laced with humor.

Since we clarified the misunderstandings—to a certain extent—and decided to move forward, the air between us has been lighter, missing the stupid preconceived notions. Just two people enjoying each other's company.

We've been talking on the phone each night, and every conversation just adds to the growing list of things we have in common, or those we disagree on yet admire the other person's view.

"My ego is proportionate to all my other important parts." His voice drops deeper and the words spread heat in my core. My mouth goes dry and my brain void.

This man. I crave him and loathe myself for it. Or not anymore. It's all too much. More I can take and all I want.

"Dan put me on probation." My words feel like a cold shower on our playful conversation.

I don't even know why the innuendo riled me up

suddenly. Hunter is more experienced than me, and as much as I want not to think about that my self-confidence is shot, so here I am, pouring ice on a fun exchange.

A beat of silence stretches.

"Is he punishing you for breaking up with him?"

"I don't know. It would have been nice if he'd done a formal investigation before drawing conclusions, but what happened is my fault, so I take responsibility however he sees fit. We need to be careful. For Caro's sake, but also because of my job." He doesn't need to know about Dan's suggestion to get back together.

"You want to hide our relationship?"

"I want you to consider it before we jump into anything. This is hard for me to say, but if you're not willing to hide for the time being, perhaps we should cancel..." My stomach tightens. "Or postpone?" I hate how needy I sound.

What if he cancels, to protect his daughter? And that's what he should do. It's not like she could switch schools again. There has been enough turmoil in her life already.

Hunter is probably running a similar assessment. One that should lead him to an inevitable conclusion that would crush me. The silence on the other side of the line is punctuated by the erratic heartbeat pulsating in my temple.

"I'll pick you up as agreed, Sydney." He hangs up.

* * *

I lay out three different outfits and stare at them. I wish he'd called me Mrs. Lowe when he confirmed our date. He uses it to play around, but calling me Sydney—in that sexy hiss of his—left me doubtful. Does he want to meet to discuss the consequences of our potential relationship, or are we still having a date?

Too late, Mrs. Lowe, we're doing it. Fuck the rules.

I hold on to his words from earlier this week. His determination seemed resolute enough for both of us. And he has a daughter to protect. Perhaps I should be the one to hit the brakes. To stop us from giving in to the maddening lust that's consumed us since we laid eyes on each other.

My phone chimes with an incoming message. I don't want to look. What if it's Hunter canceling? The doubt settles in my mind, driving me crazy. *Pull yourself together, Sydney.*

I don't know why I've been on edge like this. It might be the conversation with Dan earlier, or perhaps the lingering awareness that for the first time since Jeremy I might be under the threat of caring enough to get hurt.

I check my phone finally.

London: *Stop overthinking and just enjoy yourself. Love, L.*

I chuckle, grateful for a sister that knows me this well. I look at my wardrobe options and I dial London. Her face appears on the screen.

"You're freaking out, aren't you?" She laughs and hands some paperwork to someone. It's Friday evening and she hasn't left work. Her assistant must leave, because Lo leans back in her chair and stretches her arms over her head. "Talk to me, sis."

"You look busy. Is everything okay?" She has that frown we're all so familiar with.

"I'm just pissed at the world as usual. There is a promising research project I can't seem to find funding for. Back to you."

I turn my camera reluctantly, because I know there isn't much comfort I can offer. I let her examine my clothes and I give her a rundown of my encounter with Dan.

"First, I'm impressed with Dan."

I switch the camera to the front view again. "Are you kidding me?"

"Show me the dresses again." She waves my concern away. "All I'm saying is I didn't think he had it in him to fight. Though his motivations are pathetic. Or practical, I guess." She chuckles and I sigh.

"What should I wear?" My exasperation makes her laugh again.

"Please remind me to take you shopping on Sunday. Or tomorrow if you're not too sore to walk."

I roll my eyes. Fucking London. "Focus!"

"Wear the green wrap dress. You're going to recreate your first date, so it fits the occasion and you look great in it. Should I save you a seat for two at the gala next month?"

Oh, I forgot about London's fundraiser. It's one of the most anticipated events of the pre-Christmas season. Usually I offer to volunteer because I'm the only person in the family who can't afford the ticket.

"Don't jump ahead. This is a first date."

"After three years of yearning. You'll jump into that relationship so fast you might even tie the knot before Massi and Gina."

Our eldest stepbrother, Massimo, has recently gotten back together with his teen love and ex-wife. His mother is thrilled, but also now focused on matchmaking the rest of us. My stepmother, Bianca Cassinetti, isn't too happy about all her children being single.

"Has Bianca called you about a family dinner?" London asks.

"Yeah, what's up with that? We can barely get everyone together at Thanksgiving or Christmas, and now she insists on a weekend in October?" I wonder out loud.

"We'll find out, I guess. Are the boys coming?"

"Bianca invited everyone, I assume."

"Yeah, with a not-so-subtle threat in her voice." London drops her feet and starts typing with one hand. "I have to take care of something. Get ready, and don't think tonight. Let go just for one night, Syd."

I shower and blow dry my hair into loose waves while thinking about London's advice. Can I let go? Is the carefree woman still accessible? Could I let Hunter see her? Do I even know her anymore?

I put on my dress and apply mascara and a touch of blush. Lo would insist on full makeup, but I don't feel comfortable with that. Somehow I know Hunter would prefer me natural.

I twirl in front of the mirror by the door, satisfied with the look. Another seed of doubt blooms, and I consider if wearing the same dress as three years ago is a good idea after all. But I don't get a chance to contemplate that further, or change, because the intercom crackles.

He's early. I pick up the receiver and buzz Hunter in. "Seventh floor." I hear the front door open and close.

I touch my lips with gloss and grab my coat as the

knock echoes through the apartment. When I open the door, however, I freeze.

"You?" My eyes meet Dan's. Instinctively I try to close the door, but he leans against it. With one of his hands on the door and the other on the frame, he prevents me from closing it completely, but at least the opening isn't wide. That might change if he decides to push.

"You look good. Are you going somewhere?" The stench of alcohol reaches me and sends my nerves into overdrive. Dan has never given me a reason to worry, but right now, anxiety coils at the base of my spine.

"What do you want, Dan?" I pray for Hunter to be late. I need to neutralize Dan and get rid of him before they run into each other.

"Let me in, Syd, I want to talk to you. I miss you." Dan's eyes glisten. He rests his forehead on his forearm and wipes the droplets of sweat coating his skin.

"We already talked today, Dan. Go home and sleep. You're drunk." I lean against the door with all my strength, hoping he won't try to push.

"Syd, I need you. We were good together. I miss you, baby."

Jesus, he's never called me baby before.

"Go away, Dan." I try to push the door closed, but my resistance jolts him into action. I'm no match for his strength and it only takes him one shove and the door flies open, propelling me backward.

My back hits the coat rack and I almost lose my balance.

"Just give me one more chance, Syd." Dan leans over and cups my face. I slept with this man many times over the past ten months. He was a gentle lover, perhaps a boring one, not very adventurous, but a gentleman. Never have I hated his touch. Until tonight.

Repulsion shivers through my body. I want to push him away, but the realization that I'm at his mercy right now freezes me. I want to scream, but surprise at his action drowns my voice. His wild and desperate glare.

His breath, sour on my face, churns in my stomach like poisonous acid. The tremble of his sweaty hands sparks another wave of disgust and I finally shove him. It's like pushing a brick wall. He leans in, and I swear if he kisses me I might end up in jail tonight.

A warning—no, a threat—ripples through the air like a knife's blade. "Let go of her."

Chapter Nineteen

Hunter

Red swims through my vision. I got lucky and a neighbor let me inside. I found Sydney's name and apartment number on the mailbox and got here right in time to pull this asshole off her.

I grab his collar and it's surprisingly easy to yank him off.

"Hey." He stumbles and trips but recovers his balance. His eyes meet with mine and recognition flickers in them. "You?" The contempt in his voice wouldn't bother me normally, but after he forced himself on Sydney, his luck has run out.

"Me, dickhead." I extend my fist, turning it inward as I strike. My middle knuckle connects with his jaw in a satisfying punch that reverberates through my elbow. He blinks a few times, rubbing his face as he searches Sydney's eyes. As if she would save him after he pushed himself on her.

"Get out of here and never come back. Do you understand? Ever." I raise my fist again, not really planning to jab, just to make a point. It's clear he's not a fighter. He trips as he dashes for the staircase.

I turn to Sydney. She stares at the swinging door where he disappeared. I clench my fist a few times, the adrenaline rushing through my veins.

"Are you okay?" I step closer and Sydney drags her eyes to me. She blinks a few times, disoriented. I want to turn and catch up with the asshole and beat the shit out of him. How dare he put his hands on her?

She licks her lips and glances at the staircase door again. Fuck, now she won't feel safe in her own apartment.

"Sydney." I tame the raging animal in my chest. "He is not coming back."

She searches my face, unsure she can believe me. Ultimately, she can't. I have no idea if I scared him enough.

"Do you want to reschedule?" I ask, knowing there is no way I'm leaving her alone. I might forego our date, but she is not staying here by herself. And if I have to postpone the date, the asshole will pay. School princi-pal? What a joke.

"Could we start with a drink?" She bites her bottom lip, a blush coloring her cheeks.

"Of course, Mrs. Lowe," I drawl, and her shoulders relax.

She turns, checks her face in the mirror and shud-ders. My desire to break both of Ravinski's legs swings up a notch.

"Come here, beautiful." I reach for her. She takes my hand gingerly and I pull her into an embrace. She breathes in and out deeply, a slight tremor combs through her body. I kiss the top of her head. "You look positively ravishing tonight, Sydney."

Another wave of shivers slices through her, and this time I'm positive they are unrelated to the trauma. "We can stay in if you want," I whisper.

She doesn't move for what feels like hours. Not that I'm complaining, because holding her in my arms has just become one of my favorite pastimes.

Finally, she pushes back and looks at me with clear eyes. "He's done enough damage for one night. I'm not letting him spoil my evening even further." She smiles at me, and I can't believe how beautiful she is. Her determination is so fucking sexy.

"Excellent decision, Mrs. Lowe." I wink and lead her to the elevator.

"So much for keeping things private for the time being," she sighs as we ride down.

"I think he stepped over so many boundaries tonight, he should think twice about his future actions—inside and outside the school."

She looks at me and tilts her head like she's just noticing me fully for the first time. "You clean up nice." Her lips tug up slightly, playfulness finally reaching the crevices of her eyes.

"Why, thank you. I appreciate your choice of a dress. Very appropriate." I wrap my arm around her and pull her closer, finding her lips. I want to devour her, but she's probably still upset from earlier, so I dust her mouth lightly.

"You remember." Finally she smiles fully, and it's the most enticing sight. The small lines around her eyes crinkle, softening her face.

"I remember everything about you, beautiful."

Sydney

"I'm so full." I throw the napkin onto the plate.

"Well, then we're following the itinerary to a tee." Hunter studies me with the same intensity as he did our first time here. His gray eyes glimmer with sin and mischief. I was intimidated by his stare three years ago. Today, I welcome it. The way he lazily drags his gaze from my eyes to my lips. To my throat. Down my cleavage. I'm almost sure he can regulate my breathing and swallowing through that scorching look.

He's wearing a suit like the last time, but this time with a black T-shirt instead of a dress shirt, and somehow that careless style choice makes him even more sexy. The bespoke suit jacket hugs the planes of muscles over his shoulders, chest and arms. It's almost impossible to focus solely on his face.

The Ritz-Carlton's dining room is just as stuffy now as it was then. The place is so pompous, I fear that our conversation might scandalize people even if we're quiet. Most of the guests are eating in silence, as if annoyed by the social obligation of being here.

Hunter made a reservation at another restaurant, in case we wanted to avoid this place, but then we agreed to stick with the original plan. We definitely don't belong here, and somehow that's twice the fun. I don't know how we look to the other guests, but we are raising eyebrows with our sensual touches and telling looks.

Some things are different this time around. Instead of drowning in uncomfortable anxiety, I flirt more openly. And Hunter didn't take the seat across from me like the last time. He sits beside me at the square table. His closeness is a decadent promise of the next phase of our date.

To my relief, Hunter unleashed his charm and we passed through the dark cloud of the incident with Dan. I don't understand what got into him. Seeing him drunk and aggressive nudged at my confidence and my already hampered ability to trust people.

Again, I misjudged a person gravely. If someone would have asked me before tonight if Dan could lash out like that, I would have defended him. Because that's not the man I know. Yet here we are.

After two cocktails and Hunter's masterful steering of the conversation, I've succeeded in pushing the incident away, storing its consequences for further exploration at another time. After this date. A date that is shaping up wonderfully.

"Tell me about your family. Is London your only sister?" Hunter asks.

"We'll be here for a while because there are eight of us."

"Eight? Wow! I thought having one sister was more than enough growing up. Julia was such a princess. She would provoke me all the time and then play innocent, and I'd get shit from my parents. Always."

"Similar to us, just times eight."

Hunter laughs.

"I have three sisters: London, her twin, Paris, and

little Brook. I guess she's not little anymore, but she's the youngest. London established a foundation to support leukemia research and runs several charities related to the cause. Paris is a sought-after interior designer. Brook has extended her post-graduation back-packing trip several times now. Last I heard she was somewhere in Asia.

"My father re-married—well, they never legally married, but our families merged when I was thirteen. The best thing for an awkward teenage girl is to join a household with four boys." I chuckle and sigh at the same time. "Though Bianca became our mother and took us in like we were hers. Massi is an in-demand chef and he invests in new promising restaurants. He just got back with his ex-wife.

"Giovanni is a venture capitalist. He's the CEO of a holding company that eats up other companies or something. Andrea is a successful artist, asshole and womanizer. And little Baldo, who is Brook's age, so not so little anymore, is somewhere doing something."

"It seems they all are successful at what they do." Hunter idly draws circles on the back of my hand. The simple connection spreads peace through me.

"They've done well with the trust funds and their own skills." I swallow, my own failures blooming in my stomach. "I chose to be a teacher." A strong need to defend myself swipes through me.

Hunter narrows his eyebrows and smiles. "And you're great at it. I didn't mean to... Do you feel less than them because you don't swim in money?"

"The reason I don't swim in money has nothing to do with my capability or career choice," I blurt, regretting it immediately. I'm not ready to go this far, to bare this much.

Hunter stays silent, letting me decide if I want to elaborate. I don't. And so he bridges to a different, inconsequential topic, and after a beat or two I'm back at ease. We continue to talk, laugh and eat.

"Still a fan of Nesbo?" I tilt my head, admiring the man beside me. Hunter's chin rests in his palm as he rubs his whiskers with his thumb. It's probably a mindless movement, but it gives him an air of sexy intelligence.

He nods. "Is blue still your favorite color?" He lifts my hand and brushes my knuckles with his lips, sending delicious shivers down my spine and setting a fire in my core. This man is an arsonist.

"Yes, it is. Have your tastes changed?" I sound breathy, but that's okay. Our conversation might be trivial, but there is nothing trivial about the charged energy.

"It has, in fact. I've become a fan of green." He traces his index finger over my shoulder, luxuriating in the fabric of my green dress. Playing me like a violin.

I'm so taut with anticipation, I might snap. At the same time, I'm painfully aware that his experience surpasses mine. The awareness tugs at my self-confidence. Not that I've had any to spare to begin with, but part of me wants to bolt. Or fast forward to the morning.

"I have a slight change to our itinerary, Sydney." My name on his lips is like a dangerous promise. The way he hisses the S with a sexual undertone makes everything inside me clench.

"Will I like the change?" I swallow hard, my heart begging to escape my ribcage

"I hope so. We have to leave the hotel for this part of our date, but we'll be back to enjoy the suite." Hunter's eyes darken with the suggestion, and I wish the ventilation system in this freaking restaurant worked better. The oxygen disappeared at some point tonight and no one seems concerned. Beads of perspiration trickle down my back.

Hunter gestures to the server who promptly brings our bill.

"Let's split it," I suggest.

Hunter raises his eyebrows. "Do you want to spoil this evening, Sydney?" He tightens his jaw, frowning at me. "I'm paying." The authority in his voice shuts me up.

This isn't the first time I've faced Hunter's dominant side, but the few times he's completely controlled a situation have been in a more intimate setting. The elevator ride. His kitchen. The hallway in front of Caro's room. I'm not sure how I feel about the check situation.

The romantic part of me is swooning. Pragmatic me is screaming. And the reason isn't noble. It has nothing to do with equal treatment. I feel fairly uneasy about the source of Hunter's money. But I learned my lesson and I don't want to make assumptions.

We step outside and Hunter guides me to the left. "It's only two blocks from here. You okay to walk?"

I nod. The situation with the bill sits on me like a prickly blanket. I wish I could discuss it with him, but who discusses money on their first official date? And I certainly am not ready to talk about the disaster of my financial situation.

"I didn't want to accept the inheritance." Hunter breaks the silence, and I stop because what the hell? Can he read my mind? And what inheritance?

"You don't need to explain." I resume walking.

"Really? Are we going to play this game? You are uncomfortable I paid for dinner. Is it a question of principle, or are you wondering where the money came from?" He keeps his hand on the small of my back and I'm grateful for the tender connection, because his honesty scares me and comforts me at the same time.

I stop again. This conversation is too heavy for the walk. "I'm having such a great time tonight. Part of me wants to push it aside, but yes, you're right. You weren't rich three years ago and I wonder—"

"If the money comes from my former clients?"

Before I answer, someone bumps into me, and Hunter swears under his breath. He grabs my hand and pulls me into a nearby deli. We order two sodas and grab a table in the corner.

It's kind of comical how we moved from five-star luxury into a narrow joint with plastic chairs. Dressed up and all.

"My decision to moonlight as a male escort was motivated by my sister's—Caro's mom's—medical bills. Her treatment was expensive. It was the most money I could make in a short period of time."

Hunter sips his drink, his eyes locked on the can, though I don't think he's reading the label. I don't dare to move because I feel this is not a story he tells readily. His throat bobs up and down. Before he continues, he takes my hand and caresses it between his two huge palms.

"All that money went to her care. What was left is in Caroline's college fund. The day after you and I met, I took one of Ash's training sessions. Priscilla Stein was in her eighties, rich and lonely. She paid Ash to help her stretch and keep active, but that afternoon when I met her, I realized it was the company she sought. She didn't have any family left."

Hunter's palms are like heating pads on my hand. I remain still, letting him take his time with the story.

"I could have just shrugged and moved on, but I went back and read books for her, or just listened to her talking about her past. Soon, I accompanied her to the theater and later started having brunch with her on Sundays whenever I could. I was her escort, but I never charged her. I just... I don't know. I was lonely as well. Between Caro, Julia and my clients—fitness and escorting—I was always among people, but..."

He probably can't imagine how much I relate. I was teaching, hanging out with my sisters, recently even dating Dan, but the loneliness rarely stems from being alone. They are two different things.

I squeeze his hand and Hunter finally looks up. I hope he sees the understanding in me.

"Obviously, I couldn't date in a normal way. Or I believed I couldn't because while not many of my clients expected sex, I was dating for money. So eighty-two-year-old Priscilla was the perfect solution. We struck up an unconventional friendship. She was some-thing else." He chuckles sadly. "I even introduced her to Caro. They hit it off."

A smile lingers on his face as his eyes look nowhere in particular, deeply engrossed in memories.

"I swear I never wanted to con her out of her money. She left it all to me. The apartment and assets. A lot of it. She was cunning, though. She suspected I'd just give most of it away to cancer research in Julia's honor, so she made a significant donation and conditioned the inheritance with several clauses and stipulations that would make it difficult for me not to accept."

"It sounds like she really cared. Like you really made a difference in her life."

"I hope so. Ash was pissed at first. He couldn't believe he'd trained her for years and I was the one benefiting. He felt like I swept in and got rich on his turf. It took him months before he snapped out of it. Now we work together, so in some way he benefits from the money, too."

"I can see how Ash might have felt entitled to get a cut, but he was wrong. I don't think he'd ever use it as smartly as you, building a business that spreads health." I lift his hand to my face and rub my cheek against it.

"That sounds way too noble. But I'd appreciate it if you'll allow me to spend a negligible part of it on you, beautiful." He leans forward and kisses me, gently grazing my lips.

I don't know if I want to be treated like that by him. Clearly Hunter is now more in London's and my other siblings' league, and I don't know if I'm comfortable with that. It's not that I'm jealous of their financial success, but it reminds me of what I don't have and probably never will. Pathetic? Perhaps. Real and raw for me? Definitely.

"Thank you for telling me," I whisper against his lips. "You're a good man, Hunter Stuart."

"Don't idealize me, beautiful. After Julia's diagnosis I had to grow up fast. But believe me, I was an immature party-seeker before. I was sleeping around before the escort gig. More than when I was a paid companion."

"Jesus. Let's ease up on the honesty now." My heart gallops in my chest like a spooked horse. If I was worried about measuring up to his expectations in the bedroom before, I'm ready to run now.

Hunter throws his head back, laughing. "You got pale, beautiful. Imagine the benefits you'll reap from my training." He winks.

Jesus, this man. "What is the surprise detour?" I try to recover my composure, involuntarily doing Kegel exercises.

"Right." He pulls me up and drags me outside. I stumble and giggle all the way to our destination. Somehow this man riles me up with his brutal boldness, and then he relaxes me immediately.

Muffled music greets us as we enter a dark diner. Hunter leads me to the back corridor and the song gets louder. As we descend a flight of stairs, a thousand butterflies flutter through my chest and stomach.

Slow eighties music bounces off the walls in an intimate underground club. Several couples sway on a small dance floor.

"May I have this dance?" Hunter bows and leads me to join the other dancers. He holds me to him.

Tight. Possessive. Overwhelming.

"You remember..." I fight tears, clinging to him like my life depends on it.

"Of course. I don't want you to ever miss dancing again," he whispers in my ear.

He twirls me and pushes me away, only to pull me close again. He leads us through the rhythm with confidence and playfulness. Two people synchronized by the beat of music and its echoes in our hearts. We don't need to chase connection because it's there. Simply. Naturally. With ease and abandon.

In that moment, I realize with chilling certainty my heart is irrevocably at risk.

Chapter Twenty

Hunter

I was pissed when Sydney suggested we split the bill. What the hell? But in the end, it led to a conversation that cleared the air a bit. It also opened up another channel of intimacy between us, and who would have thought that laughing and swaying at the club would deepen it even further.

Taking her dancing could have backfired. The last thing I wanted was to remind Sydney of her late husband. But as I held her in my arms, gliding along the floor, all my worries dissipated.

I've never been a fan of dancing, but with her it might become an addiction. Everything about her has slightly unhealthy habit-forming tendencies. And we've yet to get to the bedroom. If I've picked up on

Sydney's occasional blushes and shy looks correctly, her head isn't yet completely on board with the idea.

Case in point—as we ride the hotel elevator to our floor, the air is as thick with need and hunger as the last time, and her eyes again hold that tinge of nervousness. When I trace my finger down her spine, she tenses, and an almost inaudible gasp escapes her. The sound sends a direct message to my pants and the pressure behind my zipper is almost painful.

I've waited to spend the night with her for so long. For years I denied myself even the hope that it could happen. I'm still not sure if we're heading toward disaster, especially after the altercation with the fucking principal.

But there is no denial anymore. Sydney stares at the door, practically vibrating with anticipation and a dose of hesitation beneath it. Dancing relaxed her, but she looks like she is considering bolting.

Remembering our last ride in this elevator, I hit the console. The elevator halts with a jerk and I pounce.

Stepping closer, I corner Sydney, caging her with my hands on each side of her head. Another soft gasp escapes her. "Your little sounds will be the death of me, beautiful."

My lips brush her ear as I speak, and she shudders. Why her reaction pleases me this much I'll never know. I trace my finger up her arm. Her skin is like a peach, slightly fuzzy and smooth under my touch. I want to taste her.

Her breathing comes in shallow bursts. I'm so close her nipples brush against my jacket with every breath. I drop my eyes to her breasts, admiring the hard peaks begging for my attention. Unlike the last time, Sydney is looking at me. Our eyes lock, channeling the ache we both feel. It's raw and primal. Inevitable. The air pulses with unspoken promise.

"What are you thinking?" I rasp, repeating the same question as three years ago.

Sydney groans, remembering. She licks her lips, sending lightning down my spine. "That you either fuck me now or get me upstairs quickly." Her eyes widen as though she shocked herself with the boldness of her statement.

My lips curl up. "Good girl." I step back and she almost collapses to the floor. I snake one arm around her waist and hit the button.

As we get out, I lean in and whisper, "Just to make one thing clear, beautiful, there will be nothing quick happening tonight."

Another sound from her makes the top of my future Sydney playlist. It is a squeal and a moan in one, underlined by a heavy breath. As if she couldn't decide whether to protest or cheer. Not that it matters. There is nothing that could stop us anymore.

I booked us the same suite. After we get inside, I pour us a champagne and Sydney takes off her shoes. It almost feels like rehearsed choreography.

We end up on one of the love seats. I lean closer and trail my hand down her legs. Another of her soft sounds shoots lightning down my spine and I groan. Partly in pleasure, partly in frustration. There is a beast inside my chest I'm trying to keep leashed, but it's getting harder with every touch, every look, every noise.

I reach for her ankle and scoop her feet up in one swift move. Sydney laughs, but it turns into a sigh as soon as I dig my fingers into her soles. We haven't said a word since the elevator. We don't need to anymore. The charged silence is roaring loud enough.

I massage her feet for a moment, and Sydney studies me with intrigue and what looks like hesitation. No matter how much I try to spread calm through the kneading contact, her spine remains rigid.

"Talk to me, beautiful." I ease the pressure and let my hand wander languidly up and down her shin.

"Honestly?"

"Of course."

She swallows and lets out a sigh that carries baggage heavy enough to kill the moment. I may suffer a severe case of blue balls if talking is all we do again, but sign me up. I'm willing to break the world record for the bluest set of testicles.

"I love how attentive you are. How you took me dancing. Everything about tonight. But can we just get to the bedroom and get it over with?"

I stare at her, stunned for a beat. What the hell? "Get it over with?"

"That's not what I meant." She groans and hides her face in her hands. "I'm just so nervous. You've been with…"

Jesus. I grab her ankles and yank her closer as I pivot. She is now practically under me as I cup her face. "Eighty percent of my dates were dinners, theater, and a lot of conversation. Will you think of all my clients every time we watch a movie, talk, eat together or dance?"

She shakes her head.

"So you will think about them only when it comes to sex?"

She doesn't move.

"Fuck, Sydney, I've had enough meaningless sex in my life. If you think this is in any way similar to my previous experience, you're wrong. I have never wanted a woman more than I want you. Never have I cared so much that I'm willing to forego my own release to make sure you're satisfied and happy. This is important to me. So don't you dare ask me to get it over with. It's not a pit stop we're obliged to check off."

I crush my lips against hers, channeling my frustration into a savage attack. It only takes one heartbeat for Sydney to respond, and our tongues meet in a violent dance. It's messy, sloppy, teeth clattering, but her tension is incinerated by the divine burn the kiss drives through our bodies.

"You're sexy as fuck, Sydney." I lift on to my elbows. She is flushed from the kiss, looking so delicious that an arrow of lust and joy whizzes through me. "Drop the performance anxiety because you're perfect, beautiful."

I lower my lips to her forehead, brushing her warm skin with feather-like kisses down to her temple, around her ear, to the crook of her neck. She moans and the beast in me roars to life. I need her to scream my name.

"But let's get you comfortable first." I push up on to my haunches and pull her toward me, raising her knees over my shoulders.

She yelps, shocked by the fast action, staring at me wide-eyed.

With the lace of her stocking hugging her thighs, her skirt pooled around her waist and her legs spread around me, she looks wanton. But she is anything but. Sydney packs poise, depth, sadness and burden under the layers of protective wrapping, and I need to unravel her. To find the woman she doesn't show to the rest of the world.

"Look at you, beautiful, already all soaked for me. Let's get you relaxed."

The rip of the fabric tears through the air, joined by another yelp. "My underwear," she protests half-heartedly.

"Redundant."

I drag my fingers through her wetness and a strong sense of possessiveness grips me. She is mine. I didn't lie when I told her I've never wanted a woman as much as her.

I may have believed it was the thrill of the chase. Right here, right now, it's obvious that while she might be in a very vulnerable position, there is no doubt she has me under control. Because there is nothing I wouldn't do for her.

The thought blankets me with unequivocal clarity. Overwhelming. Exhilarating. Scary.

I circle my thumb over her sensitive bud, luxuriating in the soft noises before I dive in and eat her luscious pussy. *She does taste like a peach,* is my last thought before instincts, desire, a mess of sensations and a burning ache take over.

Her hands in my hair. Her dilated pupils. Her wriggling and thrashing, finally letting go of her guard to seek the release. Her clenching muscles. She is divine.

"Hun-ter...plea-plea—"

"Do you want to come, beautiful?"

She grinds her hips, desperately seeking connection, moaning. I'm not an artist, but I want to paint her like this, to capture her essence that has the potential to make me her slave forever.

"Oh God," she whimpers.

"I'd rather you use my name, beautiful. Come for me, Sydney." I reach up and pinch her nipple. I need her naked, because the promise the soft fabric teases me with is too fucking urgent.

She clenches and goes rigid as my name on her lips carries loudly through the room. I continue ravishing that succulent wetness until her muscles slacken.

I kiss my way down her leg before I stand up, pick her up and carry her to the bedroom.

Sydney

Tiny waves of aftershock slice through my body as Hunter carries me to the bedroom. At least that's what I think he is doing, because my ability to assess reality left me the minute his talented tongue touched me.

His muscles around me feel like the safest place in the world. He stops at the foot of the bed and doesn't move, like he's considering something.

"Hunter," I whisper, my head buried in his neck. He smells like an ocean breeze and a sunny vineyard. And me. My heart somersaults in my chest. "Let's not get it over with."

He chuckles. "Good girl. Finally, you got it."

"Are you going to put me down?"

A lazy smile curls his lips. "I'm deciding if we go to the shower or test the bed."

I kiss his neck. Being in his arms like this doesn't feel ridiculous. For all I care, he could carry me around all the time. "Is the order important?"

He squeezes me tighter. "Good thinking. Let's get you fucked thoroughly on every surface here."

My stomach clenches. Part of me is scandalized by his dirty talk. I'm not used to it. But his words free another part of me. One I didn't know existed. That part is growing bolder under his guidance and luxuriates in his words.

He drops me to my feet so suddenly that I lose my balance, but his brawny arms are there to support me. Perhaps it would be safe to fall when I know he'd be there to catch me.

Hunter pulls me closer and before I realize it, my dress and bra are gone. His guttural growl vibrates through the air, sprouting goosebumps over my skin. My nerve endings are primed with a need so strong it feels like I may never relax again. Just a moment ago, I was shaking with an orgasm, and I'm at the edge once more. And the man hasn't even touched me.

He stands, studying me—no, devouring me—with his intense gaze, grazing my skin inch by inch with hunger. A threat and a promise peer right through me via those glimmering silver eyes.

The light from the adjacent room beams in dimly, leaving the room obscured. But as I stand here in my stockings, bare to his scrutiny, to his desire, to his enjoyment, I might as well be under a fluorescent light. It should be uncomfortable, and perhaps, to a certain point, it is. But somehow I also feel powerful.

Hunter watches me and then slides his T-shirt over his head. The tent in his pants must be painful. Yet he is not rushing things. Just taking his time, caressing me with his dangerous look while slowly sliding his shirt down his arms.

The expanse of muscles rippling his torso is picture-worthy. I mean, I know he is a personal trainer and I've admired the topography under his clothing many times, but fuck... he is hot.

"Like what you see?" He smirks. Bastard.

I lick my lips and refuse to nod or say anything. Yes, I'm swallowing hard as my taste buds work overtime while I'm ogling him, but I won't admit that. He obviously can see.

"Come here, beautiful," he drawls. There is no distance between us, just two steps, but my legs shake. Can I have an orgasm just from anticipation? Because I'm close.

He takes my hand and puts it on his abs. Wow! If I feared an orgasm when I stood two feet apart, this shy connection with his beautiful body is going to detonate me.

Surprising myself, I put my other hand on his chest then trail my fingers, discovering his body. My fingers draw circles around his shoulders and I move slowly around him. With one palm spread, caressing his torso, I hook the finger of my other hand in his waistband and trail around as I step behind him.

Hunter hisses when I snake my arms around him to stroke his chest. When my breasts push against his back, he grabs my hand and stills me. We stand there, breathing heavily as time stops, sucking us into a dimension of closeness and intimacy.

His heart hammers against my palm, sending vibes down to my core. His body is warm, but my skin is covered with goosebumps, the heat and the coldness mingling with devastating pleasure.

He whips around so suddenly that I jump back. The wild look in his eyes should scare me. It's the look of a predator, crazed with a hunger so strong I should fear his next move.

Yet I crave it like oxygen.

Hunter's chest rises and falls with controlled breaths. "I don't think I can give you slow and gentle, beautiful." He pushes the words out with strained effort, his face shadowed with concern.

I'm not sure if I know exactly what he is suggesting, but I'm shocked by the realization that I don't care. I trust him. Well, in this situation I do. The part of me that is used to wallowing in deeply rooted mistrust screams, trying to protect me. But those screams are a whisper compared to the need racking my body and soul.

Yes, soul. Because suddenly, in no uncertain terms, I know that breaking through my carefully safe barriers if only for tonight will burst into the freedom I so desperately need.

"Then fuck me hard." I don't recognize my voice. I don't recognize the confidence or the determination, but I have no time to analyze them because Hunter yanks his belt free and shrugs out of his pants and underwear.

"Get on the bed," he growls, kicking his clothes out of the way.

I scramble to oblige and lie on my back, panting as if it's a strenuous activity. I'm glad I wore my only pair of stockings. The lacy hems hug my thighs lustfully and the sight encourages me.

"On your hands and knees, beautiful." Hunter's voice slices through the air.

Jesus. Definitely no vanilla sex. I turn, jutting my ass up, and a wave of self-preservation descends on me, making me want to crawl away. My subtle move forward gets intercepted immediately.

Hunter grips my hips and pulls me closer. "Where are you going, beautiful?"

I shake so violently with the pent-up need for release that my teeth chatter. He strokes the length of my back, the tender touch calming my desire to bolt. What was I thinking? I want him beyond reason.

Hunter circles his palm over my bottom, and I'm sure now I can come just from the touch. I'm dripping down my thighs already, and I gain a growl of appreciation from him as he slides his hand between my legs.

He leans over me, his mountain of a body swallowing me under him. With his breath by my ear, I don't think I can stay upright for much longer. My knees shake, my elbows are ready to collapse, but I don't care anymore about anything. My entire being is absorbed by yearning.

"No more hiding, Sydney." God, that hissing of my name. "No more running. Or I'll have to punish you, beautiful."

My breath hitches as his words spread like wildfire, culminating in my center. I whimper, unable to communicate any other way.

Still leaning over me, Hunter plunges one finger into me. Instinctively, my hips sink against him, earning me another growl.

"Someone is eager to fuck my hand."

His words affect me as strongly as his finger. Or two now.

I grind against his hand, desperate for more friction, and Hunter chuckles darkly. He moves away and the sudden loss of his heat drives a frustrated huff from me.

A wrapper tears then, and his hands are on me again, bruising my hips as the tip of him nudges my entrance. He plunges into me in a move so powerful I would have fallen if it wasn't for his strong hands gripping me like a vise.

I cry out at his invasion, my body burning as I try to accommodate him. I breathe through the discomfort, but as he moves in and out a few times, pleasure grows, overpowering the initial pain.

"Jesus, Sydney, you're so tight. Such a beautiful, tight pussy. You're gorgeous."

His words make me deliriously happy. Hunter sets a punishing pace. I didn't imagine anything close to this when I asked him to fuck me hard. But the man delivers. And all the years of safe, vanilla sex seem like a waste of time.

Our bodies slap, shaking the bed. Our cries echo through the room. There is nothing tender or sensual about it, but I feel like with every thrust Hunter is setting me free, unlocking doors the carefree girl has been hiding behind. I may imprison her again as soon as this is over, but right now I let her—myself—accept and give with abandon.

Hunter backs onto his haunches, pulling me with him, my shoulders glued to his chest. His hands span my body, squeezing one nipple and simultaneously pinching the sensitive spot between my swollen folds.

It throws me over the edge with violent force. He pulls my hair, angling me so he can reach my mouth, and swallows my screams with a passionate kiss while my body trembles through the climax.

I don't have time to descend from the high before Hunter flips me over. Seriously, the man is so strong, I'm like a rag doll in his hands. On his knees, he yanks me closer, hooking my knees over his shoulders, and he continues thrusting.

I didn't think a third orgasm was possible. Nor did I think it could build up this fast. Yet here we are, and I'm thrashing and clenching again.

"Fuuuuuck," Hunter cries, throwing his head back.

We ride the wave together and collapse in a bundle

of limbs, sweat and pleasure. He shifts slightly to let me breathe. Our legs are tangled as he lies beside me. I turn and our eyes meet. He is close, and for the first time the intensity of his gaze has a new quality. It's softer. More vulnerable.

He kisses my shoulder. "Ready for that shower, beautiful?"

I burst into laughter. It's refreshing, gratifying and freeing. And I know in that moment that tonight's surrender will have lasting consequences. I only hope I can survive now that my protective walls have crumbled.

Chapter Twenty-One

Hunter

Dust particles float in the first shy rays as the light in the room changes to a softer, luminous hue. The world outside is waking up, but here, in this room, everything is still.

Sydney draws lazy circles across my chest. Tucked under my arm, spent and beautiful, she is right where she should be. Where I want her to be. Mine.

We haven't slept. We fucked on every available surface in this suite and are truly exhausted, but neither of us wants to succumb to the darkness. We've built up to this moment for too long to just let it pass in sleep.

I didn't expect Sydney to truly let go. She was shy and jumpy the first time we were here, and she was so nervous at the beginning of the night. But my girl is a tiger.

Seeing her unguarded, free, outside of that beautifulbut always warring, head of hers is an aphrodisiac. I'm unreasonably pleased she let me see that side of her.

"I'm starving," she mumbles, her breath tickling my chest.

"I can feed you my cock."

She bursts into laughter. I don't think she would enjoy that joke outside this room or this situation. That's why I don't want to fall asleep. I want to experience this unfettered, joyful version of her.

"Your cock, sir, had enough action tonight. I don't think there is a part of me that isn't sore."

I flip her over and cover her with my weight. "Have I hurt you?"

The smile lingering on her face is drowsy, but her eyes shine with mischief. "And I don't regret any minute of it. You, Hunter Stuart, have awakened dormant parts of me I didn't even know I have."

"Do you regret now that you didn't put out three years ago?" I tease and get another laugh. That simple sound affects every part of me.

"You're insufferable. At least I saved myself from three years of cockiness."

"Ten out of ten." I wiggle my eyebrows and grin at her exasperated chuckle.

"If you don't feed me breakfast soon, those points will go down fast, Mr. Stuart." She swats at me half-heartedly.

"I like this uninhibited Mrs. Lowe. Why do you hide her?" I kiss her.

Sydney looks away for a moment and her face rearranges with effort. The question must be heavier than I expected. A veil of something I can't identify shadows her eyes. Is it her late husband?

Or perhaps last night wasn't the first time the principal was aggressive? Damn it. I hate thinking about other men right now, and clearly she is not ready to talk about it. Yet, I hope.

"What do you want to eat, beautiful?" I navigate us out of the topic dimming our bubble of joy.

She scrunches her mouth to the side, and after careful deliberation says, "Anything, but a lot of it."

"That's what you came up with?" I laugh.

"I'm too tired and famished to know."

At least the veil is gone. Tucked away for now, but I'm not letting the topic go. Just parking it for the time being. Because fuck, she is right—we're both exhausted.

Fully intending to get up and order breakfast, I brush her lips with mine hastily. Sydney cups the back of my neck and pulls me closer. My cock twitches because apparently the right woman works like Viagra.

Her nails leave a trail of shivers as she drags them languidly down my back. I abandon her lips and give thorough attention to her nipples. And here it goes. Those whimpers—the soundtrack of our date. Of this night. God, I hope I hear them many more times.

Her stomach growls. "Breakfast, Hunter," she breathes, but keeps her hands in my hair and arches her back.

"You're distracting me, beautiful." I push onto my elbows and kiss her forehead before jumping out of the bed to find the room service menu.

I eat Sydney's pussy as we wait for breakfast to be delivered because it's my new favorite activity and we need to stay awake.

When the cart with our food arrives, we eat in silence in the living room. After years of constant chatter at every meal—either with Caro, with Ash, with my former clients—sharing silence with Sydney is a gift. It's not awkward or strained. It is as if the wild, carnal intimacy from the night has seeped into our languorous morning—toned down, but still very deep.

As I study the woman across from me, I realize I want to share silent moments with her beyond today. The realization spreads through my chest, but it also plants a seed of fear in my stomach. I committed to my sister and then to Caroline. Am I ready to protect and take care of another woman?

Sydney

"It's helped her a lot. Within a month she's already at the second grader level, but more importantly she's made connections with other girls. She has friends and it boosts her confidence. Soon you'll be driving her around Manhattan for birthday parties."

I'm lying naked on the sofa with a blanket carelessly tossed over me. Something I would have not believed before last night. Yet here I am, naked for over twelve hours now. And it doesn't bother me.

In fact, as Hunter rakes his gaze over me, it thrills me. Jesus. The man has unlocked a liberating recklessness in me. At least in this room. For now. And that's where it will stay.

We slept finally after breakfast and Hunter woke me up with his talented tongue between my legs again. Being awakened by burning arousal and an impending orgasm is now my favorite form of alarm. I wish I could have it delivered this way every morning.

We ate lunch and we're lounging leisurely now,

Hunter massaging my feet because we can't stop touching each other. And he is the ultimate caregiver.

"I'm grateful you're her teacher. She hasn't been this supported since she started school." He is wearing only a white towel and I'm enjoying my view of the solid mountain of a man.

"Have you taken her to an ophthalmologist since she started school?"

"Yeah, but she doesn't need glasses."

"Binocular vision dysfunction can lead to learning difficulties. In fact, it's often misdiagnosed as dyslexia."

"I've never heard of it." Concern deepens the lines around his eyes.

"It's correctable. Severe cases need special prism lenses, but many times a series of exercises helps."

"I'll take her to the eye doctor. Look at us. We're like an old married couple, talking about kids." He tickles my feet and I scoot them to me, push forward and kiss his cheek. Hunter pulls me into his lap.

"I don't mind talking about Caro. She's important to you and I'm glad I can help her out." I wrap my arms around his shoulders.

"I appreciate that, but I don't want you to work on our date." He fists my hair and coaxes me into a kiss, exploring my mouth. It's not a sweet kiss, but neither is it ravenous and desperate.

This time, the kiss is deeper, somehow more meaningful, and while I feel it in my core, I also feel it in my soul. His lips communicate beyond our undeniable physical attraction. Somewhere between our first kiss, all the miscommunication and last night, we've forged an understanding that bares us to each other.

If I thought the intensity of his stare was too much, the truth behind this kiss spreads worry through my veins.

Overwhelmed, I pull away and bury my face in the crook of his neck, tightening the embrace. I cling to him with determination and ferocity. I broke the kiss because I couldn't handle the promise of it. But at the same time, I don't want him to see my fear. So I hold on for dear life, hoping we can move past this, back to the safer, playful territory we have enjoyed all night.

I don't know what I was thinking when I agreed to this date. A casual fling has never been an option for us. This connection has been brewing for years, for fuck's sake. Can I trust the man? He doesn't know much about me. And do I know enough?

As panic grips my insides, Hunter squeezes me tighter and runs his hand down my back, soothing me like he knows what's happening inside me. And he probably does, because somehow he's more attuned to me than anyone else.

He kisses the crown of my head, cradling me like a child in his arms. Slowly, he slides his hand under the blanket loosely draped around my hips. It's all too much. His warm hand on my naked body. His gentle lips on the top of my head. The memory of trust I gave with abandon last night.

Oxygen barely grazes the top of my lungs and I chase it desperately, my chest heaving. Hunter says nothing, just holds me through my freak-out. I don't know how long I fight with my thoughts before Hunter stands up, lifting me with ease.

He puts me down on the longer sofa under the window. The sun blinds me momentarily, but a large shadow covers it as he props himself over me.

He scoops under my knee to spread me and enters me with a grunt. Filling me to the hilt, he stills, balancing on his elbows. He brackets my face between his hands and sears me with his hooded eyes. That gaze reaches deeper inside me than his cock.

If I thought the kiss before was too intimate, I was wrong. It doesn't even compare to this moment.

Hunter starts moving in and out. He sets a painfully slow pace, and every thrust feels like a promise. Of commitment. Of protection. Of more. More than I'm ready to surrender.

We fucked, we had sex, and now we are making love, and it's too much. I close my eyes, barely dealing with the pleasure crawling through my body and absolutely failing to tame the gripping fear. I'm not ready for this.

"Look at me," he demands.

I can't. If I look at him, my last protective wall will crack, and I can't expose so much to him. Not yet. Ideally never, because I need my safe cocoon to live. Well, to exist more than live.

The heat builds up and I clench around him, my body acting on pure instinct. I need the release and at the same time I don't want it. It's all too meaningful.

His lips touch my nipple and I clench again, nearing the explosion. Hunter stops moving and my frustrated whimper slices through the air between us.

I look at him and I swear he can see my soul.

"Eyes on me, Sydney." It's not a request, more a command with an undertone of a threat.

Our eyes lock and he moves again. It doesn't take long and we crescendo together, reaching a climax with such force that my vision blurs.

My high is so intense, I don't realize at first that Hunter pulled out, spraying my belly with white ropes of his seed. No condom. Jesus.

I blink a few times and a tear rolls down my cheek. He dries it with his lips, stands up and leaves. The absence of his warmth and his drowning intensity is a relief. For a brief moment. Then the familiar emptiness descends.

My loneliness is short-lived because Hunter returns from the bathroom, a towel in his hand. But even that beat of isolation propels tears. Or perhaps it's the sheer tornado of emotions. Or I'm too tired. Regardless of the reason, tears stream freely down my cheeks.

He cleans me with the damp towel, wraps me in the blanket, picks me up and sits again with me in his lap. Jesus, I'm a mess. Flushed from sex, spent from worry and hot from crying.

"Talk to me, beautiful." Hunter tucks a strand of hair behind my ear. His fingers brush my skin. It's a feather-like contact, but it rips through me, reaching the dark cracks of my heart. "What are you scared of?"

Before I can speak, I bawl. Ugly crying, snot and tears mixed, rupturing through me. The room echoes with my sobs. Hunter waits patiently, soothing me with his hands.

"I met Jeremy my last year of college. He worked at a car shop, and while he was changing my oil he charmed me into a date," I start when I finally regain my ability to speak, not even sure why this story pushed through. "We dated, fell in love and got married. Jeremy was very entrepreneurial. Always coming up with new ideas. And I trusted his instincts and gave him money.

"A lot of money from my trust fund. You see, the

Cassinetti-Lowe family is rich. All of us were set up with a solid financial foundation. Six years ago, Jeremy was involved in an accident. He died. You would think his death would be enough to break me, but it was what I found out later that pushed me right past the grief.

"Jeremy was a gambler, a high roller but an even bigger loser. There is no evidence he'd ever started any of the business ventures he talked about and appeared to foster. He had a life outside of our marriage and I was just his bank. Unfortunately, he squandered most of my trust fund, and somehow still managed to leave me with debts."

"Fuck." Hunter pulls me tighter.

"Fuck is right." My humorless laugh surprises me. "Sorry I'm tainting this perfect date with my embarrassing story."

"Sydney," he hisses, his jaw tense. "You have nothing to be embarrassed about. The asshole betrayed you, swindled you out of your money. The blame is all on him."

His conviction is like the first spring sun warming up the soil, getting ready to bring new life and hope. If only I could tell him the whole truth.

"I let him do it, Hunter. I believed him. And even if Jeremy was a perfect con artist, what about Dan? He was my friend with benefits." Hunter winces at my words. "And somehow he believed we were heading to the altar. And yesterday evening... I've known him for almost a year, and I never would have thought he was capable of practically assaulting me. I misread him. Just like I misread Jeremy. You see..." I search his face, afraid to continue, but all I find is tender care and understanding. "The intimacy between us scares the shit out of me."

He cups my face. "I know these are only words, but you can trust me, Sydney. You know more about me than anyone else. Whatever this is, I won't fuck it up. You cast a spell over me three years ago, and all I want is to be a better man for you. To be worthy of you. You can trust me, Sydney."

And I do. All my experience screams against it, but I know—deeply, unequivocally, firmly—I can trust this man. My trust in him is born out of pure instinct, but is planted in a place of absolute wisdom. It would be so freeing to let him complete me.

"It's me I don't trust."

Chapter Twenty-Two

Hunter

"But do you trust me?"

A pang of guilt swarms through me for pushing her. I file it away immediately. We've just discovered each other. Gotten the first taste. An initial image of what could be. It's addicting. Consuming.

Settled.

No fucking way I'm letting her slip away.

Her vulnerability seeps to the surface through her tear-stricken face, flushed cheeks and the misguided resolution in those bewitching eyes—her confession notwithstanding. She looks fragile at this moment. A fierce need to protect her rips through me. To claim her as mine so the rest of the world can't hurt her anymore.

As the betrayal story unraveled, it took all my willpower to control the red ogre growing in my chest. If that asshole husband of hers wasn't dead, I would kill him all over again.

"Yes?" She swallows, questioning her own conviction. "But I shouldn't." Her face contorts again, her eyes glistening.

"That's good enough for now." I pull her tighter, holding her with the determination of a warrior. Despite her words, her continuous internal battle, she's let down enough barriers since last night to fuel my belief that there could be an us.

Fuck, there is an us. And she will get on board fully. In time. Soon.

I nuzzle her neck, inhaling her scent. This beautiful woman who turned my world upside down with her chaste blushes, loyalty to my daughter, occasional unguarded humor, and stimulating conversation that challenged me. The layers still left to uncover. The mystery of her. And all those whimpers, moans and gasps.

"Would you feel better if I fuck you again now?" I whisper against the soft skin under her earlobe.

Sydney erupts with laughter and the heavy drape of our conversation lifts with the music of it.

"Hunter Stuart, you're a deviant."

"And proud of it." I smirk.

"And you're humble." She cocks her head, a little playfulness returning.

"You have the ability to unleash the best of me." I graze my teeth over her jaw. Her shivers seem to have a direct line of communication to my cock. "So, fucking it is?"

Our laughter turns heated pretty quickly and we spend the rest of the day and half of the night thoroughly discovering every inch of each other.

"I don't want to face reality," Sydney says as we reluctantly leave the room on Sunday morning.

"Nothing changes. This is our reality now, beautiful." I scoot her closer to me as we wait for the elevator.

"Only, I have a job where my boss is the last person I want to ever see, and you have a daughter who doesn't know about us. And I need to check the internal code of conduct to see if dating a parent would cost me my job. And—"

I silence her with a kiss. She tenses at first, but then melts into it. "We will solve it all. Stop worrying."

"How?"

I shrug. "Fucking."

The elevator opens at that moment and a couple of seniors glare at us. Sydney stifles a giggle.

"Is that your answer to everything?" she whispers as we descend.

"Pretty much." I squeeze her hand. "With you, anyway."

She shakes her head, a blush spreading across her cheek. I like the playful Sydney, but this half-scandalized one is beautiful too. I've been teasing her to help her relax from all the worst-case scenarios in her head, but as we step off the elevator, there is no doubt in my mind this is way more than fucking.

She winds her arm around my waist, and I put mine on her hip. Like two blocks, we fit together.

"Hello, Stuart." The piercing voice from behind us in the lobby skitters through me like a pesky insect. That's what the owner is.

"Hello, Gigi." I steer Sydney toward the exit, hoping to avoid an interaction with the poisonous spider.

"I'm surprised to see you here. With a companion nonetheless." She catches up with us.

Sydney stops, glances at me to gauge my reaction. I'm not sure what she sees, but she turns to Gigi and raises her eyebrows.

"And why would that be surprising? I'm his girlfriend. Sydney." She offers her hand and Gigi looks at it with distaste but shakes it.

"Gigi Lafontaine." She drops Sydney's hand, and *my girlfriend* wraps her arm around me again, placing her other hand on my chest. Claiming me? Perhaps.

But her hand also has an immediate calming effect on me. At least to a certain extent, because I do want to strangle Gigi.

"Hard to believe you're getting domesticated now." She cocks her head, squinting at me, waiting for the truth. When neither of us reacts, Gigi lifts her chin, her nostrils flaring.

I give Sydney a gentle shove to move away. As far away as possible from this impossible woman and my past, but Sydney mirrors Gigi's chin lift.

"Find yourself a new toy, Gigi. Nice meeting you." She grabs my hand and pulls me away.

The October air hits us with sunshine as we step outside. We walk in silence for a moment. I'm riled up from the encounter and kind of dazzled by Sydney's defense. Because I think she tried to defend me. Claim me in front of another woman. *My girlfriend.* Never had I thought I needed one of those.

"I'm sorry." My past would always hang over my head.

"Don't be. It's not like we can change the past. I'm assuming she was one of those clients that included a bedroom component as a part of your services." Sydney bites her lip.

I nod, and she shakes as if she's just swallowed slime. "Hunter Stuart, you were scoring fifteen out of ten, but this lapse of judgment just pushed you back at least ten points."

I pull her to me. "I'll work my way back up," I promise against her lips.

"I see a lot of fucking in our future."

The laugh she drags out of me is cathartic.

"I have to hurry to the gym, but come with me if you can." I don't want our time together to end.

"If you think you can make me lift weights, you're mistaken." She shakes her head with a grin.

"Come with me, beautiful, I promise the only exercise you got was the cardio this morning." I wink and pull her along with me.

The club is busy, and I lead her to the fitness studio where a group of children greet us with cheers.

"Hey, guys, who is ready to kick ass?" I call.

The boys cheer again and run to set up the stations for an obstacle course.

"What's going on?" Sydney watches the commotion.

"These are kids from families who can't afford sports or gym memberships. They come here every Sunday and we move together."

Her eyes widen. "You spend your Sunday working out with underprivileged children?"

I nod. "Can you wait, so I can walk you home properly afterward?"

"I wouldn't miss this. I shouldn't even be surprised this is what you do during your weekends, but let me tell you, handsome, this is very sexy."

"I gave you my best performance this weekend, and *this* sways you?"

Her laugh swells in my chest.

The next two weeks are a flurry of stolen dates and brief encounters at the most inappropriate places. We now know that my office desk can withstand abuse, but the sofa is not very stable. And that, unfortunately, our schedules are not very compatible to see each other as much as we would like.

I learned Sydney hates Indian food but loves Mexican. That she scratches her eyebrow when she tries to remember her to-do list. She bites her lips when she wants to do something, but her head is stopping her from letting go.

When she drinks enough she is quite a good lap dancer, and a funny and hot AF stripper. And she blushes when reminded of it once sober. She cares about her students, not only Caro, beyond her professional duties. She can't cook—I'm still waiting for the right moment to tell her. When she lets her guard down she is funny, and when she laughs I am happier.

I'm much busier since I've started dating her, but I'm also calmer. Despite the hiding, I have this unshakable feeling things are as they should be. It makes no sense since we've been together for mere days, but one of these days I might just fucking start to believe that fate is not a bitch after all.

I also find out that the school is full of gossip.

"So you like Mrs. Lowe?" Caro asks.

The sidewalk is damp from the rain and the air chills me almost as much as her words. Shit.

"I do. Don't you like her? She is a great teacher." I really hope this is what we are discussing.

"Please, Dad, of course, she is a wonderful teacher. She's helping me with reading, and she is helping Ruby with math as well. She smells really nice, and I like her hair too. But Ruby's mom said you look at her with those eyes." She stops, forcing me to look at her. "What eyes?"

"Pumpkin, I don't know what Ruby's mom thinks." Shit, have I been that obvious during school runs? "But I look at her the way she deserves. I respect her and I appreciate that she's been helping you. And yeah, she smells nice, and I also like her hair." Not a lie, but not the complete truth either. I can't tell my daughter the other things I like about her teacher.

"Don't call me pumpkin." Her glare is just short of foot stomping, but only because she probably doesn't want to stain her new purple leggings. That's another thing the new school—and I might be biased, but Sydney in particular—brought to our lives.

Caro finally ditched the dark colors and allowed some spark in her wardrobe. Though getting changed every time before we leave the school grounds is a pain in the ass, I love this new outgoing, sparkly version of my girl.

I laugh, glad that the nickname shifted her attention. We arrive at the gym, and I leave Caro with Lea at reception before heading to my office.

"What are you doing here?" I frown at Ash who is sprawled across my sofa.

"And hello to you, too. I just thought I'd make sure you don't ditch Delaney again." He pushes up to sit.

"I've never ditched her. My daughter was lost, and yes, I have been postponing the meeting, but no worries, it's happening"—I check my watch—"in five minutes."

"Can I sit in?"

"I don't see why not. Suit yourself. Things are okay at Tribeca?"

"Yeah, we're good to go ahead and start planning the opening before Christmas."

"Perfect. I'm sorry I haven't been able to get there much, but I'll come over next week."

"No problem. I have it under control. We should

discuss the budget for the new club." Ash leans back while I boot up my computer to see if there are any emergencies to deal with before the meeting with Delaney.

"Look, Ash. The deal with the company next door is taking ages, going through their internal procurement, but once that's done, we can use the financial injection and reinvest it in the marketing of the new location. Otherwise, it will be a soft opening and we'll see how things are going before we invest more strategically. Social media being the priority, I think."

Ash looks like he wants to argue. He has been dreaming big about the new location. His club, as he sometimes calls it. But he doesn't get a chance to voice his concerns because Delaney knocks on the door.

"I'm sorry again about the last time." I offer the seat across my desk to her. I don't get many visitors so there isn't another seat there, and Ash stands up and leans against the wall beside the desk. "My daughter is safe and sound, sitting outside, so there shouldn't be any interruptions."

"I saw her there. She is lovely. I think it's amazing we can give you this human story aspect as well. All hot, healthy, and a single dad. The viewers would love it." She names my attributes in a detached, mechanical way while typing on her phone. Hopefully making notes, not dealing with other business.

I'm not sure how I feel about her attributes or about dragging Caro into it. I'm not even sure if I want to do the show yet.

"I know we discussed some ideas last time, but why don't you recap for me what the idea is and what my role would be." My phone lights up with a message from Sydney and I force myself not to check it.

Delaney explains the idea and the expectations. I must admit the potential exposure would be significant, but what intrigues me more is that the show could actually impact people and motivate them toward a healthier lifestyle.

Ash jumps in with a few questions and I use the opportunity to glance at the message.

Sydney: Consulted the guidelines.

Finally. I have been bugging her about it since our weekend at The Ritz-Carlton, and for some reason she's been postponing.

Sydney: We can date, Mr. Stuart, but I need to disclose the relationship officially to management, a.k.a. Dan Ravinski. Miss you. S.

I smile, grateful Ash is keeping Delaney engaged.

Me: Would you like to be my official girlfriend, Mrs. Lowe? I hear the helicopter moms are gossiping already.

Sydney: OMG. Really? Who? Why?

I imagine her blushing and chuckle to myself. Not to myself. Delaney and Ash stare at me. Correction.

Delaney looks at me with amusement, but Ash glares as if I'm cheating with his girlfriend. Not like that would be a likely scenario.

"Sorry." I clear my throat. "Continue."

"There isn't much to say, Hunter. Are you in or should I continue looking?" Delaney asks.

My phone keeps blinking with new messages. I can imagine Sydney is freaking out about my comment.

"Do you need to take care of that?" Ash snaps.

Jesus, he really is in a mood today.

"No, I'm good." I give him a what-the-hell look. "If you're ready to make an offer, I'm open to consider it seriously."

Delaney nods and stands up. "Expect an email from me by the end of the day. I look forward to working with you, Hunter. See you around, Ash."

"Are you for real?" Ash growls as soon as the door closes.

"It went well, didn't it?" I shrug and unlock my screen, finding a missed call from Sydney.

"You fucking ignored her and texted during the meeting. What's so important? Lately, you have been distracted. Is this still about Sydney? You need to get your brain out of your pants, man, and get back to business."

What the actual fuck? Yes, I have been juggling things around, but it's not like I've been slacking. In fact, I've been working hard, planning our next location and potential launch on the West Coast. I let Ash take a more active role at Tribeca and to a certain point here, so I can focus on growing the business.

"What's wrong with you today? Do you need to get laid?"

"Whatever." He shakes his head and leaves.

I stare at the door for a moment, stunned. I haven't seen him this worked up in a long time, but I guess he's not ready to talk about it.

I dial Sydney.

"Oh my God, why aren't you answering?" Her exasperation rolls through the line, bringing a smile to my face.

"I've been in a meeting. How are you, Mrs. Lowe?" I drawl.

"Don't be cute. What do you mean there are rumors?"

"They are not rumors if they are true." God, I enjoy riling her up.

"Explain."

I chuckle. "Something Caro mentioned. I think it's time we tell her, and for you to disclose the relationship to Ravinski." Anger edges inside me at the mention of his name.

He's been avoiding Sydney since the incident,

apart from necessary work-related interactions, but the idea of her alone with him in his office doesn't sit well.

A beat of silence stretches and another unwelcome feeling creeps in. Is she having second thoughts?

"Are you sure?" she asks finally.

"You're not sure about us?"

Another beat of silence. What the hell? "No, it's just... isn't it too soon? What if, you know, things don't work out and we're exposing Caro to... well... to another change."

Part of me is grateful she puts my daughter first in this situation, but...

"So you're not sure about us? You don't want to tell Caro because you don't believe we will last. That's fucking good to know, Sydney."

Chapter Twenty-Three

Sydney

The emergency meeting at London's place is a distraction for me. Her doorman smiles at me for the hundredth time as I sit in the lobby, waiting for Paris, who is twenty minutes late. I should just go upstairs, but I've been indecisive about pretty much everything in my life lately.

I haven't seen Hunter for a week. He said I should decide what I really want and if I'm truly in. His words have rung in my mind ever since, but I'm stuck, unable to make a move. Hiding, as usual. Torn by indecision. Part of me enjoys my newly forged loneliness. It's safe, after all.

I'm not a person who hopes for the best. We don't know what's going to happen, so by hiding our relationship we can protect others from suffering from the potential break-up. We've been together for two weeks, for fuck's sake.

"Sorry I'm late." Paris flows in, an air of grace surrounding her. She is the most elegant of my sisters and the most creative one. "Hello, Cesare." She smiles at the doorman because, of course, she knows his name.

"It's okay." I stand up and trudge toward the elevator.

"What's wrong with you? You were distracted this weekend. Isn't it amazing Massi got his Michelin stars?" Paris laces her arm through mine as we ride the elevator. I don't answer because her questions are more observations, and she can go on for a while without realizing her conversation is one-sided.

I must look horrible if she picks up on my mood. I don't want to discuss my brother's achievements. I'm happy for him. But it's hard to cheer from the sidelines if my own happiness is weirdly suspended.

I know I hurt Hunter with my hesitation and he's giving me space. But I miss him. I miss his funny remarks. His smile. That intense, hooded gaze of his silver eyes. I admire the way he takes care of everyone around him, even when he doesn't have to.

Of course he adopted Caro, but he wasn't obligated to take care of a lonely old lady or give a job to his friend. Or care about people who can't afford a fancy gym in the city. But he does care. And I feel safe with him.

"What happened here?" I ask as we step off the elevator.

There are only two condos on London's floor. Both walls between the two doors are now lined with boxes.

"Someone must be moving in." Paris is about to knock on London's door.

The door across the hall opens and a tall, hot AF man steps out. In his simple white T-shirt and sweats, with his dark blond hair falling into his blue eyes, he looks like he's just stepped off a magazine cover.

"Hello. Have you just moved in?" Paris chirps and goes to shake his hand to introduce herself.

He jerks his head back, glaring at her hand as if it was poisoned. "Seriously? What the hell?" He grabs a box and returns to his place, shutting the door so hard, the walls vibrate.

"Has the jerk slammed his door?" London says as she opens for us.

I chuckle. "Come on, Paris, he thinks you were Lo for sure." The number of misunderstandings their whole life has been a source of entertainment for all of us. "You don't like your new neighbor?"

London rolls her eyes. "Let's not talk about him. We have enough to cover. You're late," she snaps, and I'm not sure if she is pissed at the neighbor, stressed about her gala, or getting into one of her darker moods that resurface once in a while.

We go inside, following her to the large U-shaped sofa that reigns in the middle of her living space. Her condo is sparsely furnished. Despite appearances, London doesn't spend much on things. On experiences and adventures, definitely, but not possessions.

"Why did you call us? We just saw you this weekend." Paris crosses one leg over the other.

Lo doesn't sit with us, and her nervous energy contaminates the air as she paces. "That's why. I've been thinking about the weird summon to the monthly family dinners. Bianca and Dad didn't just decide they want to hang out with us more, and frankly, Bianca's speech got me thinking. What if one of them is sick?" London chews on her cuticle.

All of us spent an afternoon at my parent's house this weekend which is not common in our family. But my stepmother, Bianca, insisted on the get-together, and told us it will be a regular event now because life is short.

We're a large family and coordinating everyone's busy schedules became too difficult, so at some point we stopped trying. At first, I just assumed Bianca and Dad wanted to spend more time with us, as parents do. But after her speech, I wondered myself.

"That's what I said, and Massi told me I was being morbid." I shrug.

"We need to find out." London paces.

"If they wanted us to know, they would have told us," Paris points out.

"I agree, and even if something is wrong, they can't hide it from us for too long. We should respect their timeline," I say, partially because I have enough drama in my life right now and I can't imagine adding more.

"If there even is anything going on. Maybe it really is an honest effort to get us all together." Paris smiles innocently.

Lo stops pacing and studies us for a moment, then shrugs. "Okay. Next on the agenda. What's wrong with you?"

Heat spreads through my cheeks. I was so sure I acted normal this weekend at the family lunch. Damn it.

"Hunter wants to tell his daughter about us," I blurt without preamble, because if I'm going to seek advice, these two are the ones I can count on. And London won't drop the topic until she's satisfied.

Paris shifts to face me. "And you don't?"

"It's kind of soon for that, I think." Why does the statement taste rotten?

"It's his daughter, his decision. If he's comfortable

telling her, why wait?" She searches my face, as though expecting another big revelation.

I remain silent. What can I say? Clearly, no one sees my point.

London sits next to me. "It feels like you'll be committing to one more person, doesn't it?"

Perhaps someone understands. Even though I haven't articulated the real reason behind my worry yet. Tears burn around my eyes.

"Oh, sweetie." Paris scoots closer. "You love the man. You've been into him since the first moment you saw him. And while your story is weird and not straightforward, who says how long you need to be together before you can move to the next level? Take the leap."

"It's premature to talk about love." I lean forward, burying my face in my hands.

"There is no timeline for love." Paris strokes my back.

"Also, you didn't deny it. Syd, how did you feel when Dan asked you to move in? Or when he proposed?" London asks.

"What does that have to do with anything?" I lift my head to peek at her.

"You knew you didn't want that. Is your instinct telling you to be with Hunter? Deep down, even if you don't want to label it, do you want to be with him?"

I straighten up and wipe my cheeks with the back of my hand. I read somewhere it only takes five seconds for fear and doubt to creep into our decision-making. In these five seconds right now, before fear colors my response, I know the answer to London's question with the deepest conviction. A flower of joy and hope sprouts shyly in the corner of my soul that has been wilting since Jeremy's betrayal. Doubt stomps on it quickly.

As though she could see inside me, London sighs. "Look, I don't like people and I'm perfectly fulfilled in my life without a man. But that's not you, Syd."

"You're a caregiver, sweetie. You always have been. You took care of us after Mom was gone. You became a teacher..." Paris continues stroking my back. It's comforting and unwanted at the same time. I'm the eldest, yet I've been such a mess that I need my younger siblings to console me.

"I'm scared." The words float into the room on butterfly wings. I don't think anyone even hears me.

But they do. Both my sisters squeeze me tighter from each side in a rare group hug.

"That's okay, but don't live the rest of your life from a place of fear." Lo's motto is to live every day like it was your last one. Her own protection mechanism, I guess.

"In a twisted way, you're allowing Jeremy to fuck

with you even from beyond his grave." Paris kisses the top of my head.

Her words splash through me like a cold shower, sobering me up. I'm not free to drag another person into the mess of my life. The real mess that I've been hiding successfully for years now. But I can't let Jeremy take this away from me. My chance at happiness and a genuine relationship.

"Will you be here if..." I don't want to say the words.

"We have always been here for you, Syd." London stands up. She's probably reached her limit of emotional sap.

They have been, and I wish I could be completely honest with them, because sharing the burden alone for this long has been exhausting. And lonely. But I can't. Not yet. Probably never.

For now, I have a relationship to save.

I cross the schoolyard with a determination I don't really feel. The ground is shifting under my feet. Or in my imagination. But I don't stop. I walk, ignoring everyone and everything. Somehow it's harder to walk when a set of gray eyes burns my skin.

Hunter hasn't come to pick Caro up for a week, but

he's here today. Girls run around, laughing and chattering. Relentless traffic hums its typical city score. A dog barks somewhere in the background. All the sounds are louder today when I try to focus all my senses on the man who looks at me with a dose of hurt in his eyes.

The wind, at odds with the otherwise sunny day, whips my hair around. I left my jacket inside when I ran out, hoping to catch him, but it doesn't matter because I'm sweating like it's summer. Or perhaps I'm not. I don't know. My nerves are playing tricks on me.

The corners of Hunter's lips curl up slightly. Or I might be projecting.

"Hi. Do you have a minute?" I spill the words as fast as possible to make sure I grab the chance. Equal parts from the fear he may leave, or that I might cave.

"Let me talk to Mrs. Lowe, Caro." He smiles at his daughter who was just approaching. Jesus, I didn't even see her. She stops and studies us for a beat and then hops away, rejoining her friends. Something in the way she narrowed her eyes on me hits a momentary pause on my intentions. But then who said this would be easy?

I find Hunter's eyes and the world switches to slow mo.

He licks his lips.

A shudder quakes through me.

The vise on my chest tightens.

His scent floats to me, blanketing me with a strong sense of belonging.

A new, novel form of fear settles in.

What if I lost him already?

"I miss you," I say. Swallowing is a challenge.

Hunter sighs. The sound grips my throat, strangling me. I hurt this man.

"I'm sorry. I let my fear win. It's not fair to you. Or to me, really. When I asked you to wait, I showed you I don't believe in us. That's not true."

Hunter lets out another sigh and rakes his fingers through his hair.

"I do believe in us," I continue. "But I'm scared because my beliefs were crushed before. I let the experience cloud my life. I wanted to wait to make sure that we're real. But waiting means assuming we'd fail. I don't want to start something, expecting it may not work out. We're real. I'm scared, but I'd rather have one real day with you than a lifetime of misguided security."

Thirty seconds ago, I didn't know what I was going to say, but now that the words are out, I'm shocked by their honesty. They coil around my heart with hope and trepidation.

Hunter clenches his fists. His Adam's apple jumps up and down a few times. He glances toward the girls playing.

"Fuck, Sydney." Frustration laces his words. I think. Or exasperation. But it definitely doesn't sound like relief.

My stomach twists into a painful knot. I blink, but a tear escapes anyway. As time stretches, the only reaction I get is Hunter's heaving chest.

"I understand if you don't have patience for my trust issues." *It would kill me.* I step back. The extra distance and the wind take away the scent of him and I feel lost. Cold. Sad. "Look, I didn't mean to ambush you. You have Caro to pick up."

I look at a group of younger girls skipping in a pattern. Anywhere but at his eyes.

"This wasn't a good idea or the best place to unload my insecurities on you." I keep tripping over my words, mortification burning my skin. But my shame doesn't matter at this moment. It's the painful hole in my chest and a slow, agonizing shattering of my hope. "I better—"

"Shut up, Sydney," Hunter snaps, startling me. "I'm so fucking proud of you."

A sob rips out of me. *What?*

"The past week has been difficult." He scratches the back of his neck. "I've experienced loss in my life, and you bailing on me after a couple of weeks is up there with the most fucked up situations. But the hardest thing right now is not being able to wrap you in my arms and kiss you."

Tears break out, blurring my vision, and at the same time a strangled laugh escapes. It's more like a cough, but I'm past caring.

"Wrong place. Wrong time." I giggle, I think. "Lesson learned because I really want that kiss."

He smiles and tension melts from my limbs.

"Go tell the principal about us, and then come over so we can talk to Caro. It's taco night."

I nod and wipe my nose, sniffling. "Okay. I have a few things to finish, but I'll text you when I'm on my way."

"Hurry, beautiful. We have a lot of fucking to catch up on."

Only him.

Chapter Twenty-Four

Hunter

"How did it go?" I ask as soon as Sydney walks in. She looks pale and exhausted. My chest hurts when I see her like that. I wrap my arm around her and kiss her quickly. She leans into the hug for a moment but then pulls away. Her eyes dart around chaotically.

"I'm scared." She looks at me finally and emotions spin through me like a tornado.

"What did the dickhead do?" I growl, keeping my voice down for Caro's sake.

Sydney blinks a few times. "What? Where is Caro?" she whispers.

"She's in her room watching a show. What's going on? What happened?"

Sydney lets out a long puff of air and lowers her forehead to my chest, her hands on my hips. I want to scoop her up, carry her to the bedroom and make her feel better. Make her forget. Or at least wrap her in a tight embrace so she knows she's safe. But I can't do any of it until we talk to my daughter. The last thing I want is to explain it to her *after* she catches us kissing.

I rub my hand over Sydney's shoulders. "Talk to me, beautiful. You're scaring me now."

"Sorry." She straightens up. "Sorry, I didn't mean to. On my way over here, I truly realized how important it is for me that the conversation with Caro goes well, how much is at stake, and I freaked out a bit. But, yeah, the conversation with Dan went strangely well. I didn't want to be alone with him, so I asked his assistant to join us. I wanted the disclosure to be on record. God knows what he's capable of." She sighs, her shoulders loosening a bit.

"That was smart. And it was a difficult step, so don't worry about Caro. There are two of us to handle that now." I wrap my arm around her shoulders and give her a peck on her temple. "Let's get over with it now, so you can relax."

"You're not worried at all? That she might not like it?" Sydney bores her green gaze into me. The emotional turmoil of the past week has left shadows on her face. I want to wipe them all away.

"I'm not going to worry beforehand. I don't do that. Ever." I stop and turn her to face me. "I'd have spent most of my adult life worrying and still had no control over what happened. Julia died. Caro is growing up without her mother. None of it is in my control. I can spend time making the best out of every situation, or live in constant worry. That decision is in my control. So yes, beautiful, Caro might not take it well, but we'll deal with that if it happens."

She bites her lip and exhales a long breath. "I hope some of your outlook on life rubs off on me."

There is pain, hope and skepticism mixed in her answer, and in that moment I know that I'll do anything in my power to make her believe that life should be enjoyed. That the only way for us to find peace is from within.

I know I can protect her physically from assholes like Dan Ravinski. I hope I can somehow protect her from the beliefs dickheads like her late husband instilled in her. The latter has just become my life's mission.

"It will, beautiful. I'll fuck that pessimism out of you." I wink and she shakes her head, chuckling.

I knock on Caro's door and open it. "Is your show over, sweetheart?"

She's at her desk, her nose buried in papers.

Crayons, cut-outs of some pictures and tape are strewn all over her desk.

"I'm working on my magazine now." She looks over her shoulder and swivels her chair, raising her eyebrows when she spots Sydney beside me. "Mrs. Lowe." Her eyes dart between us. "Am I in trouble?"

"No, no, silly." I step inside. "Can you leave your project for a moment and talk to us?"

She stands up. "Do you promise I'm not in trouble? Because Ruby started it first." She crosses her arms over her chest.

I look at Sydney. Great. Fuck. Do we deal with whatever the situation is with her friend, or do I come back to it?

"We can talk about Ruby later if you want. Right now, your dad and I would like to tell you something." Sydney's voice is level and friendly. No signs of the freak-out she had a minute ago.

"Okay." Caro jumps on her bed and crosses her legs, resting her chin in her palm.

"Remember when you asked me if I liked Sydney..." I clear my throat. Okay, I thought I wasn't worried. Suddenly Caro's approval is the most important thing in the world, and I start sweating. "Mrs. Lowe? I like her very much, and as it happens, I'm one lucky guy and she likes me too. We started dating."

She wrinkles her nose as if the idea was unsavory. "So, you like kiss and hold hands now?"

"We care for each other and enjoy spending time together. And yes, sometimes we kiss and hold hands." Sydney sits on the edge of Caro's bed.

Caro looks down and says nothing. The air grows heavy with silence as she intently studies the familiar pattern of her duvet.

"Do you have any other questions, Caro? Or would you like to talk to your dad alone? That's okay. I can leave the two of you to talk." Sydney stands up.

Caro finally looks up, raising her chin in defiance, her eyes misty with unshed tears. Fuck. I didn't expect her to be hurt by this. My pulse ticks up to a potentially unhealthy rate.

My mind goes blank as I dig through it for some useful thing to say. Nothing comes up through the screams of despair in my head. What if she doesn't accept this? What if she never comes around? What if she starts hating Sydney and we'd have to change schools again? Or we will have to hide our relationship?

This is why I never worry ahead of time, because my mind just constructs impossible, unsolvable scenarios. Right now, in the split second before Caro speaks again, my brain goes wild with doom and gloom options.

"Does it mean that now that you have Mrs. Lowe, you don't want me anymore? Will I go to strangers in *forest care?*"

And here I thought my mind constructed the wildest ideas. I dash to her and scoop her in my arms, squishing her as tight as possible without suffocating her.

"Caro, the day I decided to adopt you I knew it was forever. The day you accepted me as your dad has been the happiest day of my life. Nothing and no one will ever change that. You're my daughter. You'll always live with me. No foster care for you. You're stuck with me."

I kiss the crown of her head and look at Sydney who is smiling, her face wet with tears.

"My life might be cut short if you don't let me breathe." Caro tries to pry herself out of my embrace.

I laugh and let her go. "Are you okay, pumpkin?"

"I was"—she rolls her eyes—"until you called me that."

"Nothing will change between you and your dad. You just might see more of me, Caro. And if you have any more questions, we can talk anytime." Sydney smiles at my daughter.

"Will you take me for a manicure?" Caro's eyes go wide with expectation.

"Well..." Sydney looks at me, perplexed, the corner

of her mouth curling up. "If your dad is okay with that, we'll go this weekend."

Caro beams. "Can I call you Sydney?"

"When we're outside of school, please call me Sydney, or my sisters call me Syd." She smooths Caro's hair, and my girl wraps her arms around Sydney's waist.

I revel for a moment, part relieved, part mesmerized at the sight of the two most important people in my life and part still shocked about the conversation.

"Okay, Syd." Caro lets go and returns to her desk. "I'll work on my magazine until dinner is ready."

We are dismissed. I nudge Sydney toward the door, my hand on the small of her back. The touch, the gesture, suddenly represents more than before. It's not just my hand on her body—which is a turn-on—it's a sign of a new beginning. New depth in our intimacy.

She is a part of my life now. And she might not be on board with the commitment fully, but I'll do everything in my power to get her there.

I close the door behind me and crush my lips against hers. Her breath catches, but she parts her lips for me.

Inviting me.

Welcoming me.

Accepting us.

"I need a drink," we both say at the same time.

Chapter Twenty-Five

Sydney

The dress London sent me this year is over the top. She usually rents me an elegant but simple black dress. This year, a stunning dress in green that matches my eyes was delivered.

The shimmering top with a simple cowl neckline hugs my torso. From my waist the dress fans out in wafting chiffon pleats into a voluminous maxi skirt. I love it. I wish it was mine. Not that I have anywhere else to wear it, but a girl can enjoy a vain moment here and there.

I put on a set of pearls I have from my mom. I style my hair down in loose waves and apply only a little natural makeup. If I knew about the dress ahead of time, I'd have splurged on a hair and makeup artist.

As I check the mirror, I have to remind myself that I'll be working tonight. Making sure everyone is where they need to be in time for the speeches, ushering guests to their tables and running around taking care of a zillion details.

I should really get a cab to make sure I'm there on time for London's briefing before anyone else arrives. As I pick up my phone to call the car, I find a text from London from about an hour ago. I must have missed the chime when I was in the shower.

London: A car will wait for you downstairs at 7 pm. See you later. L.

That makes no sense. First, she's never sent a car for me. It would be a waste of resources if paid for by the foundation and I'd never accept something like that from her. Also, seven o'clock? That gives us no time to go over things with her assistant, so I don't have to bother her with every detail during the event.

I dial Lo's number, but there is no answer. Of course, she's too busy with the last-minute preparations. But the phone rings back almost immediately.

"Lo, what the heck? Why are you sending a car and why so late?"

"Hello, Sydney." Ashley, Lo's assistant, clears her throat. "London is not available right now, but she asked me to reassure you that everything is right on schedule and you should take the car sent for you."

"But I won't have time to get a brief from you." I sit down on my sofa, the skirt gathering around me. I must look like a jilted princess.

"I'm sure London knows what she's doing."

"But—"

"Sorry, Sydney, I really have to go. I'll see you later." She hangs up.

This is weird. I check the clock on my phone, deflated. I spend the next two hours plopped on the sofa, eating chips and drinking a ton of water to flush the salt. As I finally get ready to leave the house, someone knocks.

I open the door, slightly annoyed by the untimely intrusion, and meet Hunter's eyes. Or his doppelgänger. Hunter is with Caro tonight and he doesn't wear a tux. But the man in front of me is devilishly sexy in his black tie. He wears it as a second skin, along with a devastating, handsome grin on his face.

I blink a few times, but there is no doubt he's there. "Hi?" I squeal, my mind trying to reconcile the situation. I'm in a gown, he's in a tux. But where is *he* going?

"Would you do me the honor and join me as my guest at this year's leukemia fundraiser?"

I swallow hard. "You have tickets? Two tickets? Hunter, they are ten thousand dollars each." I shake my head as if that would somehow rearrange the confusion into understanding.

"I know how much they are. I bought two of them." He puts his hands into his pockets. The casual gesture is at odds with his formal attire and somehow the contrast makes him even sexier.

"But I have volunteer duties—"

"I took the liberty of getting you out of them." He frowns lightly. "I hope that's okay."

I chuckle, catching up with the changes. "You supported the cause with a hefty sum instead, so I guess that's okay. But why?"

"Caro's mom, Julia, had leukemia."

I plant my hand on the door to steady myself. Out of all things he could have said, I didn't expect this. It's the best reason. I can't raise an objection to that. I step closer and wrap my arms around him. He kisses me gently.

"Also, I wanted to see you in this dress." He runs his hand down my back and squeezes my ass.

"You got me this dress?" I gasp.

"Yeah and you look absolutely stunning tonight, beautiful. Would you make me the happiest man and join me for the event?" he whispers against my lips.

*　*　*

"On second thought, I don't like the dress," Hunter says as we enter the ballroom.

This year, London talked the owners of an old factory near the river into lending her the space for the gala. The transformation is breathtaking. The industrial space is lit up with fairy lights, its rough walls softened by sheer fabric pillars hung around the room from the pipes that line the ceiling.

The dance floor is on one side and a long bar is on the other, with large round tables in between.

I run my hand down my skirt. "What? You don't?"

He chuckles and yanks me closer, his hand firm on my waist. "First, you look positively ravishing in it, and I don't want to deal with all the assholes drooling over you all night. Second, the dress is amazing, but I can't wait to take it off." He presses a kiss to my temple.

"Here you are, darling. You look wonderful tonight." Bianca strolls over with my dad shuffling alongside.

"Bianca, Dad." I give them both a peck on their cheeks. "This is Hunter Stuart."

"Nice to meet you, ma'am, sir." Hunter kisses Bianca's hand and shakes my father's.

"We're very pleased to meet you," Bianca gushes, and I feel the heat making its way to my face. "What do you do, Hunter?"

Here we go with the screening. "Should we get a drink before you grill him?" I weave my fingers through Hunter's.

"It's okay," he says, squeezing my hand. "I own a fitness club and I'm about to open another one."

"So how did you two meet?" Dad asks.

Oh shit. That's not a story to share with parents. *He was a gift from London.*

Hunter lifts my hand and kisses my knuckles lightly. Shit. I've been digging my nails into his skin.

"Sydney is my daughter's teacher," he says. Oh, that's a better first meeting story for sure.

Bianca raises her eyebrows. "You have a daughter?"

Okay, not the smoothest story. "Hunter adopted his niece after her mother passed."

"Oh, I can't wait to meet her." Bianca beams. "You can't imagine how long I've been waiting for grandchildren. Seriously, with eight children combined it shouldn't be taking this long."

No matter how old I am, parents remain a source of embarrassment.

"I'm sure Caro would love another adult to spoil her," Hunter chuckles. While I'm sweating and looking for an opportunity to abort the conversation, he seems unperturbed by Bianca's suggestion that Caro would be her granddaughter.

"Hey, everyone." Paris joins us.

"Paris, darling, where is your date?" Dad kisses her cheek.

"I'm here with Gio." She rolls her eyes. "Figured

I'd spare the family from sharing the table with one of his bimbos."

"Paris, this is Hunter. Hunter, this is my sister." I facilitate the introduction as we make our way to the bar.

Half an hour after our arrival and Hunter has been grilled and scrutinized by most of my family. On the way to the bar, we run into Massi and his spouse, Gina. I also manage to give London a quick hug.

We order our drinks, finally alone because everyone got distracted saying hello to other guests.

"So, I've met the parents." Hunter winks at me with mischief.

I can't help but laugh. "Did you buy the tickets to get it over with in a safe environment with hundreds of other people around?"

"Possibly." Oh, that smirk is so sexy.

"I'm afraid a quick exchange won't be enough for Bianca. Knowing her, she's probably rearranging the name cards at our table to ensure she sits beside you and as far away from me as possible, so she can assess your suitability."

"I'm sure I can charm her." He picks up his glass and clinks it against mine.

Shit. Of course he could charm Bianca. He has some experience there. I hadn't thought about that.

About the fact that at this type of society event, he could also run into his former clients.

Before I have a chance to properly freak out, Hunter starts talking to someone he knows and Paris grabs my elbow. "Syd, look who just came in."

At the entrance stands a man who could totally audition as the next James Bond. Okay, not audition, they should just beg him to take the role. "Who is that... Oh." Recognition dawns on me. It's London's neighbor.

"That's right. Do you think Lo is going to freak out?"

Something in the way she's asking feels off. "Do you have anything to do with him being here?"

She looks at me sideways, a face of innocence.

"Oh, Paris, you didn't. London doesn't need a distraction like this."

"He is exactly the distraction she needs."

Hunter turns back to us. "What's going on?"

"You don't want to know." I chuckle. "We should find our table." I grab his hand possessively because my insecurities peaked when I realized there might be women here who know Hunter intimately. I know he only talked with most of them, but didn't he say to me once that's more intimate? Shit.

We make it through dinner, and I forget about the other women as Hunter twirls me around the dance floor. He leaves my side a few times to talk to people he knows, or to talk to one of my family members, working the room with ease, but the whole time I can sense his burning eyes on me.

Following me. Owning me. Protecting me.

My heart has been swelling with a feeling I don't want to name, but it feels damn good.

"How have you been feeling?" I ask my sister-in-law, Gina, who is fanning herself at our table.

"Wonderful, but these heels are killing me."

"No wonder. You've been stealing the show on the dance floor. I didn't know Massi could dance so well." I look over to where Massi and Gio are talking to Hunter. I hope they're not making him uncomfortable.

"Something we've had in common for a while," Gina says, her smile suggesting there is a story behind that. I'm sure there is. The two of them have been finding their way to each other through almost two decades of hate and betrayal.

"I need to use the bathroom," I say, and make my way outside the room to freshen up.

The evening has been a success for London, it seems. And I must admit that joining my family as a guest this year has been really nice. Call me shallow, but for an odd night of glamour, I feel like I belong. Like I'm not the failure.

I know my only achievement is dating a man who

could afford the tickets, but still, the sense of belonging after years of loitering on the outskirts is a gift my man gave me. Because somehow he knows what I need, and I can trust he will attempt to deliver.

I can trust him.

My heartbeat jumps in a violent rhythm. Butterflies flutter in my stomach as I recognize the feeling I've been pushing aside for what it really is.

I'm in love with Hunter Stuart. Suddenly I feel—I know—I have to tell him immediately. I don't even care if he doesn't say it back. He's been so patient with me, and I want him to know.

I return to the ballroom and scan it to find him. Massi and Gio are chatting at the bar. London stands alone in the corner, which is odd given her role as the hostess. I examine her closer and follow her gaze, or to be honest, her glower.

James Bond, her neighbor, leans casually on the other side of the bar, meeting her glare with a smile on his face. Oh my.

I cross the floor to join her. "Have you seen Hunter?"

"What?" She jumps, as if surprised there are other people around. "Hunter? I think I saw him somewhere..." She points to the dance floor. "There he is."

I spot him immediately, and my determination to declare my love to him right here and now tempers. He is dancing with someone. His shoulders are tense, but the woman is smiling and looking at him like he was the last man alive.

She might be dressed to the nines, but the venom veil is palpable from afar. "Is that—"

"Oh, shit," London says. "Gigi Lafontaine. Is she a former... never mind. I'm going to break it off." London ambles to the dance floor and elegantly extracts Hunter from the other woman.

Gigi frowns, but turns with her chin up. Our eyes meet, and while I'm ridden with insecurity and, truthfully, a dose of jealousy, she smiles at me with poisonous triumph.

Chapter Twenty-Six

Hunter

The new posh bistro is designed all in white and green, almost too bright for an evening in the city. Yet, it's inviting and promises a wonderful experience.

I will never come here again.

Tonight's visit—my first and only—will forever be tainted because of my company. I don't hurry to the hostess stand. I'm late already, but part of me, almost all of me, wants to turn around and leave.

I can't delay for too long because Gigi spots me and waves. My jaw has been so tense all day that I might need enamel replacement.

When I contacted London about the tickets to the fundraiser, I knew there was a possibility I could run into one of my former clients. But fucking Gigi. Our conversation from the gala has run through my head since that night.

Even now, the memory of her vicious smile sends a shiver down my spine.

"You announce that TV show," she told me as we danced, "and I'll let the world know about your former extracurricular activities."

"What do you have to gain from that, Gigi?" I asked, hoping nobody would pick up on the unfortunate exchange.

"That's the wrong question, Stuart. You should be asking what would prevent me from doing it?"

I've never hit a woman before, but I wanted to wipe that entitled smirk from her face with my palm.

"You look like you've made up your mind already," I told her.

"Maybe a weekend in your company would be incentive enough. Or perhaps I should talk to Delaney Rielski. We go to the same fitness club."

Fucking Ash. Did he tell her about the TV show? How else would she know?

"You think you can threaten me into a date with you?" I moved around with her, my spine rigid, touching her waist as delicately as I would barbed wire.

"If not Delaney, maybe that ordinary brunette would like to know? Or your daughter?"

Sydney knows about my past, but no chance I'd let that snake near my daughter. I wouldn't want Gigi to talk to anyone close to me.

"Are you surprised I know so much about you?" She made a grimace, attempting to smile. "Here is the thing, Stuart. People only leave me when I allow it. Not the other way around. Decide by Friday and join me at seven at this new bistro everyone raves about. I'll text you the details," she said before London wrenched me out of her hold.

Despite my better judgment, here I am, frozen on the spot. I don't want Caro to be impacted by whatever bile Gigi could spill her way, but I can't do this. Not behind Sydney's back. What was I thinking?

Gigi beckons impatiently with her hand. I don't know how I survived any time with that woman before, but I need to find a different way to deal with her threats now. I don't want to waste a second of my life in her company.

I want to be elsewhere. I need to be elsewhere.

"Do you have a reservation?" the hostess asks.

I look over at Gigi, who raises her eyebrows impatiently, and then at the woman in front of me. "I don't have a reservation, and you know what, I have better plans."

I leave without looking back. I open the app to get

a cab and then call Lea at the club. "Cancel Gigi Lafontaine's membership."

"But Hunter, we can't just cancel someone's membership. I mean she is an annoying bitch, but—"

"Just fucking do it, Lea," I snap and hang up.

It takes another ten minutes for the car to pick me up and endless minutes in traffic before I get to Brooklyn. Caro is at my mom's, so I have the entire night to fix things. Even though Sydney doesn't know there is anything to fix.

I get lucky again and someone lets me inside Sydney's building like on the night of the fundraiser. She was so breathtaking in that gown. I told her I bought the tickets in Julia's memory, but the truth is I wanted to take her out so she could have a night as an equal with her family.

I know she has told none of them about the extent of her financial problems, but I'm still upset none of them ever tried to figure out where all her money is going. That she is struggling. Clearly, they could have dug her out of her debts a few times over. Gio, Massi and London definitely, at the very least, have plenty of resources.

Sydney opens her door wearing yoga pants and a baggy sweatshirt. She raises her eyebrows and then smiles, and my heart somersaults in my chest.

Suddenly I can't find words, so I push through, kick the door closed and capture her lips.

Her arms fly up as she stumbles, but then she wraps them around me and opens her lips, her tongue finding mine in a desperate dance.

"I thought you were busy tonight." She breathes against my skin, as I nuzzle her jaw and neck.

"About that." I drag my eyes up to meet hers. "I had a date."

She blinks a few times and jerks away from me.

"Sorry. I didn't have a date. I mean, I was about to have one. A former client has been threatening to expose my past at work, and to you, but when I didn't budge, she upped the ante by threatening to tell Caro."

"The woman you danced with at the gala? Gigi someone who we met at the Ritz?" Sydney steps back.

It's just one step, but it feels like a mile. Like being close to me changed from joy to dread in a few beats.

I rake my hand through my hair. "Yes." I close my eyes, exhaling, and then I pin her with my gaze. "I couldn't go through with it. I can't stand the woman. I went to meet her because I needed to protect Caro. But it felt wrong. I wouldn't have slept with her, but even sitting there with her, talking, felt like a betrayal. I didn't even get to the table and I-I came straight here."

Sydney licks her lips and frowns. She opens her mouth, but then closes it again. She might be thinking, considering her words. Or she is formulating my dismissal. Her green eyes are dark with pain, or perhaps it's just the lighting here. I want to reach out and touch her, but I understand that privilege is now in her hands.

The seconds tick off with eerie finality, and I wish I could rewind the clock and change at least some of the past. But I can't change Julia getting sick, or me making money the only way I knew how at that time.

I can't change meeting fucking Gigi. I wish I didn't feel threatened by her. Not even for that brief moment between the fundraiser and tonight. I shouldn't have fallen for her trap. But I can't take that back either.

"I'm sorry." Desperation runs deep, but I hope Sydney won't hold this against me. I came to her. This is where I belong.

"Why didn't you tell me this was happening?" Her voice is strangled, as if my confession tightened a noose around her neck. The space between us grows, filled with pain and regret.

"I didn't want to worry you." It's true, but in the context of the distorted current between us, it sounds pathetic. "I don't want my past to get between us—"

"It will always come between us if you're not honest with me. If you go behind my back on a date. If you keep things from me." She shakes her head, in a profound but familiar disbelief. "Don't keep things from me."

It's a plea and a demand wrapped in a stifled sob, and it spears through my heart like an arrow. I sharpened and poisoned the arrowhead myself.

It dawns on me then. While my almost betrayal is nothing like Jeremy's, I kept something from her, and the degree might be different but the taste remains the same. The bitter flavor of deception.

"Sydney, I know. That's why I ran out of there before I even reached the table. I should have told you everything right there a week ago. I don't know what I was thinking." If she allows me to ever hug her again, I won't let go. Ever.

"Hunter, your past might haunt us, just like mine will. Gigi, Jeremy, Dan Ravinski—those people are part of our life. I let Jeremy impact me for way too long. We can't give those people the power to rule over it. To destroy what we have because we're not honest with each other. I'm learning to trust you. Hell, I trust you already. Don't keep things from me."

She exhales a long, painful breath and opens her arms. I don't need more encouragement. I eliminate the space between us instantly and fuse my lips to hers. Sydney pushes the coat off my shoulders and finds the hem of my shirt.

As soon as I feel her palms on my ribcage, I growl

and walk her backward to the twin bed in the corner. Shit.

We get naked faster than I'd thought possible, and without foreplay I pull on a condom and enter her. I still then, giving her time to adjust to my size, but also savoring the moment. I can't get enough of her. With her. On her. Next to her. Inside her.

Sydney hooks her legs around my waist and looks at me through hooded eyes. In this shitty apartment, freezing my ass off, on an old and definitely not wide enough mattress, I'm filled with so much warmth and happiness, I wouldn't change one thing. Having her wrapped around me like this is where I want to remain.

"I love you, Sydney." The words come so naturally, it startles me.

She gasps. Fuck, those sounds of hers will be the death of me. "I love you too, Hunter."

I move, slowly at first, my body against her soft satin skin. Eyes locked, we give and take with languid luxury, rediscovering our connection after the confession of love. But passion takes over quickly, and we become a mess of two people desperately chasing release.

Sydney gets there first and as she clenches around me, squeezing me almost painfully, I watch her face. No one is this beautiful when they come. It's that rare moment when she drops all her barriers. When she lets me in fully, without hesitation.

Watching the raw beauty, with her walls closing around me, I don't last much longer. I empty myself inside her, but it's more than that. I give myself to her, body and soul. This woman owns me.

And tonight, it feels like she is finally mine.

"Is something wrong with the heating?" I ask. I'm not complaining because her body heat is my favorite thing, but how does she bear it? We are on her sofa, a bundle of limbs under her duvet, but my nose gets cold anytime it's not buried in her.

Sydney sighs. "No. I have the thermostat set to sixty-three degrees."

"Why would you do that, woman?" I pull her closer. Her back is against my chest as she sits between my legs, pressing against my semi. My cock is a serious overachiever with this woman.

"Economic reasons." She pats my quad.

I've been nuzzling her neck, but I freeze now. This is so fucked up. Unless Jeremy spent like a small country, I don't see why her family doesn't help her. And she has me now. I can't leave things like this for her.

My stomach growls before I say anything, and

Sydney jumps up. "Let me make you something to eat."

Shit. Not that. I haven't yet told her what a terrible cook she is. "Why don't we order pizza?" I sit up and grab my phone.

"I'll make something simple. Pasta maybe? I can't compare with the likes of Gigi, but I can make you a meal." She wiggles her hips and opens a cabinet in her kitchen, her attempt at a joke falling flat.

"Come back here right now," I demand, and she whips around, her hands on her hips. She is naked and my cock twitches. I click on the app and in a few swipes, my order is in. "Here, I ordered us a pizza."

She shrugs, pulls a bag of chips from her cupboard and comes to sit beside me. I hoist one leg behind her and pull her closer, gathering her between my legs, to my chest, and covering us with the duvet.

"For the record, beautiful, Gigi isn't anywhere in your league. She isn't even in the same universe. And this is the best evening ever. If you give me some of that sodium poison."

"It's a sour cream and chives special edition, thank you very much," she huffs, but puts a few chips in my mouth. "Best evening ever, huh?" She faces me, beaming.

"We fucked, so it's up there in the top ten." I shrug and Sydney laughs.

I nibble on her ear, my hands dusting the swell of her breasts. Her laugh morphs into a moan.

"If you moved in with me, you'd save more." I don't even know where the thought came from, but as soon as the words are out, I become fiercely enthusiastic about the idea.

She shifts again to see my face. "Hunter, we've just said the L word, what's the rush? We need to let Caro adjust to this new situation before we take the next big step."

She's right. I have Caro to think about. "But I didn't hear a refusal. Just a timing consideration." I pinch her nipple and my cock wonders if there is time for a quickie before our pizza arrives.

"It's a *no* for now." As if she read my mind, Sydney turns and straddles me.

For now. I can live with that. In the meantime, I need to make sure she doesn't have to freeze here. An idea sprouts in my mind, but I have no time to consider it further because Sydney moves her hips and I get lost. Lost in the woman I love.

Chapter Twenty-Seven

Hunter

"Hello, Mrs. Lowe. How was your day?" I kiss her passionately, dipping her backward like we're on a movie set and not in the middle of a busy sidewalk in front of a popular SoHo restaurant.

Now that our relationship is official I can't help it, and show over the top affection at every opportunity. It's so much fun how these kinds of gestures rile Sydney up. If I didn't know better, I'd have thought she was ashamed of me.

While we're official, we're waiting a bit longer before Sydney spends the night at my place. Given Caro's worries she'd be replaced by Sydney, I don't want to rely on my mother too much in this next phase.

Needless to say, my cock is screaming in protest because we've spent the last few nights apart.

Tonight, however, Caro is at her first sleepover, and we are having a date night. Sydney got us a table at Casa Cassi, a restaurant that belongs to her brother.

"Stop it." She laughs and swats at me, but gives me one more kiss before we pull away. "I had a good day. What about you, Mr. Stuart? How are things at the Hunter Club?"

I pull her to me and kiss the crown of her head. "Things at the club are great. In fact, I have something to share. How would you feel about dating a TV star?" I curl my arm around her hip, snuggling her under my arm as I prompt us toward the entrance.

"What do you mean? Did you find me a better boyfriend?" She bites her lip as she looks sideways at me.

I pinch her where my hand is resting—not that it does anything through the thick layer of her coat. Sydney squeals and laughs.

"I got an offer to star in a reality show, helping celebrities get into shape."

She stops. "Oh my God, that's amazing. Congratulations." She coils her hand around my neck and pulls me down for a kiss.

Our lips are still connected as I pull the door open

with one hand, the other occupied with holding her as close to me as decently possible.

"Get a room," a male voice growls as soon as the door shuts behind us.

My fist clenches as Sydney jumps away from me. "Gio, what are you doing here?"

Her brother stares at his phone. "Getting dinner, what else? Nice to see you, Syd." He raises his eyes from the screen and nods.

"Hunter, do you remember my brother Gio?" She grabs my hand and pulls me to the hostess stand where he waits. Expensive watch, tailored suit, a coat of arrogance. "You met at the fundraiser."

"Nice to see you again," he mumbles, but his phone chimes and shifts his attention. Sydney rolls her eyes and shrugs.

"He's always glued to his phone. Don't take it personally." She unbuttons her coat and I help her take it off.

A hostess appears and takes our jackets, and another woman, a petite blond with a smile that could power the entire city, strolls toward us. I've seen her somewhere before, but I guess most of Sydney's people were at her sister's gala.

"Sydney, I'm so glad to see you," she says and hugs Sydney. Clearly this is a family place.

The room has an industrial feel with its brick walls,

dark wood and copper features all around. It's teeming with activity. The chef, Sydney's brother Massimo, has recently gotten two Michelin stars, so I guess we're lucky to get a table.

"Hunter, this is Mila. She works with Gina. Is she here as well?"

"No, she isn't tonight. Nice to meet you, Hunter. I think I saw you at the fundraiser. I was so happy to work the event. Let me get you to your table." She consults the book.

"And I've been standing here for ten minutes," Gio grumbles and Mila's smile dies on her lips. It's like she's just exhausted all her sunshine and there is only room left for clouds. But she recovers quickly, and the sun comes—more like an artificial tanning bed beam, but she tries.

"Well, excuse me, I thought you just wandered in off the street not realizing where you are. By the way, you've been staring into your phone since you entered. It looked like you mistook us for a bus stop."

Gio looks up for the first time since she joined us. "Can I have my table, Ms. Ward?"

Mila rolls her eyes again and exhales, but then she bites her lip and asks, "Are you here alone, Mr. Cassinetti?"

"My date is late," he snaps, glowering at her. Mila, to her credit, doesn't waver.

"Do you want to join us while you wait?" Sydney asks and mouths sorry to me.

Well, not the date I was imagining, but I smile at her. It's not like he would stay with us for too long.

"No, go ahead. She'll be here any minute."

At that, the door swings open and a tall woman walks in. Short skirt, long legs, beautiful figure—she is very young looking and staring into her pink phone.

"Well, and here she is," Gio says.

Before we are ushered to our table, I glance at Mila. The disgust she throws Gio's way is so palpable I almost wince. He doesn't notice as his attention remains on his phone.

"Why does your brother need a date when he's perfectly happy with his device?" I ask as we sit down.

"He works all the time. It might look like browsing to us, but I think he's watching markets, reading reports and whatnot. I know it's strange, but before, when he started building his empire, he wouldn't even leave his office, so we're kind of glad he gets out now."

"No offense, but he seems self-absorbed."

Sydney shrugs. "I guess we all wear a mask." She looks over to where her brother sits now. He and his date are both staring into their phones.

"What's your mask, Sydney?" We've talked enough about other people for one night.

She snaps her eyes back to me, wide-eyed for a

moment, and then looks away as though she'll find the answer among the other guests. Or courage. I didn't even realize how loaded my question was.

The server interrupts, reciting the specials and taking our order.

"Tell me about the show." Sydney uses the interruption to switch to a lighter topic.

I decide to go with it. I'll uncover her mask in time. Sipping the wine, I explain the idea behind the TV show.

"It sounds amazing, Hunter. I'm so happy for you. What does it mean for your clubs?"

"I'm hoping only good things. I have a five-year plan of opening clubs across the country, but I'm treating Priscilla's money as a loan, so I'm being prudent with the expansion. The publicity of the show could help with the growth. I hope."

She raises her glass. "To my TV star boyfriend, then."

"You lucked out, Mrs. Lowe, what can I tell you?" I wink and we drink. "It will be busy for a while. My concern is Caro... and now you."

It might be too soon to talk about us in this context, but I want every opportunity to make sure Sydney breaks through her trust and commitment issues.

She beams at me, and it's a sight I want to

remember for the rest of my life. "I'm happy to step in and help with Caro."

Out of all the things she could have said, offering to help with my daughter shoots straight to my heart. I'm speechless for a moment, just savoring the intimacy that has been growing between us.

"Have you always wanted to be a teacher?"

Our meal arrives and we both get distracted by the presentation, the smell of garlic and thyme, the succulent steam rising from our plates. We both ordered the special, which is fish, and before taking a bite, I'm already sure this is going to be an experience.

"I'm not sure about always, but for as long as I remember. My mom died when I was eleven and I started helping dad with my sisters. Most people felt sorry for me, having to step in as a caregiver, but I actually enjoyed it. Later, I saw what schools can do to kids.

"Take Gio, for example. He's rich and successful, but he was failing miserably at school. Massi struggled as well. Now Bianca was strict but always fair and she supported them. But what happens to kids that don't have parents like Bianca, or you? They lose self-confidence and grow up believing they can't do anything.

"And so I wanted to teach, to make the system work for the kids that are unique. I even planned to open my own school, or a learning center for kids who require—and deserve—alternative approaches to learning. There are systems in place now, but it's still a struggle for parents. And it depends on the individual school, as you know."

"Frankly, I knew I needed to get Caro out of her former school quickly, but I was lost as to how else to help her. We're lucky to have gotten you. Both of us are benefiting."

She smiles and crimson spreads across her face. "I can't complain either."

"Why haven't you pursued the idea of the learning center?"

"My plans got derailed with Jeremy's betrayal, but I'm happy where I am now." She swallows and I get the feeling it's not the complete truth. I guess tonight is the night to wear the mask.

A murmur among the diners catches our attention and we both turn. The chef ambles amongst the tables with a cocky smile.

"Massi," Sydney says and waves. He winks at her but gets intercepted by someone.

"He seems to enjoy the attention. I like him. We had a pleasant chat at the fundraiser. He might even consult on the show from the nutritional point of view. He'd look good on camera." I watch as he shakes hands and jokes with his customers.

"He wasn't always like that. Until recently, he

growled at everyone. It's his wife that lures out his kinder side."

I reach for her hand and kiss it. Sydney also draws out a side of me I didn't know I had. The man who wants to be a better person, a better father, a better everything to protect her, to make life easier for her, to make her happy and carefree.

"Syd, I can't believe you've finally come." Massi makes it over and shakes my hand. "Hey, Hunter, nice to see you again. Thank you for dragging my sister out of her cave. I've had the restaurant for fifteen years and I can count Syd's visits on one hand."

"The honor is mine." I wink at her. "This dinner was one of the best things I've ever eaten."

"Thank you, man. You look good, sis."

"A night of compliments." She blushes. "The meal was splendid. Send my regards to Gina. Did you know Gio is here tonight?"

"Yeah, I better go and say hi. Thank you for coming again." He kisses her cheek and shakes my hand before moving on.

A well-dressed man with a couple of bulky guys who look like bodyguards walks by on the way to their table. He nods to Sydney and she tenses.

Looking away, she fidgets with her napkin before placing it on her plate.

Before I get a chance to react, Gio strolls by.

"Enjoy your evening, Syd. Hunter." He bows his head quickly and then frowns, looking at something behind me. "Do you know him?" he asks Sydney.

Gio puts his phone into his pocket. I don't know Sydney's brother that well, but the fact he puts away his phone spikes my attention, and the hair on my neck.

I turn to see who he's talking about. The stocky man in a dark suit who has just passed by raises his whiskey in our direction, but his eyes are not on me. I spin back around.

If it was possible, Sydney would blend in with her chair, or at least that's what her body screams as she shrinks away, her eyes darting around, her face flushed.

"Of course I don't know him," she snaps at Gio.

"That man is bad news, Syd, and he's been staring at you. What the fuck?" her brother demands, his voice low.

"He must have mistaken me with someone else," she says through her teeth.

"Elliot McFadden is a dangerous loan shark, Syd. I don't understand what you've been doing with your money, but I hope it has nothing to do with him." Gio leans in, speaking into her face.

"Chill, man," I growl. "She said she doesn't know him, so leave her the fuck alone."

Gio straightens and glances over my shoulder

again, then he looks at me. "If you care about her, you better find out what the hell is going on."

Gio storms away, the blond supermodel behind him.

"Who is he?" I ask softly.

Deny all she wants, it's clear she knows the man. Sydney straightens, ready to tell me off, just like she did with her brother.

"No hiding, beautiful, cards on the table. Why does a dangerous loan shark know you?"

I can sense she is considering bolting. I've seen her like this before, even with me when we first met. She swallows a few times, licks her lips and then bites them.

"Because I owe him money."

Chapter Twenty-Eight

Sydney

Hunter holds my eyes and then throws his napkin on the table. "Let's get out of here."

We ask for the bill and leave the dessert—courtesy of my brother—on the table. By the time we exit the restaurant, I'm trembling. My nerves are primed to spark and explode. Hunter's hand on the small of my back is a comfort, but who knows how long it's going to stay there once I tell him the whole story.

He has a daughter to think of. Why did I even try to pull him into a relationship, putting him in danger? Giving Elliot McFadden another card to hold over me.

Hunter hails a cab. He doesn't speak, just holds my

hand. It provides safety and makes things graver. I focus on that point of contact where his rough hand swallows mine as if it's the ultimate source of energy on Earth.

We get to his building and take the elevator in silence. I'm grateful to gain this time without unraveling the complete truth, but anticipation of the conversation is leaking like acid into my stomach, burning a hole.

I don't want to tell him anything, and at the same time he's the only person I'm willing to tell. I've never told a soul. Not even London knows. What a stupid chance encounter, and of course Gio had to go all ballistic about it.

Why would McFadden even acknowledge me? Was it a warning? I have never missed a payment.

Hunter helps me out of my coat. His entire body hums with tense energy. With silent anger, perhaps?

"Are you angry?" The question catches in my throat. Our eyes lock and I relax slightly. There is kindness in those eyes. They have always been filled with kindness.

"I'm angry, but not at you. I'm pissed at the situation, and I don't even know what the situation really is." He pulls me to him. Wrapped in that strong, warm embrace, I regain the ability to breathe easier. "Come on, beautiful, let's talk."

"I'd rather fuck." I make a pathetic attempt at a joke.

"Believe me, so do I, but talking first." Hunter kisses the crown of my head and leads me to the kitchen. "Sit down and I'll make us tea. Probably a digestive one." He sighs.

I sit at the breakfast nook. "I might need wine, or something stronger."

"Oh, I'm spiking your tea, no worries." He smiles at me. It's a sad smile, his muscles all tight, but he's trying to make me feel better. Warmer. Cared for.

I sit in silence until he places two mugs on the table. I expect him to sit across from me or stay by the island, keep his distance. Instead, he scoots to my side, pushing me farther along the bench.

"Leave nothing out." His voice is silky as always, but it has a sharp edge.

"You know Jeremy dipped into my trust fund significantly during our marriage. He lost all that money and got even deeper into debt, and not with a bank, but with people who are dangerous. They didn't care about his passing. They came to collect the day after his funeral. They found out about my family, and they assumed they could score."

I hold the mug, seeking comfort in its warmth, staring down blindly. Hunter puts his hand on my back, stroking slowly. The touch weaves a fine thread of courage.

"They threatened me and my family, and I needed to come up with half a million fast. So I did." I bury my face in my hands.

"Borrowing from Elliot McFadden." Hunter finishes for me. "Why wouldn't you talk to one of your siblings?"

"My siblings?" I face him. "You mean the people who took the trust money from our parents and turned it into successful businesses or institutions while I blindly gave mine to a man who lied to me?"

Hunter glares at me, a storm brewing behind his eyes. "I think they would have understood. They would have helped. Some of your family members are snobs, but they don't judge. I'm pretty sure even Gio would have helped."

"Yes, perhaps you're right, but I was too scared. Betrayed, heartbroken, depressed." Tears prickle the corners of my eyes. "I was ashamed. And after I made the mistake of taking money from McFadden, my shame deepened. I was stupid the whole time with Jeremy, and I got even stupider after him. They all felt sorry for me already and I couldn't... I... I—"

"Oh, beautiful." He cups my face. "You can't blame yourself for trusting Jeremy. Has anyone in your family suspected who he really was?"

I shake my head. They didn't.

"So he fooled them all. He took advantage of you, and in the lowest moment of your life you made a desperate decision and borrowed money from the wrong person. How much do you owe him?"

"Over four hundred thousand," I whisper, unable to look away because somehow there is understanding in his eyes. Not pity. Not anger. Not disappointment. Understanding.

"Jesus. I assume most of it is interest? How are you even paying that from your salary?"

"Slowly." I shrug.

He kisses my forehead. Then my eyelids. The butterfly touches of his lips act like drumsticks reverberating through my chest. "When I first let a woman pay me for sex—because the first time it was just sex—I was ashamed. When I realized how much I could help with Julia's medical bills, I got over myself and dove into it. I'm not comparing the situations, I'm just saying that sometimes we make decisions out of desperation, but that doesn't define who we are."

A sob escapes me loud and broken and Hunter seizes my lips. I don't know how it's possible that each of his kisses feels different, but that's how it's been since that first burning kiss at The Ritz-Carlton three years ago.

Tonight his lips give reassurance, absolution, care. I love this man. I love him more every day.

Hunter stands up and pulls me with him. He presses his lips to mine again immediately as he walks me backward. He lifts me to sit on the island and moves his lips lower, nuzzling my neck.

I bury my fingers in his hair as my head falls back, a whirlpool of pleasure swirling in my core. He finds the hem of my shirt.

"Too many clothes," he growls against my skin. His words spur frantic action as we both shed our tops. Hunter doesn't even take off my bra, just pulls it down, my breasts jutting out, the peaks tender with need.

"I need you," I demand as he sucks on my nipple. "Now." I'm crazed with desire.

My problem hasn't gotten resolved tonight, but sharing the burden with someone has unleashed something crazed inside me. I need to wipe out all that lonely struggle with something wild and cathartic.

"Bossy tonight, beautiful. Does my girl need to fuck? No lovemaking tonight?" He growls, his eyes burning through me while he trails a finger over my ribcage. Just one finger, but oh what it does to me. I nod hungrily.

"Speak up, Sydney. What is it you need?"

"I need you to fuck me," I scream, and the words don't even leave my lips before Hunter yanks me off the counter, pulls my skirt up, spins me around and pushes me back to the marble surface.

My breasts ache at the contact with the cold stone, but the rest of me is burning. He rips off my underwear and hikes my leg up, flattening my knee on the counter. His other hand is pressed between my shoulder blades. I'm completely at his mercy, unable to move. Unwilling to move.

Hunter fills me to the hilt in one deliciously destructive move and starts a punishing tempo. The edge of the counter bruises my hips, but I don't care. I need him like this. Like it's punishment. Only it isn't. It feels like a reward or atonement. Cleansing.

I take with abandon, moaning loudly against the marble as the heat spreads through me and awakens all the parts of me with a divine pleasure. And with a realization that hits me in the middle of my heart.

I'm no longer alone.

Chapter Twenty-Nine

Sydney

"Okay, I'll see you later. Love you, beautiful." Hunter hangs up and I stand with the phone to my chest, smiling like an idiot.

Things have been fantastic. Hunter even survived lunch with my family. We're trying to squeeze as much time together as possible right now, because he shoots the show in January and things will get even busier.

We agreed I'll move in after Christmas as a trial. Okay, the trial is for Caro's benefit. We told her that with the filming, it's easier for me to stay there so I can take care of her. We're hoping that will create a natural transition for her.

Hunter's mom is leaving for Florida right after

Christmas. It's been a dream of hers to spend winters there, but she refused to leave before because Hunter needed her help.

We have been doing all these cheesy touristy things with Caro, and I love every minute of it. Next up is skating tonight at Rockefeller Center. For the first time in years, I'm enjoying winter in New York.

The trees I saw as bare before now sparkle with Christmas lights. We've been visiting markets, window shopping, writing to Santa, and taking advantage of the sizzling city life, bundled in our coats.

I would have hated all of it before. But with Hunter and Caro, Christmas cheer spreads through me along with the growing love I feel for both of them.

The only shadow on all of this is my dad. Our concerns materialized and he finally told us he was diagnosed with cancer. He is staying at London's during his treatment, and I'm grateful I can visit him as often as possible.

I'm even more grateful for having Hunter in my life now, because dealing with this news alone would have spiraled me into a dark place. Hunter has been my rock.

"Are you leaving soon?" Lara sticks her head into my classroom door, startling me.

"I think I'm going to stay behind and grade a few papers. Are you done for the day?"

"Yes." She enters and leans against a desk in the first row. "I meant to ask you. Is there something happening between you and the principal?"

What? Dan has been avoiding me since the incident. Things have been awkward, but I didn't have time to delve into that. If he needs more time to process the situation, it's fine with me. "Why are you asking?"

"Listen, I probably shouldn't say anything, but he's been asking about you a lot. Not just me, other teachers as well."

"What do you mean? In what way?" I've put the Dan issue to one side. He seemed sufficiently mortified by the incident at my place, and I didn't think he would still pursue a chance with me.

"Like he's trying to find out if you... I don't know, I might be making things up, but like he's building a case to challenge your performance."

Her words reach me in a disconnected way. I understand every single one of them, but my mind refuses to comprehend the meaning. Could Dan bide his time to take revenge and cost me my job because he feels jilted?

"You think he's trying to get me fired?" Even as I say the words, they sound foreign to me. He wouldn't, would he? But then, I wouldn't have expected him to assault me either. Shit.

"Look, Syd, I don't know, but his questions are not

a normal check-in. I mean, has he ever asked you what you think about my class?"

I shake my head. "But I only teach reading in your class."

"And I only teach music in yours, but he's asked me twice already if I think your class is performing to the school's academic standards. He masked it with 'It's her first class here, I want to make sure,' but it didn't sit well with me."

I don't know her well enough to trust telling her about my former relationship with him, so I let the information stew and thank her for telling me.

"Of course, Syd. I wouldn't want him to go behind my back to gather info about my work. The second time he approached me, he was even asking about specific kids. So odd. If he cares about students' results, that's what we have the conference for. Or he should ask you." She shakes her head. "Anyway, I miss our old boss." She stands up and heads to the door.

"Any particular student that interests him?" I ask, my heart hammering in my ribcage.

"He asked me about Janey Clement and Caroline Stuart. That's your boyfriend's girl, isn't she?"

My heart pulses in my temple. It might be nothing. Janey has behavioral issues and Caro has learning problems, so his interest is warranted to a certain extent, but why wouldn't he ask me?

"Thank you for telling me, Lara."

She leaves and I sit down to grade the students' work, but I can't concentrate. I consider running to Dan's office and confronting him. I fight the idea for a moment. I pick up the phone and almost dial Hunter, but I don't want him to come over all caveman-style. The last thing we need is another altercation between the two of them. I should have reported Dan after he came to my place. Shit.

I pack up my purse. I think about calling London for advice, but as I walk down the corridor, something stops me. I should find out what the hell is going on. Turning, I take the steps two at a time, anger fueling my determination.

"Hi, Sydney," Melissa greets me as I barge into the administration office. "How can I help you?"

"I need to speak with Dan." I glance between his door and her desk, tension coursing through me.

"He's left already. He had a meeting with the chair of the board. Do you want me to schedule you for tomorrow?"

"No, that's okay." Oddly deflated, I leave.

Maybe Lara is exaggerating. Dan could be asking around about all the teachers and students who require extra help. He might not be going about it the right way, but it's his job after all.

I check the time on my phone. There's no point

commuting back to Brooklyn only to turn around for our skating adventure. I open my purse to protect the phone from the light snowfall outside and see the envelope. Shit, I almost forgot about my monthly deadline.

With a sigh, I start the dreaded walk of gloom, as I *cheerfully* call it, and take the subway to Elliot McFadden's offices. There is nothing good about borrowing money from a loan shark, but it would be nicer if I could make online payments.

But McFadden's business doesn't uphold human decency, let alone the law, so all transactions are cash only. No paperwork. No trail.

His offices look almost like a normal office, but reek of despair and hopelessness. And maybe blood, because my overactive imagination has painted brutal beatings happening behind the back door.

A bodyguard gives me a menacing once-over and the receptionist asks me to wait, so I take a seat. Two people cross the hallway, laughing. It really feels like a normal place of business. Only the ethics and tactics might not be normal.

The receptionist straightens up, looking like a deer in the headlights, as the entrance opens and the room gets dim with the arrival of the boss and his minions.

"Mrs. Lowe, I'm surprised to see you here." Elliot McFadden offers me his hand.

I frown. I despise the man with all my heart, but

it's not like I can share that sentiment, so I just nod and remain silent.

"Do you need money again?" A sly smile lights up his red face, raising the hair on my nape.

I stand up, reveling in my height as he steps back so he doesn't have to crane his neck so much.

"I came to take care of my monthly payment."

His phony smile spreads wider. "As much as I'd love to have you as my client, Mrs. Lowe, your debt has been paid in full."

"What? I-I-that must be a mistake." Is he trying to trick me?

"Mr. Stuart paid off your debt. But I hope we can do business again soon." He laughs and strolls toward his office where I sat crying and desperate six years ago before I signed my freedom over to the devil.

The gust of wind chills me to the core as I stumble outside. I lean against the wall and breathe, trying to collect my thoughts. But they roam freely around my head, laughing at me. This can't be right.

Somehow I make it back downtown. Without thinking, I go to the club, hoping to find Hunter there.

He went behind my back.

A small part of me keeps arguing it's an amazing gesture. I should be happy to be rid of McFadden, it's a needed financial reprieve.

But the woman who once loved and trusted, and

then lost it all, the Sydney I thought was finally buried with Jeremy, is as strong as ever.

"Sydney," Caro calls and runs to me as soon as I enter. They are here. He's here.

"Hey, darling." I caress her head, trying to focus on the space around me but failing. As much as I fought the tears until now, they are winning.

The music echoes loudly in my head. Feet thump on cardio machines, the air conditioning hisses above all the hushed conversations, beeping and metallic clacks and clangs. My heart thuds inside my temples, deafening the cacophony of the place.

The city blinks with cheerful lights behind the steamed wall of windows. The world continues to turn as my own tumbles slowly.

"I finished my homework." Caro tugs at my arm. "Are you excited about the skating?"

"Hunter is in his office, Syd." Lea studies me with narrowed eyes. I guess my internal turmoil is visible.

I exhale, surprised how painful breathing is. "Caro, I need to talk to your dad."

"Come and help me make the smoothies," Lea calls out, reading the situation.

I walk around the mirrored wall, afraid to look at myself because I'm worried the woman I'd see is just a shadow of the widow from six years ago.

I knock and open the door. Hunter looks up from

his computer and his entire face, his entire being, lights up as if his life improved just by my entrance. Almost immediately he frowns.

"What's going on, Sydney?" He leaps to his feet and pulls me in, closing the door behind me. I step back when he leans closer to kiss me. Stupid tears play their get-out-jail-free card and stream out.

"I asked you to never keep things from me." The words struggle around the lump growing in my throat.

Hunter squints, trying to decipher my state. "Sydney?"

"I went to the McFadden office and learned I'm no longer a client." I don't recognize my voice.

Hunter sighs and smiles. "I was going to tell you tonight. I wanted to surprise you..." He steps closer.

"You went behind my back and you kept it from me. It's humiliating enough to go to that office once a month to relive my mistake and its consequences, and today McFadden enjoyed my little surprise."

"Forget about him. You never have to see him again. I took care of it for you. And for me as well. I looked into him after our dinner at Casa Cassi and the man has a reputation. He's out of your life now. Out of our life. What if he threatened Caro?"

His words punch me in the stomach as confusion swirls through me. Of course, I don't want people like McFadden hanging over my head, especially now when people I care about are involved. He is right about that.

"You didn't tell me. You decided to make a significant financial transaction behind my back. How can I trust you?"

"No, no, no, Sydney, I helped you out. To protect you. Are you suggesting I lost your trust by helping you out? If I told you I would pay your—Jeremy's—debt, you'd have never agreed."

"No, I wouldn't, because I'm not a charity case. I made mistakes and I'm paying for them, but I don't need your pity."

"It was a fucking practical solution to a problem that fucking impacts my life. It's a lot of money, but I won't miss it and it makes a huge difference for you. Why can't you just accept I want to take care of you and protect you from assholes like McFadden?"

"Behind my back!" I yell, anger pulsing through me, poisoning my reason and my words. "What else have you been doing without telling me? Picking up dates with Gigi Lafontaine?" I regret the words, driven out by a need to hurt, as soon as they leave my mouth. I don't even know what my point is.

Hunter yanks his head back as though my words hit him physically.

"I can't do this." I run out and don't stop until I reach the street.

Chapter Thirty

Hunter

It's been two weeks since Sydney ran out of my office. Christmas is in a few days, and I've been in such a foul mood that most people have been avoiding me. Hunter the Grinch.

I've stewed for a week. How dare she compare me to her husband? How could she even remotely compare those two situations? She can't possibly blame me for wanting to get rid of McFadden, especially when she would be moving in with us.

If she's moving in with us. I throw a pen across my office and it lands with a dissatisfying plop, not even falling apart. I'm the only one falling apart.

I've been working on payroll for the past two days.

At this pace, people will get their Christmas bonus next summer.

I can't even sulk and steam in peace, with a tumbler of whiskey, because Caro's presence in my life doesn't allow for such luxury. She's been asking questions about Sydney since that night when I canceled the skating trip, because I was seeing red and couldn't imagine spreading cheerful joy around. I still owe Caro that skating outing.

Fuck. Fuck. Fuck.

The worst part is I miss her. I miss her so fucking much. I'm blind with sadness. A thousand times a day I have something I want to share with her, but she's gone.

After my initial anger subsided, I called her, but she hasn't been answering. And Caro said she hasn't come to school. Her class was told Mrs. Lowe was sick and a substitute teacher has taken over.

But now it's been two fucking weeks. The worst weeks of my life.

To add insult to injury, things at work haven't been going well either. We had to push the opening at Tribeca to next year, and there have been a few more membership cancellations than usual.

Yet I can't focus on the business, because my mind is constantly struggling to veer away from the green eyes and soft sounds she makes.

I'd have hoped Ash would step up, but he's been avoiding me and acting weird. I really need to focus on getting the house in order before the shoot starts, but I can't think straight until things with Sydney get resolved.

She hasn't been answering her phone. She hasn't been going to work. I imagine her suffering alone in that cold apartment and pain sears me. She was so hurt when she left. Fuck.

I check my watch. It's eight o'clock in the morning and I have to leave for the photoshoot with Delaney soon.

My entire being wants to go to Brooklyn, but Sydney needs to realize she overreacted. Has she, though? As more days, hours, minutes pass without her, the more I can see how I betrayed her trust. I shattered the confidence that was fragile to begin with.

I promised to never keep things from her. But in my mind that promise blanketed bad, hurtful shit. Not helping her out. I don't even know why I went behind her back. I was focused on the result, not the execution. All I saw was relieving her of an immense burden.

Goddammit. I gather my things and make my way out.

"I have to go," I tell Lea. "Call me if you need me. I might not come back today."

"Sure, boss. Can't wait to see the pics." She smirks.

I get into the car the studio sent for me and dial the number I should have called sooner. It rings six times and I'm about to hang up when a raspy voice answers.

"What the hell, Hunter, you woke me up. Is Sydney okay?" London sounds as if she smoked a pack of cigarettes in her sleep.

"That's why I'm calling. Is she okay?" I hate this, but I doubt she would see me and I need to know she is okay. And, shamefully, part of me needs to know she is as miserable as I am.

"Why are you asking me? She's been canceling on me because she's with you all the time," London scolds, but then she probably wakes up fully. "Why are you calling *me*?"

"I paid Sydney's debt and she got upset. I haven't heard from her in two weeks. Could you check on her?"

"Jesus. What do you mean you paid her debt? What debt?" Sheets rustle in the background.

"Jeremy's debt. Not my story to tell, but I'm worried and she hasn't been answering her phone. I'll bang on her door tonight, but could you please check on her?" The worry crawls up my neck.

"Of course I will. Not for you, though, for her. Why didn't you call me earlier?" she snarls.

"Because I'm an idiot. It only occurred to me now

that she probably retreated from life overall. She's been on sick leave from school."

"Jesus Christ, Hunter, you should have called me sooner."

"Obviously I can't do anything right," I snap, tired of all the should-haves.

"It's nice of you to take care of her debt. Though I can see how that triggered some of the old baggage. I'll talk to her and text you." She hangs up.

I groan. How am I going to survive this day? I reach the destination, a large warehouse, and try to put on a normal face.

I hate that I have to be here.

I hate that I haven't gone to Sydney sooner.

I hate that I didn't at least call London earlier.

"Hunter," Delaney greets me with a cheer. "You dog." She punches my biceps. "I spilled my coffee this morning and was ready to kill you, but the network loves the story and plans to spin it to capitalize on the publicity."

What is she talking about? What story?

"Don't look at me like that? Is it true?" She bounces on her tiptoes in glee. "No, no, don't tell me. It doesn't matter, anyway."

"What are you talking about?" I growl. Fuck this day.

She scrolls on her phone and turns the screen to

me. Red spreads at the edges of my vision as something inside me dies. Mother-fucking Gigi.

My own face smiles at me from Delaney's phone with a headline that I've been dreading for years now.

Owner of Manhattan Fitness Club Former Gigolo.

I run my hand down my face. "I'm sorry, Delaney." And then her words register. "What do you mean the network wants to spin it?"

"They're leaking info about the show and your involvement, hoping to get some free publicity, and frankly it's kind of cool. Are you really retired?" She winks, but the smirk disappears under the heat of my glare.

If there was a chance this would die unnoticed as a tiny mention by some inspired blogger, it went up in flames when I signed up for the show.

I need to talk to Caro. What am I even going to say? But it has to be me telling her sensibly rather than one of the helicopter moms with *well-intended* cruelty.

"And imagine... for a moment I considered giving the show to Ash." Delaney shakes her head and continues swiping through the coverage. "This is gold, Hunter. You'll be famous before we air. Let's get you ready."

I stare at her, my head on the brink of a nuclear explosion. I've feared that one day I'd have to explain my former gig to Caro and face the judgment of strangers. Never did I imagine that when that day came, it wouldn't even be my top worry.

"What do you mean you considered Ash?" I follow her as we walk toward the makeup station.

"When he came to me saying you felt bad telling me no but that you didn't really want to do the show, and how he would love the opportunity. But you accepted the offer that same day, so I forgot about it."

Before I even have time to process the information, I'm pulled into work. Makeup, change of clothes and endless standing, posing, smiling. The last one is the biggest struggle. Delaney complains, but the photographer says my brooding is a turn-on and people will love it.

By the end of the shoot I feel like a piece of meat, chewed up and spit out. I hope shooting the show will feel less vain, more impactful. Though I shouldn't judge the work by today because my head has been anywhere but here.

I give the network's driver Sydney's address.

My phone rings and I snatch it up, my heart swelling with hope it's Sydney or at least London with some news. When I see the caller ID I consider declining the call, but then I decide I couldn't have gotten a better punching bag if I was looking for it.

"So I see the cat is out of the bag," Gigi sings, turning my stomach upside down.

"I hope you're satisfied. I'm still not sure what you wanted to achieve because I wouldn't sleep with you before and I sure as hell won't do it now. Ever."

"Oh, I don't need you to warm my bed, Stuart. Or is it Hunter? Ash has been doing a pretty good job in that department."

Like a punch to my gut, her words spread pain through me. *Ash?*

"You see, I think he's great in the sack. I don't need you anymore, but he deserves more, and you've been taking everything from him, so now he's taken from you." She cackles.

"If you're referring to yourself, you're delusional." Fuck this shit. I wish I had Sydney to calm me down, but she doesn't want to be by my side. I don't know the extent of Ash's betrayal yet, but its hurt is negligible compared to the misery Sydney's absence has carved inside me.

I hang up. Yelling at Gigi brings no satisfaction. I'm about to put the phone away when it chimes again. I read the text and almost throw my phone out of the window.

London: She's not ready to see you. Stay away for now.

"Fuuuuuuck."

The driver looks at me over his shoulder. "Bad day?"

"More like a lifetime."

We're almost at the Brooklyn Bridge and I reluctantly obey London's advice, giving the driver the Tribeca address since it's not far anymore. I might as well deal with Ash.

The gym is dark when I arrive. I check my watch. Strange. We've been paying the construction workers for overtime to compensate for the delay. Finding my key, I enter. The place looks just like it did the last time I was here two weeks ago.

I call the foreman.

"Hunter," he answers on the second ring. His voice is nearly drowned out by the banging and chugging of machinery in the background.

"I'm at the Tribeca location and it seems like no work has been done here since the last time. What's going on?" Clearly he's at another job.

"What do you mean? Ash told us there are no funds available and he'd call us after New Year's."

"Oh, yeah, he probably didn't get a chance to tell you to come back," I lie. "Are you available to return now?"

"Sorry, Hunter, we took another job, but we can come back the first week of January."

"Okay. I'm taking over here, so you'll deal with me from now on. I'll see you then. Merry Christmas."

I don't expect the driver to wait for me, but he's still

outside. I may as well take advantage of the network's perk. They are taking advantage of my media coverage, after all.

The drive back to the Madison location is taken up by a lifetime of snapshots in my mind. Ash talking to Gigi. Sydney laughing at my joke. Caro's disappointment about skating being canceled. Ash talking to Delaney. The hurt in Sydney's eyes the last time I saw her. The way she felt in my arms when we danced. How she read with Caro. Her hair fanned out over my pillow. Her lips on mine.

No matter how shitty my life is, she steals all my thoughts.

I enter the gym, hit by the usual commotion, familiar smell and typical sounds that I take for granted. The soundtrack of my life, but my favorite sounds are currently missing.

"How did it go, boss?" Lea asked. "I thought you weren't coming back."

"I have a few things I need to check." I make my way to my office, barely acknowledging the patrons who greet me. I shut the door and exhale. This day is certainly winning the longest day contest.

I sit at my computer and open up the bank statements and financial spreadsheet. It takes me about an hour to connect the dots. Ash has been careful, but I can see he diverted the funds for the remodeling of Tribeca club to another, personal account.

I'd prefer to confront him face-to-face, but I want this to be over, so I can focus on what matters. Even though right now that amounts to pining over the woman who refuses to see me.

I dial and half-expect to get his voicemail, but he picks up after two rings. "Hey, man, what's up? How did the shoot go? Did you have to wear makeup?" He chuckles.

Looks like his new lover didn't tell him she's already spoken to me. "You're fired. Lea will have your stuff delivered to you."

One beat of silence. Two. Three. I should just hang up, but I don't. Damn it, I should have a lawyer present.

"What the hell, Hunter?" Ash finally finds his voice.

"You stole money from me, you deliberately sabotaged Tribeca's opening, you went behind my back to Delaney, and you sank so low that you fucked Gigi to get information on me and then used it, hurting my family—"

"You stole from me first, asshole," he yells. "That inheritance should have been mine. I trained that old hag for years. That juicy past of yours is going to get me the show to even up the score."

I hang up. I'm so done with this shit. Even as I was summarizing his betrayal, I felt little. It all seems fixable. There is something—someone—more important than any of this. Two people in fact. I need to talk to Caroline.

Leaving things as they are, I lock my office for the first time ever and give Lea strict instructions to change the codes and have Ash escorted off the premises if he attempts to come in. She stares at me wide-eyed but doesn't question or protest.

I send the driver away and walk home, hoping to clear my head. I wonder what Sydney is doing. I want to call London to find out, but I stop myself.

"Mr. Stuart," Karl greets me. "Welcome home. Mrs. Stuart and Caroline are upstairs already."

"Thank you, Karl." Shit, if I don't get Sydney back, I'll have to cancel Mom's trip to Florida. Or hire a nanny. The thought pisses me off further. I don't want to be thinking about not having Sydney in my life. I don't want to be thinking about logistics around my family if she's not a part of it. "Is Suzanne looking forward to the holidays?"

"Yeah, her whole family is crashing at our place. I took an extra shift." He winks and I chuckle. "Is Mrs. Lowe coming later? I haven't seen her in a while."

Yeah, you and me, Karl, you and me. Even the doorman misses her.

At my silence, his face falls. "I'm sorry, Mr. Stuart. I didn't mean to overstep. I should be—"

"It's okay, Karl. I pry into your life with Suzanne all the time."

"Well, for what it's worth, I hope Mrs. Lowe will be back soon."

I nod, crushed by the weight of it all. I don't know how to fix things if she is not willing to talk to me. Stubborn woman. Damn it.

I take the elevator and open the door, forcing myself to put on a neutral face for the other two girls in my life.

"Daddy." Caroline runs to me. I pick her up and hold her tight. Having this little girl in my arms makes the world brighter, better, bearable.

My mom leans against the kitchen doorway at the end of the hallway, looking at me with concern. She must have seen the headlines.

"Let me go wash up, Caro, and I'll come to your room in a minute, okay?"

I join my mom in the kitchen.

"Is it true?" Her question doesn't carry judgment or disappointment. Yet guilt ripples through me.

I nod and she exhales. "I'm sorry I let you down, Mom."

Her breathing hitches with a swallowed sob.

"Hunter, sweetheart, you didn't let me down. All the money for Julia's care?"

I nod again.

"I chose to never ask where it came from, Hunter. And frankly, I'm relieved it wasn't something worse. At one point, I was afraid you were a drug dealer."

That confession scrambles my brain. "What?"

"I mean, you had a lot of cash. What was I supposed to think? Is that the reason Sydney hasn't been around?"

Hearing her name again is another burning jab into my heart. "No, she's known from the beginning."

"You should talk to Caro." She pats my shoulder. "Ruby's mom already hinted at something."

I kiss the crown of her head and turn toward Caro's room.

"Hunter." Mom stops me. "Are things with Sydney fixable?"

I shudder and pinch the bridge of my nose. "I really hope so, Mom."

Caro's lying on her bed, her hands behind her head. She is never this still and my stomach tightens. I drop beside her and she tucks her head in the hollow of my shoulder.

"Talk to me, kiddo." Because I have no idea what to say.

"Ruby's mom said you're disreputable and she

doesn't want Ruby to have playdates with me anymore." She sighs with the weight of her entire existence in that breath. I should be the one fixing things for her, improving her life, not screwing it up even more.

Fuck. How to explain this. If Sydney was here, she would know what to say.

"Dad, what does disreputable mean?" Caro tilts her head, looking at me.

"It means something people consider not right. I used to have a job that many people think wasn't proper, not a good thing to do. I had to do it because I needed money and it paid well. Everyone has found out now and they think less of me. I'm sorry Ruby's mom doesn't want you to play with her anymore. I've never wanted you to deal with this, Caro."

"Did you like the job?" She snuggles back into the crook of my shoulder, her small hand over my hammering heart.

Out of all the questions she could have asked. "It was okay, I guess."

"Sydney says it's important to love what you do. So I guess if you liked it, I don't care what others think. Ruby likes that we can be secret friends anyway." She scoots closer, half hugging me with her short arm.

"I didn't love the job, Caro, but it was the only way

I could get the money we needed, so I did it anyway. I love my job now, though."

"That's good." There's sadness in her voice and I hate that I've caused it.

"Is there something else you want to ask, Caro? I like when we talk about things." I need her to understand as much as possible, so the assholes in school don't blindside her.

She lets out another heavy sigh and I want to punch the wall. She hasn't sighed with such gravity since Julie.

"Is Sydney going to die like Mommy?" She raises her head, her huge eyes full of concern.

I sit up and pull her into my lap. "Caro, sweetheart, no, she won't. How did you... Why do you think that?"

"She canceled the skating and hasn't been around, and they told us at school she is sick. Mommy had to cancel things all the time and went away to the hospital for a long time and..." Her lips tremble.

"No, Caro, Sydney is fine." Ignoring the topic and not talking to Caro about Sydney's absence has caused too much fear and pain. "We're both a little heart-broken right now. I wanted to surprise her with some-thing, but she didn't like the surprise and she's mad at me."

Caro jerks away from me, the bed bouncing as she pushes to her knees, her hands on her hips. "What kind of surprise? Why would you upset her? Did you cook her Indian food? She doesn't like Indian, Dad. You have to apologize."

I chuckle at her enthusiasm. I fucking wish I had cooked Indian. That would have been easier. "I will do that, Caro. I'll go tomorrow after I drop you at school."

"But get flowers and chocolates." She jumps off the bed. "I'm going to make a special edition of my magazine to show her how amazing she is." She looks at me, all practical. "You know, in case you screw up the apology."

"May I help with the magazine?" That seems like a better plan for the evening than sulking alone in my bedroom.

"Find pictures on your phone, and let's see what we have to work with."

Today beat the hell out me, but Caro's innocent belief that we can win Sydney over flows over me with an abandon only my daughter can spread.

Chapter Thirty-One

Sydney

The spider in the corner hasn't moved in hours. It's certainly stayed in the same spot it was in last night. And the day before probably. The morning sun breaks in with laser-like beams, rendering the web's thread prismatic. Perhaps it hasn't moved for longer.

I've been watching the spider from my place in bed for long enough to know, but I don't know. I know little lately. I hate that it's morning. I hate that I have to face another day.

Another day consumed by this agonizing ache inside me. Every night I promise myself that tomorrow will be better. That I'll make an effort and start functioning like an adult, but I don't.

I shouldn't have taken time off work. Work would have given me purpose and eventually I would have gotten better. But I couldn't face Caro every day without thinking about Hunter. Not that staying away from the school has helped with that particular predicament.

I didn't even know one person could hoard all my thoughts. He robbed me of my heart, my ability to trust, my newly-discovered joy.

But I lived through a similar experience once. The thing about broken people is that we know we'll survive. It might take time, but I will survive. Staying away from Hunter might hurt like hell right now, but staying with him is much scarier. I can't linger in the place that keeps me vigilant and worry that he'll go behind my back again.

I will survive this and move on.

The only problem with my theory is that with every day away from him, things don't improve. They don't even stay the same. I could deal with that. Instead, I feel worse every morning. It's exhausting.

"Good morning, sunshine."

I bolt out of my bed, my hands in front of my face in a combative stance.

Lo raises an eyebrow. "You need to brush up on your self-defense skills, Syd. Do you want coffee or wine? We're out of vodka, but I can get my assistant to bring us breakfast and more booze." She takes two cups from my cupboard.

Jesus. I forgot London was here. "Did you stay the night?" I can't picture London curled up on my couch. On anyone's couch.

"Apparently." She scratches her head. Her hair is all tousled and she is wearing my T-shirt. "Your couch was designed by a villain determined to eliminate the world's population by spreading soreness. I need to book a massage."

I plop onto said sofa. London hands me the mug and sits on my bed, cross-legged.

She purses her lips as if deciding something and then opens her mouth. I wish she wouldn't.

"Okay, I gave you love and support yesterday, alcohol-induced reset last night, and now it's time for tough love. You're being stupid. That man with his little girl —and I don't even like children—is the best thing that has happened to you for a while. Or in your life. He loves you, and you love him."

Her factual tone is annoying. Her fucking truth is annoying. Painful. Mean. Tears pool in my eyes.

"Arguably, my experience in that department is minimal, but I've observed the two of you together, and I'd bet a significant amount of money on the fact he's it for you. Don't be stupid, Syd. Not all of us get the luxury of spending life with someone we love." She looks away, blinking, and I'm shocked to see my sister emotional.

It's not my plight that moved her, but rather her lost love, but still her words hit hard in my heart, cracking at my determination to protect myself.

My phone chimes and I look for it because it's something to do and I need to break the moment Lo has built. She harrumphs and climbs off my bed, gathering her clothes.

Lara: You should come. Ravinski is trying to get Caroline expelled. They have a meeting in an hour.

I call Lara right back, but she has no more information. I sit and stare at the white wall of my pathetic apartment, my mind idling. London comes out of my bathroom, dressed.

"What's going on?" She frowns.

"Dan is trying to expel Caro from school." I say the words slowly, letting them settle into some sort of comprehension.

"On what grounds?" Lo shakes her head and snorts dismissively. "He can't do that."

"I need to get there." I stand up and open a drawer, trying to find clothes. Shit, what do I wear? I've been in my leggings and T-shirt for two weeks now. At least London forced me to shower yesterday.

"Isn't this against your *I need to forget them* goal?" She leans against my counter, smirking.

"Fuck you." I jump on one leg, trying to put my jeans on. "Can I use your car?"

"I sent the driver home last night. By the time he comes back and drives you all the way to Manhattan, you might be better off taking a cab or a train."

"Okay." I grab my keys and my purse. "Let's go. How are you going to get back to town?" The idea of London on a subway is as preposterous as her sleeping on my couch. So I guess anything is possible.

"I'll have my boyfriend pick me up." She shrugs.

"You don't have a boyfriend." I lock the door behind us and rush down the stairs.

"Of course I do," she says casually, and it would have made me stop in my tracks if I didn't have a more important mission.

I make it to the school in decent time. I text Melissa to find out more information and pray she's willing to disclose something.

Melissa: Mr. Stuart has a meeting with the chair of the board and the principal in ten minutes. He's been summoned.

I dash to the teacher's bathroom and pace for a moment. Should I just crash the meeting? Should I confront Dan before it? They wouldn't have summoned Hunter and invited the chair if they didn't plan something drastic.

I wash my face and lean against the sink, breathing. The door opens and Lara enters.

"Are you okay?" She rubs my arm.

"Yeah. I should join that meeting. What the hell is going on?"

"I think he's going to use Hunter's reputation to—"

"What do you mean, his reputation?" My heart is trying to escape my ribcage.

"Well, the coverage about him..." Her eyes dart around. "His past job."

I pull my phone from my back pocket and type in the search bar. The list of results is staggering. My knees buckle. Poor Hunter. Poor Caro. They have been dealing with this. Jesus.

"You didn't know?" The worry in Lara's eyes doubles.

"I didn't know it was out. Never mind, that's not important. I need to get to that meeting and help Caroline."

"Let me know if I can do anything. I already went to HR about his sneaking around and unofficial performance questions."

I squeeze her hand and run out.

Melissa stands up as soon as she sees me. For a moment, I worry she might try to stop me, but she opens the door to the small boardroom instead.

Three heads turn my way. But it's only one face

that registers. Dark circles accentuate Hunter's beautiful eyes. His face is pale, his jaw clenched, and he looks exhausted. And so handsome it hurts.

We stare at each other for a moment before Dan clears his throat. "Sydney?"

"Yeah." I try to refocus. The whole time I was rushing to get here, I considered everything but the fact I'd have to face Hunter.

Seeing him after two weeks of agony is harder than I imagined. What was I thinking, believing I could get over him? What was I thinking, leaving him without giving him a chance?

A wave of emotions knocks me off-balance, but as the other two people in the room shift with impatience, I force my eyes away from him and look at the chair of the board.

"I understand this meeting is about Caroline Stuart, who is in my class, so I believe I should be here."

"That won't be necessary. You're on sick leave," Dan says.

"I think Mrs. Lowe's presence is important," the chair interrupts. "Thank you for coming. I hope you feel better."

Dan straightens the paperwork in the folder in front of him and clears his throat. "As I was saying, we're concerned Caroline's academic performance is not up to the standards of our school. In addition, your reputation… we feel that you're not the right match for this institution."

"You can't—" Hunter starts.

"What are you trying to achieve here, Dan?" I challenge, sitting down and glaring at him. "Because you've never discussed Caroline's academic results with me. In fact, she started in September practically illiterate and with major learning challenges, the result of the school system failing her. In a few short months, she's improved significantly. So, correct me if I'm wrong, but if her academic shortcomings were not a concern at the time of her admission, I find it hard to believe we would want her to leave the school now, when she's advancing in the right direction."

I turn to the chair. "Isn't inclusion and fairness a point of pride for this institution? Children like Caroline who need different teaching approaches should be at the forefront of that mission."

The chair assesses me with narrowed eyes and moves her attention to Dan. "Would you like to explain your concerns?"

Dan's face pales as he tries to flip through his papers.

The chair lets out an impatient sigh. "There is still the concern over the current reputation issue you're facing." She looks at Hunter. "I've been fielding multiple calls from parents who are worried about their children alongside your daughter, given your lack of morals."

Hunter drags his hand over his face and shakes his head, looking resigned.

I burst to my feet, my chair tumbling behind me with a deafening crash. Everyone at the table instinctively recoils. Or I think they do.

"Sydney?" Hunter's voice cuts through me like a knife. God, I miss my name on his lips. It caresses me like a touch of silk, boosting my determination.

"Let me tell you something about the character of Caroline's father." I no longer look at Hunter or Dan. I'm making my case to the chair because she needs to hear me out. "Did you know he is not her biological father? He adopted her after her mother, his sister, succumbed to cancer. In fact, the *immoral behavior* is related to that... but that's beside the point. Knowing him, how generous and kind he is, how he supports his family, makes me question the characters of all his accusers."

I narrow my eyes briefly at Dan, and then return my attention to the woman across from me. I should probably stop at this point, but I'm past reason or playing safe.

"He might have not chosen the most socially acceptable way to make money, but he did it for his family. He also spent time with a lonely elderly woman, not because he had too much free time, but because she had nobody. And when he opened his first club, instead of capitalizing on his location and catering to top dollar clientele, he made sure the gym is accessible to others, including underprivileged children."

The words spill from me like a wild river. "So if you're concerned about reputation, perhaps think about what it says when this school turns its back on families like this one."

"That's enough, Sydney." Dan stands up, closing his folder with a thud.

"I agree." The chair stands as well. "We've heard enough. Mrs. Lowe, thank you for joining the meeting. Mr. Stuart, please accept my apologies and I hope Caroline can continue her progress in this school." She walks around to the door. "Mr. Ravinski, in the future, don't waste my time with meetings based on thin air. We'll talk more about this later. I have parents' phone calls to return now."

She opens the door and turns to Hunter. "If you don't mind, I'll just tell the parents your little scandal is not true."

"But it is." Hunter is the last one to rise from his chair.

"Yes, but it's your mess and I don't want to deal

with it." She wrinkles her nose as if the idea rotted on her tongue, shrugs and leaves.

I'm stunned, unable to move for a moment.

"I take it you're back from your leave?" Dan asks, not even trying to mask his bitterness.

I blink a few times, my body too aware of Hunter's closeness. "Tomorrow is the last day before the holiday break, Dan. I can't wait to be back in January."

I turn and walk out. Part of me wants to run and hide, process everything. I've just defended a man who I claim I don't trust. Who I blame for... helping me.

"Sydney." Hunter's voice stops me. He approaches and goosebumps run down my spine. "Can you look at me?"

The silence in the long corridor thunders in my head as I pivot and meet his eyes. I've always thought the intensity of his gaze was burning, baring, devastating. I can see now it's way more. It's protecting, caring, loving. It's too much, and not enough at the same time.

"Thank you, Sydney." He hisses my name in that sensual tone, and it tears me apart.

A tiny gasp escapes me as the three simple words shudder through me. "I'm sorry." I'm not sure what I'm apologizing for, but that's how I feel. I'm sorry for all the hurt I caused us because of my fear of commitment.

"I'm sorry I went behind your back," he replies. "I realize how my gesture looked vile in the light of your previous experience, but you need to understand I acted out of love."

"I don't want to go back to the twenties," I blurt, and Hunter jerks his head up, taken aback and frowning. "I don't want to go back in time to the Art Deco era. I'd like to go back to the day we were going to skate, and instead of everything else, I'd very much like to skate under the Christmas tree at Rockefeller Center." I sniff, biting my lip.

"We don't need a time machine for that, we can do that tonight if you want. Sydney, the only thing that matters to me is protecting you and Caro, loving you, taking care of you. Because my life is better with you in it. It's so much better. Without you, I don't seem to function anymore, Sydney."

My breath catches. "I think we have a lot of fucking to catch up on." I smile hesitantly.

He shakes his head and chuckles. It reaches his eyes and I know the look of those gray eyes on me is more important than anything else I've accumulated in my life.

"Though I'd love to spend a day with you and Caro first. I've missed you both." Hope swells in my chest.

"She would love that. We made a special edition of her magazine for you."

God, I want to run into his arms. But he hasn't opened them yet.

Hunter closes his eyes, lets out a long breath and then looks at me again. "Damn it, beautiful, you promised not to get into these things here at school. I need to kiss you."

I want to wipe away my tears, but there is no point because they run with abandon. Only now they are tears of joy and relief.

"Then kiss me."

Epilogue

Sydney

"We'll be late, Hunter. What is so important right now? Where are we going?" The bare trees of Central Park glisten with frost as the car takes a turn in the opposite direction of the Tribeca club.

"Stop stressing. We have an hour to spare and I want to show you something." Hunter squeezes my hand.

"But where are we going?" Caro asks, her eyes glued to her phone.

"As I said, it's a surprise." Hunter rolls his eyes.

Uneasiness trickles through my veins. Trickles, not yet floods. It's Valentine's Day and the past two months have more than proved I can trust the amazing, handsome man beside me. We spent Christmas morning together as a family, and we've been just that ever since.

I've kept my Brooklyn apartment, but I'm giving them notice by the end of this month. It's a big step for me to let go of that place, and I catch myself still forging scenarios about why I should have a backup home. However, it represents a different era in my life and, for once, I'm hesitantly looking into the future with hope. And even joy.

"Am I going to like the surprise?" I bite my lip.

"I don't know, beautiful. You either like it or hate it, but I'm showing it to you today, so if you don't like it, you'll have to let me down gently, since it's my big day and all." He winks and my stomach tightens.

"That almost confirms I won't like it."

Hunter laughs. "No, but the last time I wanted to surprise you... well... we all ended up suffering. This time I'm hoping to just tease you with the opportunity, and then we can discuss everything together."

"And you're using today's opening at Tribeca in hopes I'll be easy on you?"

"Exactly, beautiful. You can't be mad at me. I'm opening a new club and about to become a celebrity, so I'm hoping you look kindly on my attempts to improve your life." He smirks and I'm about to scold him, but he captures my lips.

And, as always, every kiss is a unique experience. This one teases, filling me with warmth. How could I get mad at him? Whatever he's planning.

"Stop that. Gross," Caro interrupts us.

"Interesting that you miss half of the conversations and things happening around you during your screen time, but you notice this." Hunter bumps her shoulder.

Hunter's mom got Caro a smartphone for Christmas to ensure she could talk to her all the time while in Florida. We've been testing the waters in terms of screen time, but it's been a struggle to say the least.

The car pulls into an underground garage and the driver stops near the elevator bank. Hunter holds the car's door open for us.

"Ladies." We get out. "Caro, please put away the phone," Hunter says, and then smiles at a man who leans against the wall by the elevators.

"Jackson." Hunter shakes his hand. "This is Sydney and Caro."

"Nice to meet you. Are you ready?" Jackson calls the elevator.

"No, not at all," I say, and Jackson frowns and darts his gaze between me and Hunter.

"It's a surprise," Hunter tells him, and Jackson—whoever he is—smiles knowingly. *What does he know?*

We take the elevator to the second floor and step out into a carpeted reception area.

"Jackson is helping me find a new location for my next club," Hunter says and intertwines his hand through mine, dragging me around the place.

The long corridor is lined with small classrooms and a few offices. There is also a larger classroom. All semi-furnished, natural light streaming through the tall windows. It feels warm and inviting, but I'm at a loss as to what I'm inspecting.

"This seems small for one of your clubs." I trace a student desk, feeling strangely at home. But then, I'm a teacher.

"It used to be a language school and the former owners are looking for someone to take over the lease. Every room is set up with outlets and technical requirements for state-of-the art technical set-up, video streaming and whatnot," Jackson explains.

"Let's explore the other side." He leads us through the space. "The layout is slightly different here, broken down into small rooms for individual classes and a large common area for students. There is a kitchen with a small eating area and two large offices. Since the owners are pressed to find someone to take over the lease, the rental conditions are better than expected. Definitely for this location."

"So what do you say?" Hunter looks at me, his eyes sparkling.

"I think it's mean to take me to a school on Saturday." Caro puts her hands on her hips and glares.

Hunter chuckles. "Sorry, pumpkin."

"That's it. I'm out of here." She marches out of the room.

We're standing in the middle of a corner office, Central Park in the distance.

"I'll give you a moment and go check on the young lady," Jackson says and leaves.

"So?" Hunter takes my hands.

"I don't know what you're showing me. Great location. The place feels good, but what do you want to do here? Besides, it seems like it has its purpose already. I'm sure there are more open, larger spaces for your club."

The corners of his lips tip up. "I'm sure there are, and I'll find one soon, but I like the purpose of this space."

I frown and look around again. I like the space too. I love it in fact. It would be perfect down the road if I ever get to open my learning center. *My learning center?*

I snap my gaze to his.

"For you, Sydney." Hunter smiles, but worry shadows his expression.

I narrow my eyes as his words sink in slowly. My heartbeat ticks up a notch. I look around the office again and through the door into the empty hallway. I would hang large prints of happy children on the white walls there.

The idea startles me. The first thing I think about is how to decorate the space? What's wrong with me? It's not even mine. I can't afford to start a venture like this.

"But I can't... You know I have no money, Hunter. I can't start a business. And I'm not letting you pay. We've been through this." I shake my head, wishing there was a way. Damn him. I love the place.

"But what if you could afford it?" Hunter hugs me and kisses the top of my head. I want to wiggle away because it's hard to remain reasonable when his scent wraps around me. But he holds me tight, not allowing me to protest freely. He knows me too well.

"With my history, no bank would back me up." I put my hands on his chest, annoyed he'd dangle this treat in front of me. But he was right, I'm not going to make a big deal out of it, not on the day of his opening.

There's no fight left in me because disappointment seeps through as I reluctantly let go of the idea of the pictures on the walls. Of me sitting at the desk with this view.

"A bank, no, but what if you had private investors?" He doesn't let go of me. In his arms, I want to believe in everything, but this is too much.

"Remember how that ended up the last time I tried?" I won't repeat the Elliot McFadden mistake.

"Casually, over drinks at your parent's house last month, casually—not behind your back—London suggested she would be interested in such a venture and Gio confirmed as well. London believes there is also government funding that can be accessed. In that case, you'd set it up as a not-for-profit, but that's all up for further discussion. I'm happy to channel some of our money into this. And before you protest, I would mostly do it for kids like Caro. Parents with kids like Caro deserve someone like you in their life. Let us help you to help them."

Damn him. Tears push into my eyes. "Gio agreed to consider. He said as much."

"Well, I texted him the following day to make sure he was even listening, so I have a phone message to prove that to you."

Let us help you to help them. Jesus, this man. "Okay." I nod, equally scared and excited.

"Yes!" He seizes my lips. Thousands of emotions flood my entire system, and most of them are wonderfully dazzling.

Hunter grinds his hips against mine and a current

zips through both of us. He pushes me against the floor-to-ceiling window, his hands roaming from my hips to my breasts. I moan and he hisses, our breaths syncing in panting.

"Are you coming?" Caro yells from somewhere in the space.

I giggle and Hunter swears under his breath.

He lowers his forehead to mine. "You should sign the lease tonight, so we can come back to finish this."

I laugh and call out to Jackson. "I'm in."

"I can't believe you're really dating." I keep shaking my head as I make a plate of fruit and veggies for my dad.

Our father has been having a great few weeks, and we're all cautiously optimistic his health is turning for the better. I'm thrilled he could be at Hunter's opening.

"Yeah, whatever." London growls.

"Is it serious?" I ask.

"Is what serious?" Bianca appears from somewhere.

For some reason, I decide to mess with London. "London is dating," I explain.

"Of course it's serious. They are perfect together."

Bianca smiles and Lo shrugs, the emotions on her face as far from joy as possible.

When Bianca and Dad walk away, I glare at Lo. "Am I the only one who hasn't met him yet?"

"You were busy with your own shit."

"Why didn't you bring him?"

London glares at me for a moment and I swear there are tears in her eyes. Before I can find out what the hell is going on, she shakes her head and walks away. I can't imagine London getting attached, but by the looks of it, something is not right.

"Hunter tells me you found the space for your learning center." Gio startles me. I turn and meet his eyes, which surprises me even more because usually I would see his frowning forehead as he focuses on his phone. Is he off the screen?

He looks dashing in his bespoke suit that hugs his strong, muscular figure. He's not as tall as Massi, but he's impressive, nevertheless.

"More like he found it, but it's perfect. Thank you for offering to loan me money."

He shrugs. "Rather me than fucking McFadden. What is she doing here?"

I follow his frown. "Mila? She's one of the best event planners we know and was able to get this all together on a short notice. What's your problem?"

He groans and pulls out his phone. The conversation is over. I know Gio has a caring side because I've known him for a long time, but Jesus, he really can be a jerk.

"Hello, beautiful. I think everything turned out well." Hunter sneaks his arms around my waist from behind, nuzzling my throat gently.

I whip around in his arms to face him and kiss his cheek. "I'm proud of you."

"Has anyone given you a tour yet?" he whispers.

I laugh. "I've been here several times already."

He wiggles his eyebrows, takes my hand and leads me away. We climb the stairs to his office and Hunter locks the door behind us, then draws the blinds on the inner window that overlooks the party below.

"Hunter, everyone saw us coming up here," I protest, but my core contracts and my heart sets a dangerous tempo.

"It's my office, Sydney." He hisses my name in that sensual way only he can. "I'm expected to take care of business here." He pulls me to him and walks me backward.

My back hits the door and my objections die with his lips on mine. Hunter grabs my wrists and pins them above my head, imprisoning them in one of his large hands. The other hand finds my breast as he continues ravaging my mouth. My jaw. My neck. My clavicle.

"And it's my business, Mrs. Lowe," he mumbles against my skin, "to take good care of you."

With his knee, he spreads my legs wider. "Keep your arms up," he demands.

My body succumbs to a violent quiver, but I obey.

Only Hunter Stuart can order me around like this. Because despite his occasional domineering, he always takes care of me. It *is* his business, and he takes it seriously.

He hikes me up and I wrap my legs around his waist. He pushes my panties to the side and sinks not one, but two fingers into me. I whimper with lust and desire, and immediately, outside of my own will, my hips grind against his hand.

"Oh, yes, beautiful." He squeezes my ass, takes his fingers out and brings them to his mouth. He sucks my juices off them and then moves his lips to mine again.

"Hunter, I need you," I cry out, tasting myself on him and forgetting the party below.

"I thought you'd never ask, beautiful." He thrusts in and we both groan. I don't even know when he undid his pants.

Our bodies move in perfect unity. Familiar yet new. Exciting yet devastating. Punishing yet rewarding. We reach release together, falling over the edge with abandon.

"I love you, beautiful."

* * *

London

I watch Syd with Hunter disappear upstairs and I swipe at an angry tear. I'm pissed off. Not because they're clearly squeezing in a quickie in between entertaining their guests, but because I don't want to feel this stupid envy.

I had something similar to what they have. I don't anymore. This feeling of loneliness and desperate need is so stupid and useless, and yet I can't shrug it off. It has lingered for a week now, and I don't know how to move on.

I didn't want to come today, but that would spur concerns from Syd, or God forbid Bianca, and I can't deal with that anymore. I thought my plan for a fake boyfriend was the perfect way to get everyone off my back.

Instead, I jumped head-first into vulnerability. It hurts. It fucking hurts so much. I was better off shielding myself from potential heartache all these years.

God, I miss him. But I wasn't enough for him to stay. To choose me.

Who is London missing? Start reading Reckless Dare on the next page.

Thank you for reading Reckless Desire. Both Hunter and Caro have a surprise for Sydney. Read about it in this bonus scene at www.maxinehenri.com/desire or scan the code below:

Reckless Dare

London

"So what's your next adventure?" My brother alternates between swiping and typing on his phone, not even looking at me.

I sigh. Since we're at his upscale gentleman's club and he's paying, I should just endure his antisocial behavior, but sometimes I wonder why I even bother.

"Northern lights."

He looks up for the briefest second and then returns to his screen. "You're escaping New York's winter by going to the Artic Circle?"

"Oh, how you always find a way to criticize me," I quip. "I'm going to find my own personal Loki and fuck his brains out." It's not unlikely, but I say it more to provoke him.

"Yell it louder, so you get escorted out and they revoke my membership." He shakes his hand while typing again. "I thought women were into Thor."

And there it is—a tiny, almost invisible grin on his face. That's why I like Gio. He's annoying as hell, but deep down, he cares.

"Why thank you for your suggestion. The jury is out until I return from my adventure."

My adventure. Most people believe I leave every winter to escape the dreadful weather, or to blow off steam after my biggest event of the year. There is some truth to that, but my motivation has its roots elsewhere.

I started traveling in memory of someone who can't experience it anymore. But it's become my church. It makes me alive. The crazy adrenaline sports, reckless parties, nameless hookups where I can let go completely are acts of rebirth for me. Moments in time to find peace despite the wildness of the actions. The thrill of it grounds me and liberates me at the same time.

"Are you going anywhere this winter?" I ask, but keeping this conversation alive is a genuine struggle.

Okay, it's not like we need to catch up on anything, but it would be nice to talk while we wait for our food. After we placed our order, I tried to spark his interest in a new project I want to finance. After that failed, I moved onto a recent political scandal, the price of gold and a mining crisis in Brazil. I even tried discussing our siblings' sex lives. Not that I know much, but I certainly know more than him.

Gio stares at his phone. We must look like a couple who has lunch out of obligation and has maxed out their daily quota for discussing life's logistics. He works and I try not to be bored.

Nothing. I get nothing. If I don't count hums, nods and a few other acknowledgments. Though I suspect his *animated* reactions relate to the issue at *his* hand. Or on the screen, in this case. Finally, he glances up for a millisecond.

"You know I only travel in summer."

The lack of patience in his voice would irritate me, but I have too many other grievances in my life.

"Sorry to break it to you, bro, but spending a month at your house at Lake Como while still working is not a vacation. It's another level of workaholism."

"We all enjoy different things." He holds my gaze for a moment and it's unnerving. Perhaps it's better when he stares into his phone.

I look around and spot Finn van den Linden, the billionaire playboy, entering the restaurant. Satisfaction washes over me. It won't be a wasted lunch, after all.

The hostess walks him to his table, practically tripping over her own feet in an effort to draw his attention. He acts with the detached politeness of people with his pedigree and takes a seat.

He's alone. Perfect. I snatch the white linen napkin from my lap and place it on the table. There will only be a brief window before someone joins him.

"I'll be right back," I tell Gio, though he probably doesn't hear me. He never looks up.

For some outlandish reason, I wonder if that's the case even during sex. Yuck. I shiver at the idea of my brother having sex. Gross. He's my stepbrother and we're not related by blood, but still...ugh.

A few eyes follow me as I head to Finn's table. Good thing I chose the curve-hugging dress this morning.

I care little for things, but I dress for success. My clothing ensures I look the part I'm playing. It's all just wrapping, but it helps me get what I care about and that's what matters.

The Madison Club is quiet at lunchtime. Hushed conversations full of pretense hum through the air. I've never understood why men feel the need to socialize in member's only clubs. At least this one allows women as guests. Not that many of them use that benefit. It's a boys' club.

While the rules here are a century old, the decor isn't the stereotypical, stuffy mahogany darkness with marble undertones. The floor-to-ceiling windows bring a lot of light into the beige and birch wood restaurant. It's a large space where members enjoy high-end cuisine and the only room where guests are allowed.

"Finn, it's been a while." I turn on my biggest smile, fake but ample. It might dislocate my jaw, but my work smile garners attention all the time.

He looks up and frowns, his shoulders stiffening. Is he going to pretend we don't know each other?

"It looks like you haven't bought a table at the fundraiser yet," I chirp. "Perhaps an oversight?" I bat my lashes at him. Van den Lindens have never missed the event.

"London," he almost yelps as recognition settles over his expression.

"Of course." He stands up, smoothing his yellow tie. "My assistant must have forgotten. My family has always proudly supported the cause."

"Great. There are many research projects benefiting from your generosity." I might fake my smiles, but the words are honest. The efforts to find a cure for leukemia need all the money I can find.

"Sure, of course. More causes need a"—he pauses a moment—"dedicated ambassador like you."

"I appreciate your support." *And I believe you should do more.* But I learned a long time ago that shaming people into donating only works short-term. "But if you have time later this week, I'd like to tell you a bit more about a project I'm currently sourcing funds for."

He scratches his neck, making me brace for an excuse. I've worked on many members here already and very few get truly excited about leukemia research. It's not a sexy topic, but I don't give up.

Finn clears his throat. "Why don't you call my people and let's have coffee later this week." He bows his head and sits down, dismissing me, but at least he agreed to buy a table at the biggest annual event my foundation hosts and didn't reject a future conversation. Yet.

Fucking van den Linden. He could sponsor a research lab for decades without even noticing the dent in his finances, but people like him diversify their donations.

Frustration coils around my stomach, but I maintain my smile. "Thank you, Finn. It was nice to see you again."

I return to my table and watch Gio work until our meals arrive.

Unsurprisingly, he digs into his meal while swiping over the screen. He ordered pasta, probably due to his unwillingness to put his phone down, and eats with one hand. Lunches with him are tedious, but I gain access to the members here, so I endure.

I don't want to eat in silence. "What do you think is

behind Bianca and Dad's sudden summons for regular family meals?" I take a sip of my sparkling water.

My sisters and I are meeting in a few days to discuss it also. The unexpected insistence on spending time together smells sinister to me. I'm worried either he or his wife, Bianca, who is Gio's mother, is sick or something. They served us the life-is-short speech as an appetizer and I can't shake the odd feeling about the whole situation.

"Hmm." Gio nods his approval to *my question.* Screw it. Is access to this dining room really worth being ignored for a whole meal?

Despite his abhorrent manners though, he has supported my projects in the past and helped me wisely invest my trust fund. It's allowed me to donate my salary to the charitable arm of the Justin West Foundation, an institution I founded and have been managing for almost ten years now.

Gio shows up when I need him and while he constantly questions how I spend my money, he does help me all the time.

"You have blood on your shirt," I say just to mess with him.

His eyes snap down to his chest and he reaches for his collar as if he could find the stain by touch. When our eyes meet, I'm pleased his irritation mirrors mine.

"So you do listen," I mock him. "Good to know." I

give him a smile. Not the one I use when chatting with people like van den Linden. I don't pretend with Gio. We grew up together, so he gets my glaring smile.

"For fuck's sake, London, let's not pretend this is a pleasant family lunch. You don't do that. I don't do that. You schedule these *lovely* occasions to get access to the other members. To pump them for money or to hook up. I'm just the asshole who has to sit through a meal with you."

"I don't come here to hook up." Indignation spreads through my veins. How dare he. I'm no prude and I love sex, but I'm not stupid enough to mix work with pleasure. "I'm sorry these lunches are such a waste of time for you. Why do you even indulge me?"

He drops his phone and takes another bite before he pierces me with his gaze. He chews in silence, perhaps contemplating his response.

"This pasta is actually fantastic."

I halt my fork halfway to my mouth. "Asshole," I snarl and Gio laughs. Like throwing his head back, full-on laughter.

"I'm just teasing you, London." He shakes his head at me. "I've been preoccupied with a merger in Europe, so my head is elsewhere, but I *indulge* your company here because I think your work is valuable and important. Because while I don't understand your way of life and how your remarkable altruism goes hand in hand with that bubbling anger and hatred you harbor under your well-put-together appearance, I believe you're doing an important job, a service really. And people like me and my peers here need to be reminded to distribute our wealth beyond investments that multiply our return. Into something that matters."

His words stir a fuzzy feeling inside me. I don't know when something—or someone—last rendered me speechless. Outside validation of my mission isn't normally important to me, but hearing the praise from my brother means more than I would have suspected.

"Thank you." My voice comes out hoarser than usual.

Gio nods and picks up his phone, so I jump in quickly. "Perhaps I can tell you about a project—"

"Don't push it, London," he growls.

Got it.

We finish our meal in silence, but this time I don't mind it. While he works, I make a mental list of things to finish today. The gala is in a few weeks, so the list is long. I have two wonderful assistants, but this still is the busiest season for me.

Before we wrap up, I identify one more target. Gilbert Sutton is the heir to a global food conglomerate, and we've never been introduced. I consider my options while Gio signs the bill.

"Let me introduce you to Sutton," Gio says when we stand up.

"How did you—"

"Seriously, Lo, I might be distracted, but I'm not completely absent-minded." He gives me a disapproving look, like he hasn't just spent an hour staring into his phone.

I bite my tongue. The Suttons have never come to my fundraiser and if I can do anything well, it's keeping my eyes on the prize.

By the time I leave the club, I have commitments for two more tables, which makes me cautiously optimistic. I call my assistant, Ashley, to ensure she follows up and closes those ticket sales. One goes for ten thousand dollars and provides enough funds to support several long-term research efforts and my staff. Not enough, though. It's never enough.

Two months ago, the lead researcher on a project at Stanford University presented an encouraging theory. If the drug works, it would revolutionize the treatment of leukemia. It would take years to prove the concept and run all the testing before the clinical trials on people can start, but it would be the first significant improvement in decades.

Unfortunately, they ran out of state funding and private partnerships are hard to come by, unless you want to be married to the pharmaceutical industry.

Instead of steady progress, they have encountered hurdle after hurdle. I've only managed to drum up moderate support commitments over the past eight weeks.

The walk to my building gives me too much time to think, and the high from selling the gala seats evaporates by the time I reach the front entrance. The familiar helplessness hugs me tightly again. It doesn't matter how much I try—I don't seem to make any progress. There is always more money needed, more people desperate for help.

I'm failing you, Justin.

The elevator door slides open on my floor and frustration bursts in my chest.

If I thought I had maxed out my daily dose of irritation during my lunch with Gio, I was wrong. Oddly, it pleases me because having someone to blame for all my issues is the best medicine.

A very temporary one, but still.

There are only two condos on this level. The hallway between them has been lined with boxes for two weeks now. I haven't met my new neighbors yet, but I'm confronted with their fucking boxes on a daily basis.

I march to their door and knock. No, I bang, my palm curled into a fist. Nothing. They must be at work. I decide to bang one more time just to release some of my frustration, not really caring that it's not directly related to my neighbor.

My hand connects with the wood. And then it doesn't.

Losing my balance, I tumble into a wall of muscles.

Two strong hands steady me and I look up. I'm not short, but I have to crane my neck to meet this man's eyes.

My center clenches involuntarily and I regret— briefly—my rule not to hook up with people I might run into afterward. My new neighbor is a descendant of Greek gods.

His black T-shirt stretches across broad shoulders and a chiseled chest, exposing arms with defined muscles. He's wearing black sweatpants that hang low enough to draw my attention and briefly fantasize about the bulge suggested in between his thighs.

"May I help you? Other than keeping you upright?" His voice is laced with annoyance and something I can't identify. It could be a sarcasm or amusement. The emotion aside, his baritone is like a decadent caress.

I jerk back as if his touch burned. And it did. A little. Or a lot.

His eyes are mesmerizing, those dark irises too seductive. And so is the stupid sly grin on his face. And the lazily tousled dark blond hair, falling into his eyes. I don't even like facial hair and yet, here I am oddly attracted to whatever is happening on his face. It's not even a sexy three-day stubble. He is sporting a full-on hipster beard.

I take one more step back and hit a stack of boxes. The impact snaps me out of my temporary brain fart and reminds me why I'm here.

"The boxes," I bark. "It's been two weeks. Get rid of them."

He cocks his head. "Who are you?"

"I live next door." I gesture to my door on the other side of the hallway.

"Oh, my neighbor." He smiles, an x-rated kind of a smile. "Finally, we meet. Dominic Cressard." He offers me his hand.

I raise my brow and put my hands on my hips.

He leans against his doorway casually, unaffected by my animosity. "I would invite you inside, but I'm afraid I have nothing to offer you. In fact, I don't have any chairs yet."

"You have no furniture?"

"Practically none," he drawls.

I smile. "Wonderful. These fucking boxes must fit inside, then. Take care of it."

I turn on my heel and march to my door. And though I can't see him behind me, his gaze still burns holes in my back. Shit. This interaction was far from the intended outlet for my frustration. And why can't I find my keys, damn it.

"It was nice meeting you, *neighbor*."

For some—not very mature—reason, I'm proud I haven't introduced myself. I finally unlock my door and before I can close it behind me, I glance back. Dominic, the picture of nonchalance, smiles at me.

I flip him off.

Also by Maxine Henri

Untamed Billionaires Series

Tempted by the Billionaire (A Fake Relationship Romance)

Chosen by The Billionaire (An Enemies to Lovers Romance)

Chased by the Billionaire (An Age gap/Innocent Heroine Romance)

Stolen by the Billionaire (A Forbidden Love Romance)

Reckless Billionaires Series

Reckless Fate (A Second Chance Billionaire Romance)

Reckless Desire (A Single Dad Billionaire Romance)

Reckless Dare (A Fake Relationship Romance)

Reckless Deal (A Grumpy/Sunshine Bosshole Romance)

If you loved this book, please spread the word and leave a review. One sentence is enough to help other readers and make me very happy.

Acknowledgments

Dear reader,

Thank you for making it this far. I hope you enjoyed Sydney and Hunter's story.

When I got the idea of a male escort being the love interest in my book, I got too excited and couldn't drop it.

My initial plan was for Hunter to be a playboy and an asshole, but well, he came out completely different. While dominant, he is also caring, so I didn't fight it and let him lead me through the story.

When the manuscript came back from my editor, several places were marked with a single comment: "poor Sydney".

Okay, I admit, I put her through a lot, but she needed to snap out of her hermit way of life and trust people and herself again. I hope you could empathize with her and root for her.

You, my dear reader, are the reason this journey has been so rewarding for me. Thank you for allowing me to share my stories with you.

Mr. Henri has been my rock for twenty years and without his support I'd have never tried to share my words.

They would have been locked in a drawer. As they had been for years. I know, my darling, that this often feels like a sacrifice to you, but I can't stop😊.

Editor Jess, thank you for patiently listening to me when I blabber about my story, trying to make sense out of it.

I appreciate your invaluable input and your excellent editing skills.

Dan, thank you for your keen eyes on all the typos.

Jaycee DeLorenzo, I love the covers. Both of them. I love that you smile even when I ask for yet another minor design change.

To all my author friends who make this journey less lonely and more fun, but who also keep me focused and productive.

Kat Bammer, D.E. Haggerty, Mila Kane, Sienna Judd, Gabrielle Sands, Mia Sivan you're all very talented and inspiring.

And let me loop back to you, dear reader. It's you and only you who make me continue with this wonderful passion. Every single one of you matters to me.

About the Author

Maxine Henri is a contemporary romance author who infuses her stories with steamy passion and complex characters. When she's not crafting stories, she can usually be found sipping on a cup of black tea while reading a good book. Or traveling to new destinations.

Maxine believes that stories matter. They facilitate emotional journeys, inspire and entertain. And when it comes to books and fiction, stories are a great escape and probably the most beneficial addiction on this planet.

Her billionaire romances are the perfect escape, offering a taste of luxury and adventure. Maxine introduces heroes who may have a dark past, but are always balanced by a lighter side. And her leading ladies? They're strong, independent women who may be a little broken, but always find their way in life.

You can connect with her on any of these platforms:

facebook.com/maxinehenriromance

instagram.com/maxinehenriromance

bookbub.com/profile/maxine-henri

amazon.com/author/maxinehenri